GILDED WINGS

FALLEN FAE GODS 1

JAYMIN EVE

For those who wanted to follow Alice down the rabbit hole, and wished it was an R rated version with dragons and gods.

p.s Don't pet the bunny.

EASTERN REALM OF RISEST
Fallen Fae Lands

WILDS OF S

SEAS OF VERDIN

FAE ACA

CRATERS OF LASTOA

TOIA

LAND OF OCHERAN

KE

ISLE OF DENILLE

TRENCH

CHAPTER
ONE

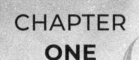

T he pile of returned books teetered precariously before I managed to straighten the few spines that had been sticking out at an odd angle, throwing the whole stack out of alignment.

"Holy sailors' tatas, Morgan, that was close," Lexie grumbled. My best friend, and the only other person employed to help take care of Dragerfield Private Library, stumbled closer, her arms full of a pile of books almost as tall as the one on the table. "You know how mad Simon gets when we damage any of the *precious tomes*."

Oh, I knew. I freaking knew. Simon was the caretaker of Dragerfield Estate. He was a stately man, with dark skin that didn't show his age, but he had a few wisps of white hair on his head to indicate he was quite a few years older than my twenty-five. He always wore a black suit and carried a heavy cane that he loved to smack against our legs whenever he discovered a new crease in a spine. Thankfully, he rarely made an appearance here.

Well, except when we fucked up. Somehow he always knew when we were being less than careful with the books.

Lexie dropped her pile as gently as possible next to mine to be sorted and reshelved or repaired, depending on the condition they were returned in. It was totally fine if the people who borrowed the books damaged them. *That* was allowed.

She wiped a hand across her brow, her short cropped dark hair showing off the gorgeous bone structure of her Japanese heritage. With her looks and height–a few inches taller than my 5'8–my bestie could have been a model, but instead she'd chosen a quiet life with me. Books, both new and priceless ancient tomes, filled our days, and I couldn't be happier about it. My double degree in English and history had led me down this path, and there was literally no other career for me.

The Dragerfield Private Library was housed in a huge building on the outskirts of Biddeford, Maine. I was from Portland, so it wasn't a huge change to move into this area, but it got me away from my parents, who were just a touch on the smothering side. They were my only family and I loved them, but I needed my own house and privacy, despite my mother's groans about it.

"Are we still getting drinks tonight?" Lexie asked as we sorted the piles. After two years of this, we had it down to a fine art. Check the front, back, spine, and binding before opening to ascertain that no pages were loose. Then, if everything was in order, it went into the reshelve pile. If it was damaged, we had a repair section.

"We are absolutely getting drinks tonight," I said while we worked. "That new bar is open now. Their seafood is supposed to be to die for."

Lexie smiled wistfully, as if the mere thought of a decent meal was cheering her up. I could relate. My curves were testament to my near obsession with food in all shapes and forms. "Give me *all* the butter and garlic shrimp." I almost had to wipe away some drool. "And mashed potatoes and thick cut fries. I'm here for all of it." It was close to quitting time and I was starving.

"Stop," she said, pointing a finger in my face. "You know I don't curse, but I will find some very colorful phrases to throw your way if you mention garlic and shrimp and mash while we're stuck at work."

She was the queen of colorful non-cursey phrases, so I believed her.

"Let's just get this done and we can knock off ten minutes early," I said, picking up the pace. Her smile picked up too, and we moved even faster.

Most of the books in my pile were from the newer section, but there were two large tomes near the bottom that would require more of my attention. When I reached them, a tingle of energy raced across my hands, but I was so used to it with these older pieces that I barely even reacted. This private library was owned by some anonymous billionaire, and whoever borrowed the books only did so at night when we weren't here. A lot of the collection should be in museums—it was that rare and special—and I always felt as if their ancient prose was infused with just a touch of magic.

The first time I'd felt the spark, I'd jumped a foot in the air, thinking there was an electrical issue in the room. But nope, it had been the books. Usually only the most ancient zapped me, but occasionally some of the newer ones too.

Thankfully these two, written in a text and language I didn't recognize, were returned in perfect condition, so off I went into the upper level of the library to re-shelve them all. It was a three-story building, curving shelves around the second and third balconies, all of which looked down onto a large ballroom on the ground floor. There were also these incredible white, hand-carved stone pillars that spanned up through all three levels and into the ceiling many stories above.

Lexie and I guessed that at one point the marble floor below had been used for fancy balls, before they built the balconies above to house all the books. There'd been no balls or dances held here in our time, this building only ever utilized as a library, and I was curious why they hadn't renovated the lower levels to add more shelves. Could you ever have too many bookshelves?

Well, that was a stupid question.

You definitely could not.

The tiny apartment I shared with Lexie was literally lined in shelves, every spare wall, nook and cranny crammed and over-flowing with books. As I'd said, we lived and breathed our jobs.

By the time I'd trekked between the second and third level multiple times, my calves and arms ached, and I'd already mentally decided I deserved three cocktails as well as a double serving of the shrimp. I mean, it was Friday. No one started a diet on a Friday.

That was a Monday job.

"Come on, Morgs," Lexie called. "We need to get out of here and into that bar. Garlic shrimp is calling my name."

"I'll meet you outside in a minute," I called down, peering over the edge of the third story to see her standing on the marble ballroom floor below, bag over her shoulder. "I just have one final book to shelve." She waved up to let me know she'd heard. Our voices carried well in this massive building because everything was so open.

Pushing on, I went to the very farthest section of the third floor, where you needed a special key to even enter. I didn't have a key, nor did Lex, but there was a small return slot to leave books. Simon would ensure they were reshelved correctly.

It wasn't my place to question why this area was off-limits, since I could effectively do my job without entering that space. Come Monday, when I returned, there would be no books in the slot. There never had been in the years I'd worked here.

As I turned away, a low, husky female voice, unusual enough to stall my steps, said, "Thank you, human." Swinging around, I examined the barred door and small slot in the middle. I leaned over to peer into the gap. It was dark on the other side, with no sign at all that another person was back there.

What the hell?

Okay, clearly shadowy corners and desperate hunger had me hearing things.

It was time to get out of here.

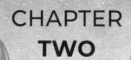

CHAPTER
TWO

After that *weird as fuck* incident, I found myself walking faster than usual toward the exit, keeping an eye out for anything out of place. As much as I enjoyed my free weekends, it was hard to leave the books for two full days with no one to care for them. I'd never admit it, but when I stepped into this building on a Monday, it was like coming home.

One day I'd worry about the level of ownership I felt here, considering I earned just above minimum wage and could barely afford the apartment I shared with Lexie. There was no way in the world I was ever going to own a place like this. No matter how much I loved it like my own.

But a girl could daydream… maybe the zap of energy in the books would rub off on me and I'd finally hit those lotto numbers.

When I reached the ground floor, I moved toward the employee entrance, grabbing my bag and coat from the cubbies on the side. From here, I hit the lights to shut everything down in the entire library, and after shrugging on my thick wool coat to ward off the December chill, I left the building, locking the door behind me.

The main entrance to the building was around the other side, but no one ever seemed to use those huge, double-entrance gilded doors. One more section of the library left to sit unused.

As I stepped outside, the wind grabbed up the waves of my long golden-brown hair, tossing them around my face, until I wrangled the mass into a band. When I reached the black, beat-up Jeep Lexie and I also shared, I slid into the passenger seat, thankful she had the heat blasting. Rubbing my hands, I gave the old building one last look. There were no windows, just those two doors—the small employee entrance and the huge golden ones. The outside walls were shaped like a stadium, with turrets and carved images depicting battle scenes through the white stone of the three-hundred-year-old structure.

I'd almost died when Simon told me its age. While we tried our best to preserve our buildings in Maine, with the inclement weather a lot of our historical pieces were nothing more than rubble. But the Dragerfield Library was in near pristine condition. It was special, unable to be replicated, and my love of history was probably half the reason for my love of my job.

"Finish your last look, girl," Lexie said with a smile, shifting the jeep into drive. "I know you miss this place over the weekend."

She knew me better than most people in the world, including my parents. Their overbearing nature made it difficult to share freely with them. The only way to survive was to keep them at arm's length, otherwise they would control every aspect of my life. It was a painful lesson I'd taken years to learn. The covert narcissism of my mom, Dianne Starrer, had almost cost me every opportunity and friendship in my life.

Lexie was the only one to stick it out. Through freshman year of college until now, she never gave up on me, and it had been her support that helped me break free from the life I'd been trapped in. There was no one more important in the world to me, and the fact that I was now living independently with my own money, making my own choices, still shocked me.

"Where did you go?" Lexie asked as she drove down the four-mile-long driveway that led out to the double gates of this large parcel of land. The gates were never closed, but no one ever visited. At least not while we were there. Those who borrowed the books at night had to get here somehow, so it was only empty in daylight hours. Or so I assumed.

"Just thinking about home," I told her, relaxing as the heat blasted the wintery chill away. "About how lucky I was to get away from a toxic situation. I couldn't have done it without you. You're the best friend anyone could ask for."

Lexie shot me a sad smile. "Girl, you know how well I under-stand family trauma. My parents are so busy, overseas all the time, that I've all but raised myself. I feel like we lived opposite lives in that way, and yet we both needed each other."

It was a truth that could never be denied. She'd stood up to my mom when I couldn't, and she was still the bravest person I'd ever met. Not just brave but strong, beautiful, and kind. One day soon she'd be snapped up by some amazing man and I'd lose my wing woman. But we'd always be best friends. We were lifers.

"Should we just head straight for Pattie's?" Lexie asked. "I mean, our work uniforms are fine for a bar, right?"

The plain black slacks and white button-down shirts we wore when working were more than fine. "Let's do it," I said, feeling my spirits lift. "I'm not sure my stomach can wait any longer for food. No one cares what we look like."

Lexie snorted. "Bish, you have to be kidding yourself. You have your Marilyn Monroe curves, your long golden-brown hair and big blue eyes. You're never going to escape notice, whether you wear a white shirt or a hessian sack. Just own it."

It was my turn to snort-laugh. "Says the lady with cheekbones to die for, perky boobs that don't destroy your back, and skin that's so damn perfect it hurts me a little to stare directly at you. Yeah, okay. How about you own your hotness, and then we can both enjoy our shrimp."

No one else was hyping us up in this town, but that was okay. We were our own damn cheerleaders.

Lexie's lips twitched before we burst into laughter. We caught our breaths as the lights from the town came into view; the library was ten miles out, across some of the more rugged terrain.

"Truthfully, I think it's more the lack of any quality men in this town than the fact we aren't hotties," Lexie said. "We're both rocking all the right things, and we're well-read and educated to boot. It's a them issue, not us."

I didn't argue, because she was right about one part. For her, it was a *them issue*. But for me I had never easily gelled with another person. I'd been on dates. I'd had sex. I'd even wondered if I was into chicks, but after my date with a lovely surfer girl from California ended with a kiss that did nothing for me, I knew it was more than just *I was confused*.

I was different. My heart and soul weren't the same as others I'd met, and outside of Lexie, I'd never found another who fit into the odd shapes of my existence. It was probably the trauma of my upbringing. But whatever the excuse, in my situation, it was a me thing.

At least I had my books.

That would have to be more than enough satisfaction, hence

why I liked them on the spicier side to go with my decent array of vibrators.

A girl had her needs, and if no one else could fulfill them, I was damn sure not missing out.

CHAPTER
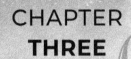
THREE

The food at Pattie's Bar and Grill more than lived up to its reputation, and by the time we got home—in the only Uber in town since we'd indulged in an array of cocktails—I was exhausted and ready to crawl into bed. Our small apartment was part of a two-story walkup a few blocks from Main Street. There were eight apartments with the exact same layout as ours, but we rarely saw the other occupants. At least half worked at night to our day, and the rest were on trawler boats, coming and going sporadically.

We had a ground floor, and it only took three attempts to get the lock open, before we fell inside.

Literally.

Lexie tripped in the opening and I took a tumble after her, both of us landing on the thick rug in the entryway.

"Ouch," I groaned. "What the shit? I think I broke my vagina."

Lexie went into a spiral of hysterical laughter. "You wish, babe. That would be the most exciting thing to happen to your vagina in years."

If only she was kidding. I wanted to be annoyed, but laughter kept spilling out from between my pursed lips, dispelling the notion that I was offended. "Someone break my vagina," I begged the universe. "Is... is it re-really too much to ask f-for?" Laughter and drunkenness had me slurring and stuttering my words, and by the time I was done, we were both howling. Drunk chick style.

This had been the best night I'd had in ages.

Lexie dragged herself up and I followed, managing to slam the door behind us, and even slide the deadbolt into place. We stumbled into the tiny living area with its three mismatched but comfy couches and a small TV we rarely bothered to watch. The kitchen was just off the side, the L-shaped design giving an illusion of more space than we actually had.

I stopped off here for some water, already regretting the morning hangover. It might take a lot to get me tipsy, but when I got there I paid for it dearly the next day. Drowning myself in water before bed was, on occasion, my saving grace.

"Two cups at least," Lexie called, before she ambled off into the bathroom. A second later the water started and I knew she'd be in there for a while. If anyone was unconcerned with conserving water, it was my bestie. I preferred baths myself, but unfortunately, this apartment barely had a shower. No space for luxuries like a bathtub.

Starting on my second glass of water, I heard chiming, and it took me an embarrassingly long time to realize it was my phone. When I pulled it out of my bag, I squinted suspiciously at it, to find that it was the library's number.

What in the world?

I'd never received an after-hours call from them. Actually, I'd never received a single call from this number. The only reason I knew their landline at all was from the rare times I'd had to call in sick. Simon always answered and was short and to the point, accepting my absence without question.

Why would the cantankerous caretaker be phoning me tonight though? Had something disastrous happened? *Did the library burn down?*

Even knowing it was a terrible idea after drinking, I wouldn't sleep until I knew what had happened, so I slid the answer button. "Hello?" I said hesitantly, turning that greeting into a question somehow.

"A book is missing."

I'd been walking toward the couch, and as the deep, orgasm-inducing voice rumbled from the phone, I tripped for the second time in ten minutes, smacking my head on the side table as I fell. That was not Simon. Not even close.

By the time I had shaken off my confusion and the pain in my head, I had missed his next words. Catching only "…immediately what happened!"

Orgasm-in-a-voice was mad, lashing out at me. Was he using some sort of machine to deepen his voice or something? Because *damn,* I'd never heard anyone sound like him.

And I was still not listening to his actual words.

"I hit my head," I blurted out suddenly, interrupting his next sexy snarl. "Just then. I might have a concussion." Or was drunk and mesmerized by deeply graveled tones.

"There's a book missing from the special edition section," he started again, slower, to compensate for what he must be assuming were my additional needs. I dragged myself up from the floor, forcing my brain to pay attention. "It was returned last night, and you should have logged it in today, but it's not here."

Special editions… There had only been one from that section. "It was logged in through the slot as always," I told him, sobering up a touch as I wondered if this was the moment I lost my job. "A female voice thanked me as I walked away, which, come to think, was odd. I've never heard a voice in there before, but clearly she received the book. I mean, what else would she be thanking me—"

The call died, and I blinked again, lifting it from my ear to stare down at the main screen. "What the fuck?" I gasped. "He hung up on me."

I knew that, in general, there was a bit too much *ramble* in my personality, but this was a whole new level of rude. Deciding not to worry about it tonight, or this weekend at all, I stood on shaky legs, ready for my turn in the shower.

"It's all yours, jellybean," Lexie said as she emerged in a cloud of steam, butt naked because that's how she liked to sleep. We'd been naked around each other so much it wasn't even weird at this point. "I'll see you in the morning."

"Night," I called, forcing myself to sound normal. Thankfully Lexie was either too tired or too intoxicated to notice anything odd in my tone or movement, and I was able to escape into the bathroom before she caught on. The shower was lukewarm, and we had shit water pressure here, but it was enough to scrub off the day's grime and makeup and refresh myself before bed. I drank more water straight from the faucet, uncaring that it was gross city water and even grosser hot water system water.

It was better than the hangover I had coming if I didn't.

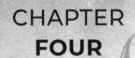

CHAPTER
FOUR

When I'd finished with the bathroom, face scrubbed clean, teeth as well, dressed in my favorite flannel pjs, I snuggled into bed and picked up my phone, prepared to read a few more chapters of my current book. It was book three in a series I'd been loving, and it released two days ago. With work I'd only been able to sneak a few minutes to read, and it was killing me slowly not to know what happened to *Hannah,* especially with the whopper of a cliffhanger the author left in the last book.

As I went to open my reading app, my eye caught the phone image, and that deep voice filled my mind once more. He had a distinct tone, *really distinct,* and I was certain I'd never met anyone with it before.

Had I just spoken to the mysterious owner of the library? *Dragerfield.* I still had no idea if it was the owner's name or random library name.

A book is missing. How was that possible? Had I overlooked another special edition somehow? Or had I accidentally sent the one I'd had through the wrong slot because I'd been in a hurry to get out of there? The shadows had freaked me out for some reason, and I'd all but bailed when I ditched the book.

Or was this to do with that odd female voice? Did they take the book and now I was about to get fired? And even worse, could I get Lexie fired too? She'd probably quit on my behalf anyway, but I couldn't do that to her. Not when we had the most perfect job in the world.

Especially for our little town.

There was not a single other job option that I could think of, especially if we wanted to remain on dry land. I refused to accept us losing our jobs because of one stupid screwup.

Right? There had to be a way to fix this with Mr. Sexy Voice.

By now, the alcohol had worn off and I was heading into the migraine territory. If I didn't have more water and take some painkillers, I'd regret every part of my existence by the time morning arrived.

Dragging my ass out of bed, I threw on an overcoat over my pjs, needing to stay warm against the chill of our uninsulated home. The furnace was on its last legs, and we were not equipped to deal with these wintery months without some extra layers. In the kitchen, I stared at my phone again and cursed at the conversation which continued to run through my head.

Before I could think it through, I was downing two tablets, another glass of water, and pulling up the Uber app. I called in for a pickup before my addled brain even registered what the hell I was doing, and then I was sneaking out of our house, still dressed in pjs and a coat—no bra of course. If you slept in a bra, you needed to seek professional help.

When Uber-Fred pulled up in front of the house, squinting at me under his heavyset, weather-beaten brow, I almost changed my mind and ran back into the house. "Missy?" he said as he lowered the window. "Did you forget something at the bar?"

Fred called all women *missy*. It was a dreadful habit that we'd all tried to break but eventually conceded to. He was too old and stubborn to change at this point. "Uh, n-no," I stuttered, bouncing from one socked foot to the other. "I have a work emergency. I need to head out to the library."

This wouldn't be Fred's first trip out there, but it was definitely his first at midnight. "An emergency at the library?" he said slowly, his accent drawing out many letters that didn't require emphasis. "That don't sound correct."

It really didn't, and yet here we were. "I misplaced a book," I added, my face near numb at this point. "If I don't figure out what happened to it, I'm going to get fired. And then I'll get Lexie fired, and then we'll live on the streets, until one of us has to prostitute ourselves to make a dollar, and Lex is so much better looking than me and I don't want it to be her…"

This whole ramble-when-I'm-nervous thing was starting to become a concern, and I was fairly sure Fred regretted even asking where I was going.

"Get in," he finally shouted when I was mid-way through our dual pregnancies on the streets, raising tiny hooker babies. "Just as long as you shut up."

"Right, right," I said, stumbling on the edge before managing to open the passenger door and drop inside. "I promise I won't be long if you'll just wait for me."

Fred grunted, already taking off before the door was even fully closed and seatbelt on. "Dude," I gasped. "Safety first."

This time he definitely muttered some four-letter words, and it was nice not to have to interpret Lexie's "frogs" and "jibblenuts" in place of legit curses. Fred believed me a fucking weirdo, and he said it plain as day.

The car was silent after that, Fred zipping around the quiet town, taking every shortcut in existence so we were out of the main area and on the road to the library in minutes. It was very dark, with only his headlights to keep us on the road and off the rugged terrain on either side.

I'd never seen another car on this road, and tonight was no exception. Strangely, I'd been expecting traffic though, because this was the time when books got borrowed. *Right?*

The gates were open, as always, and Fred didn't even slow, mere inches from knocking his right-side mirror off on the post. He clearly didn't give a shit about his car, hoping to ditch the *fucking weirdo* as soon as possible.

When we got closer to the library, I blinked at the illumination casting a glow around the building. I'd never seen it at night before, and it was lit up like we were in the middle of Times Square. But strangely… not a single car in the grasslands around the entrance.

"That's odd," Fred finally muttered, both of us leaning forward to peer through the windshield as he slowed. "Is there a party happening?"

"I have no idea," I breathed. "If there is, we weren't informed."

Which was kind of rude, if you asked me. I mean, I'd been curious why the main ballroom was never used, and here these assholes went using the space and not telling us.

Dragerfield. That deep voice. Maybe he was back in town… and that was why he'd called me.

"You still going in?" Fred asked, and I noticed that he'd come to a halt a few yards from the side entrance, where he usually dropped us. "I'll wait ten minutes, unless I get another Uber request. Then you'll have to hang out here until I'm free to pick you up again."

I nodded, still staring at the building, blinking at how odd this night was becoming. "That's fair, Fred. Very fair. Thank you."

He just grunted, and when I still didn't move, he leaned over me and opened the door. "Get out. Fix your mess."

What a sweet grandfatherly figure. Seemingly with no choice, I got out in my pjs and socks, closing the door gently behind me. From this angle I could see that the great double doors were finally open, but I decided that the side entrance was still my best bet.

The aim was to sneak in and out and find the damn book, returning it before morning.

Maybe the party was exactly the distraction I needed to ensure no one found me out before I finished my task.

It was a great plan. Zero flaws.

And with that confidence in my stride, I hurried toward the side entrance.

Ready to save the day.

CHAPTER
FIVE

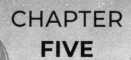

I made it inside with ease. The side entrance was locked, but there was a spare key hidden under a rock just off to the side, for those early mornings I forgot my keys. When the door silently opened, I entered the dark room. No one was back here, and that gave me the advantage I needed to shuffle inside and get the door closed behind me.

It was darker than I'd ever seen it in the entrance, but I'd walked through here so many times I knew exactly where everything was. My slightly damp—*ew*—socks kept my steps quiet, and when I reached the stairs and made my way up to the next level, a few slivers of light filtered around me, the ballroom ambience making itself known.

The noise I'd heard outside was louder inside, naturally, with music and laughter the most prevalent sound, followed by a lower thrum of conversation. I found myself prancing up each step in time to the fast-paced, instrumental music, and with each step my anticipation of what was happening below grew.

This was Dragerfield at night—a secret nightlife that Lexie and

I had no idea of—and while I knew it was stupid and reckless to be here when I wasn't invited, another part was desperate to discover this other side of *my* Dragerfield.

This delusion of ownership would be a great conversation for therapy, no doubt.

When the dark landing leveled out, I was thankful that no one appeared to be on the higher floors. Inching toward the edge, I peered over the side, and the light reflecting off the marbled floors burned my eyes after being in darkness for so long. All I could see were what looked like glittering spotlights and a room awash in dresses and suits.

I closed my eyes to help them adjust to the light, but when I opened them again, it was the same view: light and color and no way to make out who exactly was down there, or what sort of party it was. Almost as if the view from this level was hiding the scene below, and I couldn't figure out how that would be happening.

Shaking my head, I decided that I'd deal with the missing book first, then I'd go full spy mission on the event. If I had to view it from the ground level, then I'd just have to sneak a peek when I was leaving.

My eyes watered briefly as I turned away from the railing, the discomfort easing as darkness once again surrounded me. Keeping my head lowered and my steps light, I first made my way toward the desk that held the box where all returned books were found.

The box had a couple of new books in it, but there was no sign of any special editions. I then checked the table above and below, in case there'd been another special edition I'd missed in reshelving. Still, nothing. I used the light on my phone to double check in the darkness, but the area was clear.

The music continued in the background, songs I had no knowledge of, but I was humming and swaying as I searched, reluctantly enjoying the ambience. These assholes having a glittery ball and not inviting us was the top of my shit list for this year. And that was saying something considering what my parents had pulled to get me back home earlier in the year—pretending they were struggling to cook and clean and function without me, even though they were both in their fifties and in perfect health.

It had scared me, but I'd stood my ground and asked for them both to see doctors first before I made any decisions. Funnily enough, I'd never heard another word about it.

A narcissistic use of guilt did not go over well with me, not these days. Even if old habits and a lifetime of conditioning was hard to break. Now that I saw through their games, it did make it easier to stand my ground.

Abandoning this area, I found my way up to the next level, where the special editions were returned, creeping along still, but with less cloak-and-dagger ducking and weaving. No one was interested in books tonight.

When I reached the door with the slot that I deposited books through, I did something I never had before. I turned the handle.

In all seriousness, what the fuck was up with me tonight?

I wasn't a rule breaker. I lived a boring life and was okay with it. Boring meant safe, and safe meant that I wasn't about to be emotionally manipulated into living someone else's happiness.

I'd never do that again.

When I pushed the handle down, there was a click, and the door opened.

Well, shit.

Never in a million years had I expected that the forbidden room, completely off limits to Lex and me, would be unlocked. I mean, had they legitimately been banking on our ability to follow the rules and do as we were told to keep these contents from being discovered?

How did they know we wouldn't sneak a look?

Why hadn't we snuck a look?

Okay, yeah, mostly because this was a great job and we didn't want to lose it. As long as we weren't in danger here, they could have their secret rooms and weird hours of borrowing and returning books. Who was I to question the rich and eccentric?

But now that a book was missing, and I was at risk of losing my job anyway, there was really no choice but to open this damn door and search for the book. *Right?*

When the door was completely open, hesitant to walk inside, I used the light on my phone to shine in from the entrance. From the threshold I couldn't make out any details; it looked as if the room was empty. I shuffled a little farther inside and a tingle raced across my skin, almost as if I'd just brushed a low voltage live wire.

"I'd stop right there, if I were you."

I swore a little pee came out as I discovered I wasn't alone up here. Even worse, that command had been issued by the same deep, sexy rumble who had phoned me and set this entire chain of events into play.

The same damn voice.

Was I about to meet Dragerfield? For real?

CHAPTER
SIX

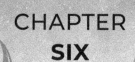

It took me a moment to realize that the voice wasn't coming from behind me, but from the room I'd almost stepped into. That rumbling tone filled the air around me until I felt like I was surrounded.

From the darkness before me, a giant of a man stepped forward.

And I do mean giant.

In the illumination of my phone it appeared that he stood at least seven feet tall, the shadow he cast almost obliterating its light. "Fuck," I squeaked, realizing that I was in a fairly dangerous situation, alone, in the dark with a complete stranger who was near twice my height and width, and from what I could see, built like an ancient warrior.

Backing up a few steps, I found my composure and started to move toward the reading table, hoping to use it as a barrier between me and *whatever the hell had just appeared in the darkness—* a guy I was assuming was Dragerfield, but who the fuck knew.

Keeping the phone light up before me, I managed to make it

behind the table before he even moved. Not because I was lightning fast or anything, but he apparently wasn't aiming to scare me by chasing. At least not yet.

The light wavered as I trembled, waiting for him to emerge from the shadows. When he did, the trembling only increased, because the moment he stepped free from the doorway, some other natural illumination came into play and I could see every part of him. *Oh, hot damn.* The illumination was him. The darkness could not hide a being made of light, shining from his bronze skin.

As he got closer, I noted that his golden blond hair was shaved close on the sides, longer on top. As I moved from his hair to his face, I had to physically stop myself from reacting verbally.

If I hadn't clamped my mouth shut, who the fuck knew what sort of moaning gasp would have emerged, because his face was not of this world.

"What are you?" I whispered, the words spilling out from between my clamped lips. *Shit.* I should have said *who* are you, but *what* was way more appropriate.

This *man* had a face built of hard lines and perfect angles, topped by sinfully full lips. His eyes were narrowed on me, but from the light of his skin I could see that they were a piercing green and gold, the shimmery gold closest to the iris and brighter than any pigment I'd ever seen. He also wore armor, with a golden shield across his chest, and straps emerging from the edges to wrap around very muscular arms. The front of his thighs were encased in a similar sort of armor that followed the line of his dark pants, finishing up with heavy combat-style boots.

Yep, it was definitely a *What are you?* kind of day.

He stopped on the other side of the table, and I brandished my phone like a weapon. "Don't come any closer," I warned. "I'm recording everything, and it'll go straight to the police."

He tilted his head, as if he couldn't understand my words,

when I knew he spoke English perfectly, albeit in a gruff tone designed to make panties wet and women stupid.

"You're the one who works here?" His eyes traced along my body, and if I hadn't been so muddled I might have felt embarrassed to be in my pjs and robe. But we were so far beyond that at this point.

Come on, Morgan. Get it together. He asked you a question.

The best I had was to nod vigorously, as if it was an Olympic sport and I was going for gold.

"You lost my book?"

Wait a freaking minute. "I did not lose your damn book," I shot back, some of the thrall of his voice fading under my anger. "That's why I'm here. You didn't give me a chance to finish speaking on the phone, but I wanted to reiterate that it was absolutely, one hundred and fifty percent, no doubt at all, returned to the slot in this doorway. Just as all special editions are."

"Absolutely, one hundred and fifty percent," he repeated, sounding amused, even if his expression remained scarily grim.

"Correct," I choked out, my hand shaking again.

"And yet you are here, sneaking into the room that is expressly forbidden for you to enter."

Ironically, my attempt to keep my job had probably just gotten me fired.

I dropped the phone to the table, and the light nearly blinded me, but I wanted both hands free in case I had to fight. "I never made it inside. Technically, I didn't break the rules."

His lips thinned. "You were going to, and that's as good as breaking them for me."

"You're Dragerfield?" Might as well ask my questions, since it was clear I was getting fired. *Or worse.* "The one who owns this library and the land it's on?"

His smile was sinister, and as he tilted his head back a touch, I noticed a sliver of what I assumed was a dark tattoo just visible on the side of his neck. "I am Drager. A sun god from the realm of Risest, and I use this Earthly portal to strengthen myself. Your sun here on Earth has more power than mine, and with this safehold gathering and storing its energy for me, my land and fae grow into a power that cannot be defeated."

I blinked at him. Once and then again. Had he just said he was a sun god from another realm?

Run, girl. Get the hell out of there. That was Lexie's voice in my head, and I knew that my fear of being fired had dulled under the knowledge that I was standing in the dark with a mentally unstable man who called himself a *sun god*. I mean, he was glow-y and clearly confident, but his statement wasn't just a big ego; he legit believed what he was saying.

Spinning on socked feet, I took off, slipping and sliding my way along the wood floors, wishing that I had boots on instead of these death traps. But I never expected, when I dashed out of my apartment not even an hour ago, that I'd soon be running for my life from a deranged lunatic.

Where had he said he was from… Reset? Like… reset the fucking channel, because this shit was too whack for even the sci-fi streaming service.

I couldn't hear anything behind me, and I was too terrified to look back, because that was how you tripped over in the dark, hit your head, and got eaten by the big bad monster. In this situation, it was a gorgeous monster at least, but unless he was eating me in ways that had orgasms rolling in, I was fairly keen to skip the next part.

A sob escaped when I made it to the stairs, my eyes adjusted enough to the dark that I managed to make it down without injuring myself. On the final step, I went to jump onto the wood floor, adrenaline pumping through my veins, only to slam against what felt like a rock, sending me shooting back into the stairs. I caught a glimpse of those green and gold eyes seconds before I crashed to the floor.

As predicted, the hit was hard enough that my head cracked against the edge of the step—its second bashing tonight—and everything went dark.

CHAPTER
SEVEN

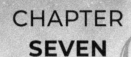

Consciousness returned with a painful throb, the jolt of pain in my head intensifying when I attempted to open my eyes. As I did, the events that led to me being unconscious on the floor returned. *Drager had been chasing me.* And then somehow appeared in front of me, knocking me back into the stairs.

Despite my best efforts, I'd managed to live out my very own, *stupid heroine in a horror movie* moment. Lexie would be so proud of me.

As more of my senses came back online, a terse argument happening nearby started to register. One voice was the *sun god*— the distinct rasp of his words would stay with me for the rest of my life, however long or short that was going to be. And the other sounded a lot like… *Lexie?*

What the fuck?

With a groan, I pushed myself up. Or at least attempted to. I was no longer on the hard winding stairs, resting instead somewhere infinitely softer. The noise of the party was still prevalent in the background, and if anything was a little louder here, so I'd hazard a guess that we were on the ground floor in one of the side breakrooms. There were beds and showers there, not that Lexie or I had ever used them.

Whatever noise I'd made pulling myself into a sitting position drew the attention of the pair arguing in the doorway—one a stunningly beautiful chick with a familiar pixie haircut, and the other a dangerous, sexy-as-sin "god."

"Lexie?" I rasped, shaking my head, wondering why she suddenly looked a little glow-y as well. Had to be a concussion. "Is that really you?"

She rushed to my side, dropping down to land on the floor next to me. "Morgan! You're in so much damn trouble, bestie. How could you run off into the night without me? You could have been killed."

Blinking more rapidly, because a glowing light was definitely seeping from her dusky skin, I tried to make sense of everything. "You just said damn."

That was all that managed to slip out before another strike of pain in my head had me hunching forward.

"I think this situation calls for something a little stronger than ibuprofen," Lexie murmured, her cool fingers brushing across my temples. The pain subsided briefly as she touched me.

Tonight was just becoming too much.

Could any of what I'd just experienced be true? Could my library really be some sort of supernatural haven, a portal to another world?

This had to be the concussion speaking, right?

"I'm so sorry, Morgs," Lexie whispered, still stroking my head with her cool touch. "I never wanted you to find out like this. I wanted to ease you into the truth."

Pulling away from her, I swallowed roughly. "You think you're one of them too. A god from Reset."

"Risest," she said with a lopsided smile. "But close enough."

The way she said it, it almost sounded like *resist*, but with more emphasis on the e.

"I just… I don't…" I shook my head once more. "How can you expect me to believe what that lunatic was saying? I mean, it's more farfetched than most of the books we read. *And they're high fantasy!* How can our library be a doorway to another world, and that dude over there…" I tossed my head toward the doorway filled by Drager. "…is a fucking sun god?" A snort escaped me. "Oh, and even better, you all speak English."

The twitch in Lexie's lips grew, and I was starting to understand how she was so otherworldly beautiful. And how she never displayed any obvious cultural signs of being raised by Japanese parents, despite clearly agreeing with me when I'd guessed that was her country of birth. Apparently, she was just happy I was too stupid to see through her lies and deception.

She was not Japanese. She was not even freaking human.

"I might have… embedded… our language into your mind long ago," she said with a shamed expression. "Since I occasionally slip into it without thinking. Figured it would be easier if it sounded like English to you. You even reply in faerie to me sometimes, and it still sounds like English to you."

Violence wasn't my nature, but right that second I wanted to hit her. The betrayal slammed hard and hot into my center, leaving an icky, oily feeling behind. My chest hurt bad enough that breathing stalled for a few seconds, but I knew there was no time to fall completely apart.

These crazy *creatures* or whatever they were still posed a rather immense danger to me. Hitting them would only hasten my death, and I still hoped to avoid that altogether.

Forcing my voice to stay even, I said dully, "I'm going to need you both to explain everything to me really fast, and then I want to go home and pretend none of you exist."

Lexie's face fell. "Morgs. Please. You're my best friend and no truth changes that."

It changed it for me. I'd been lied to for years, and I didn't know what to believe or who to trust.

Crossing my arms, I scooted away from her and she let out a sigh. Standing, she dropped her hands to hang listlessly at her sides, and turned to look at Drager. "What can I tell her?"

He shrugged. *God* of many words apparently. "Enough that she understands but not too much that I have to kill her."

That was the first plan I'd heard since coming here that I could get behind.

Lexie paled, and I realized that I'd been wrong before about the arguing I'd thought I heard. It must have been a discussion that sounded heated in my frazzled head, because she was clearly afraid of this guy. He was not her equal in any way. He was her superior.

When she turned back to me, there was no smile. "I'm sorry that I kept the truth from you, but you'd never have believed me without proof. Not to mention it was—and still is—way safer for you not to know about any of this."

Possibly true, but that didn't make it any easier to swallow that so much of our friendship was built on lies.

"My name is Lexical Lightsbringer," she said with a sigh. "I'm not a god, as you said before, but a fae from the land of Risest. There are only a few gods in Risest, and they're our leaders. I was born in the land of Ocheran, which resides under the call of Drager the Sun God, and when he ordered me years ago to Earth to keep this portal functioning, I went without hesitation. We aren't a submissive group, but we never refuse an order from the gods."

"You went to my college," I whispered, shaking my head. There was no physical pain now that she'd done her *faerie magic* on me. Yep, it was as ridiculous as it sounded, but I couldn't deny that I'd been suffering from what felt like a concussion, and now I was completely pain and nausea free.

Lexie shrugged. "I was curious. After some time with humans, I decided I wanted to assimilate further. It was all part of keeping this property as safe as I possibly could."

Looking past her, I found Drager watching me closely. "And you were happy with her prancing off into the human world? Weren't you worried about keeping your secret?"

His expression was cool. "Lexical knew the rules, and she's one of my best and brightest fae warriors. She begged for you to be brought in to work the library. I was against it from the start, but she insisted you could be trusted. Boring. Without ambition. Content to shelve books."

Reverting my gaze from him back to Lexie, I noticed that her cheeks were slightly pink, eyes downcast. "That's not exactly how I phrased it, but I was more interested in ensuring you could work with me. That you could stay where I'd protect you."

"Why?" I shot back. "Why would you bother? I'm just a lowly human. You are both clearly filled with some sort of energy or magic. Humans must be like animals to you."

"No!"

"Yes."

They answered at the same time. No need to wonder which one of them thought of us as the baser species.

"I should go," I said, sliding my ass to the edge of the bed, dropping my legs over the side. "I honestly don't think I can handle one more revelation. You can keep your magical library, where Reset *faeries* pop over during our night to borrow books and bulk up on energy, and I'll go back to my parents and allow them to smother me until I forget this shit ever existed."

Lexie stomped her foot. "Not a chance. I will never allow you to go back into those manipulative narcissists' house. They gaslight you into doing everything they want."

Pushing myself to stand, I met her near eye to eye. "Pot meet fucking kettle," I sniped. "Lexical Catfisher is your new name."

She arched an eyebrow. "Catfishing and gaslighting are not the same thing."

"I fucking know," I shouted, throwing my hands in the air. "I. Fucking. Know. You did both, and you're a shitty person—fae, whatever—and that's all that matters."

Apparently there was no one in my life who wasn't a shitty individual, and maybe that said more about me than anyone else. I was the problem.

Lexie let me move around her, her expression crestfallen but she made no attempt to stop me. When I reached the doorway, Drager remained exactly where he'd been—filling the entire exit with his bulk.

"Excuse me," I said shortly. "You're in my way."

A low rumble rocked his chest, and I heard Lexie move closer, only pausing when Drager leveled a dark look on her. Then he returned that glare to me. "You're not afraid of me," he said with soft menace. "Why?"

Tilting my head back, and then farther again because he was one tall *sun god*, I let out a sad snort of laughter. "Dude, I'm terrified of you. But I'm also tired, confused, a little broken, with no idea what my future is now. Most of that is equally as terrifying."

He examined me closer, and somehow I didn't squirm. "What's a dude?"

Oh shit. "Uh, a very cool person," I shot back quickly. "A very, *very*, cool friend."

He didn't seem to believe me. "Tell me about this voice you heard in the room when you returned the book."

The segue almost gave me whiplash, but I managed to contain my surprise. "It was just a feminine voice saying thank you. Though she did call me human, come to think on it."

"Was there anything else?" he pressed, and it felt like he moved closer, even though he clearly was in the same position. Somehow I felt more crowded.

"Uhhh—" I honestly couldn't think of what else to tell him. "Nope. That was it."

He was definitely closer now. "Would you recognize her voice if you heard it again?"

I didn't even have to think about that one. "Yep, for sure. She had a very distinct sound, and it's still clear in my head."

I had a great memory for voices and faces; it was names that often eluded me.

Drager clapped his hands together, and more light burst from between his palms briefly. His skin remained in its normal low simmer of glow. "Fantastic, you will accompany us to the party and speak with the ones I suspect. We should have our traitor by morning."

Traitor? By. Morning?

Shit. *Was this really happening?* And did I really believe that this was actually a gateway for the supernatural, or was I about to be taken advantage of by a bunch of delusional beings?

If Lexie wasn't here, confirming what Drager had said, I'd be running and screaming again.

But despite all evidence telling me I shouldn't, I still trusted her, and that meant I had no choice but to believe what had been said.

Supernaturals existed, and it seemed I was about to go on a hunt for one.

The list for my therapist was just getting longer and longer at this point, but to survive what was about to happen next, I had to go with the flow.

Tonight I'd pretend this was all part of a story I'd read, and then tomorrow I could run screaming for the hills.

CHAPTER EIGHT

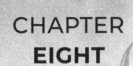

D rager moved out of the doorway, allowing me to finally squeeze by.

"Okay, so how will this work?" I asked. I didn't consider myself a super anxious person, but I also thoroughly researched all new situations so I'd be as prepared as possible before stepping into them. Preparedness saved a lot of inner turmoil and embarrassment.

Drager's expression as he turned back to meet my gaze indicated that he had a bad taste in his mouth, and I was fairly certain that taste was caused by my presence. Well, tough fucking luck, sun boy. It wasn't as if I'd asked to be here at his mercy.

"I need to dress you for a ball," he said shortly. "No point tipping them off to your humanity. The magic of the clothing from my realm will mask the obvious signs."

Ah, there he went with the grimace again. It almost amused me that he found my presence so distasteful, since there was little else I could do to irritate him.

"I can dress her!" Lexie piped up.

Drager shot her a dark stare. "You are compromised by your feelings for this human. I'll keep her in my sights for now."

Lexie shot me a commiserating smile.

"Am I safe with him?" I asked, completely uncaring that the sun god could hear me.

"Uh..." She hesitated briefly, before sucking in a deep breath and nodding. "While he has use for you, you are safe. I make no promises after that."

Great. Just fucking great.

Shifting my stare up to his face again, I shook my head. "If you kill me, I will come back and haunt your every waking moment until your brain is frazzled and your nerves are shot. Humans can do that, you know."

From the corner of my eye, I caught sight of Lexie swiping her hand across her throat in the *stop whatever you're doing* gesture. Too late at this point. "Did you just threaten me?" Drager said, voice deceptively calm, but *was it getting hot in here?*

"Me?" I squeaked, backing up a step. "Never. You must have misheard."

His skin's glow intensified, and it burned into my retinas as my eyes watered like they were literally leaking. "I never mishear. I never make a mistake."

"God of the sun," Lexie called, raising her voice to be heard over his power. Which was weird, right? Power shouldn't have a sound. "Don't forget that she's the only one who can identify the spy in our midst."

He turned toward her, and I felt the mildest reprieve in not being his sole focus. "I never forget."

Drager leaned in close, but he didn't touch me. "Follow me," he rumbled, and despite the very real danger he presented, my body still chose that moment to remind me that it had been a literal year since I'd had sex. My multitude of vibrators and spicy fantasy books got me by, but they weren't the same as a man.

I knew I should fear the sun god, and I did, but there were other emotions at play here too. He was the sexiest, scariest, most desirable *being* I'd ever seen.

The fact that he was more inclined to kill me than fuck me and I still found him sexy was something to add to the list for therapy. If I survived the next few hours, I would finally make that appointment.

Drager left the room then and I did as I was told, scurrying after him, not even sparing a look for Lexie-the-traitor. If she'd just come clean with even a tiny bit of her true identity and reason for being here, I'd have never risked my life and barged into the library tonight. Would I have believed her without the very other-worldly presence of Drager? Who the hell knew, but she could have at least tried.

Some of the fault here lay with her, and I had already added her to the list of people I would have to haunt in my murdered afterlife. Because we all knew that as soon as I was done being useful for this sun god, I was getting fried into a human roast.

I followed him from the room and into another small storage closet that I'd never used, but I remember it being referred to as for *miscellaneous equipment that you don't have to worry about* by Simon during my orientation tour. The door opened for Drager before he touched it, and despite the light emanating from his skin, the darkness inside the closet remained completely impenetrable.

"This is another portal to Risest," he told me. "The same as the room where the special editions are returned. Don't ever try to use them without me, or you'll be destroyed the moment you step into the vortex of power."

I nodded rather frantically. "No intention of ever entering either room on my own," I verbally confirmed.

Drager huffed like he absolutely didn't believe a word I said. Probably because I was a *dirty, stupid human.*

He continued into the room, and I followed as close as I could without touching him. The darkness remained for one second, and then it was like walking through a curtain and we were suddenly bathed in light, the obvious signs of a large closet around us.

Blinking, I tried to take it all in, from the beams of warm light shooting through the skylights above, to the floor-to-ceiling shelves holding row after row of clothing.

"This is my home, *Lancourt,* which floats above the land of Ocheran, in Risest," Drager said shortly. "I like to be in the sky, closer to the sun, to increase my power. Your human form will probably handle the energy of Lancourt for no more than thirty minutes of time as you understand it. Which means we must hurry."

Thirty. Minutes? Was he fucking serious? "Why bring me here at all?" I squawked, looking around like the walls were about to crash in on me. I could feel it on my skin, the energy he spoke of, tingling and caressing my exposed hands, neck, and face.

"Because wearing clothes made from my power would destroy you as well," he said without inflection, "and I need you to live long enough to finish the task."

"How magnanimous of you," I shot back, smiling my sweetest smile. Sweet with *screw you* undercurrents.

Hooded eyes locked on me. "Just because I choose not to use sarcasm doesn't mean I don't understand when it's being used."

"Good for you, bro. Good for you."

Drager just shook his head, and I had my suspicions that he was mentally reminding himself that he needed me alive. I was essentially safe until I found his traitor. So I'd say whatever I wanted.

"We only have thirty minutes," I reminded him. "Better dress me up like your own personal doll."

That got me a withering stare but he didn't bother to reply. Turning away, he strode toward the end of the closet, which was loaded with clothing. "There should be something left here by one of the ladies of my court," he muttered, ignoring my presence.

Finally we reached the back shelves, and tucked in amongst some armor, were a few long dresses. One was red, another white, and the final a deep rich burgundy. Peering around his bulk, I eyed the three of them. "If you can create clothing, you know, for those not so weak and gross like humans, why do you have a closet?"

"I don't create clothes for anyone but myself. This room is used by the rest of my court. The cloak room."

The cloak room. Okay then. *Sure.* Just a room that was the size of my apartment back home was the cloak room to his court. "Why would a god have a court? Aren't you an isolated sort of creature, more content to sit alone and count your power?"

He might not do sarcasm, but he had the withering stare down fucking pat. "Gods require worship to elevate our natural power. I cultivate my worshippers here and in the library. Between the building storing energy, and those who borrow my books sending me energy each time they do so, I have more than enough." He paused. "To count."

His hand whipped out past me and I flinched, but he was just grabbing the deep burgundy dress. "Even you, little human. I know your essence since it's touched so many of my books. I could find you anywhere."

He thrust the dress into my hands then and I forgot to breathe for many seconds.

Was that another threat? If so, why were my damn panties so wet?

I really needed to get my priorities straight.

Tonight, was about surviving, not fucking a sun god. Judging on the size of him, he'd kill me in one... uh, blow.

Yep.

No blows for me. Shame.

CHAPTER
NINE

The sun god refused to leave me alone to get dressed, so I just turned my back, dropped the pjs into a pile, and shimmied my way—sans bra—into the dress he'd pulled from the hanger. I might not be hugely experienced, but I wasn't shy. Not like I had to worry about him checking out my curves and wanting to bang me—sadly.

Stepping into the dress, at first it appeared that the burgundy number was just a normal ballgown, with a corseted top and full-bodied skirt that spread out around me. Until I pulled it tighter against my body and the impossibly soft, silkiness of the material reminded me that all of this was very far from *normal*.

The tingling across my skin increased as I attempted to lace the back, and I felt the resignation of Mr. God as he moved closer.

"Do not move," he ordered. "Your wiggling is going to get you killed."

Would I die from the burn of his energy? Or the burn deep in my body? Drager's presence was an aphrodisiac, and I was half tempted to ask him if we could just quickly screw and get it out of the way. Of course, the whole *he thinks of you as an animal* put a bit of a damper on that plan.

"It's the power," he rumbled suddenly, and I was jerked out of my own head and the sexual fantasies there.

"Excuse me?" I gulped.

"The reaction you're having to me is purely due to my power."

He didn't sound angry. It was a clinical sort of statement, and weirdly it helped calm the ragged nature of my thoughts.

"So, I haven't just suddenly turned into a bitch in heat, needing to rut against any other creature around?" *Dammit, Morgan!* Why did I have to use an animal analogy when this asshole already thought of me that way? I was my own worst enemy.

"No… it's just because you're human and weak. Nothing else."

Ah, there he went, putting me firmly in my place.

But at least I understood now I wasn't losing my mind. This was all his damn fault.

Excellent. I loved to place blame exactly where it deserved to go.

He laced me up in a split second, faster than would be humanly possible, faster than I would have thought was possible for any being, even those supernatural. Did a god count as a supernatural? Or were they even higher in the hierarchy of powerful beings?

I had so many questions, my mind burned and hummed with everything I didn't understand, from Risest to this land here— what had he called it… Lancourt? How did it all work? Was Risest the country or the world? Did this world consist of only one land, maybe? Hence why it was all called Risest. Did he rule a lot of fae, or were those other gods Lexie mentioned more powerful than him?

The need for knowledge was a driving force, but it would have to wait, since Drager was apparently done. Without a word, he moved toward the exit of this closet, and I hurried to follow him. As I walked, I felt a brush of heat along my spine, and then black boots appeared on my feet, followed by my bedhead hair falling into long perfect curls.

"You can withstand my energy for a short time in small doses," Drager called over his shoulder. "These little touches shouldn't bother you."

Little touches needed to convince the fae that I was one of them.

When we exited through the door of his cloak room, we stepped through the portal back to Dragerfield. When I returned to the library, under the guidance of Drager himself, I felt like a twenty-ton weight lifted from my chest. I hadn't even realized how cloying the energy from Lancourt had been until we returned.

The fact that all of this was nearly unbelievable hovered in the back of my mind, but I refused to let my shock and disbelief emerge. If I truly thought about what was happening here, my human brain would crumble. For now, this was just a really cool story I was in the middle of reading.

"Okay, your mission is simple."

Drager gave me his full attention, and I almost missed what he said under his mind-boggling presence. "You will take a few turns around the room, have Lexie introduce you so you can hear their voices, and if you find my book thief, you let me know. I will send a few fae your way as well, since this will also be about eliminating members of my land as suspects."

I opened my mouth, but there was little point, since he'd already turned and walked off into the main ballroom, leaving me standing in the wings. A few moments later, Lexie pranced into view, dressed for a ball too. She wore white with lots of lace, and while her gown wasn't as puffy as mine, it had a lot more intricate detailing across the corseted top. The light color highlighted her complexion perfectly, and without needing any makeup—should have known this bitch was supernatural—she looked stunningly beautiful.

"Morgan!" she exclaimed as she came to a halt beside me. "You look incredible. It was almost as if the fae clothing were made just for—"

"Let's get this over with," I muttered, interrupting her. When her cheerful expression fell, I felt like an absolute asshole. I managed not to apologize, despite really wanting to, mostly because she might think of it as forgiveness. And we weren't close to that yet.

Far from it, actually.

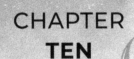

CHAPTER
TEN

As I'd predicted when peering over that balcony—what felt like hours ago now—there was no way to really take in the ball until you were standing there, on the main floor.

Down here, the lights weren't particularly bright. If anything, there was a mysterious air in this huge space, with purple, pink, blue and silver lighting making up most of the illumination.

The room was full of people—well, I guess not people, but magical fae.

"You doing okay?" Lexie whispered, staying close to me as we pushed into the room.

A few curious faces turned our way, and when I really paid attention, it was clear that many bore little resemblance to humans. Complexions were tinted in shades of yellow and green, with eyes ranging from pure black to glittering gold—and every shade between—all without a sign of defined pupil and iris. Many had pointed ears and extra appendages, and there were a lot of fae who wore no indication of race, gender, or even species.

Maybe they didn't even have race, gender, or species. I knew fuck all about these creatures, but I was clearly no longer in the human world.

"Morgs?" Lexie pushed, reminding me that she'd just asked how I was doing.

"Fine," I bit back tensely, wanting to freak out, but forcing myself to deal as best I could. "Let's get this over with."

She swallowed her frown, a strained smile appearing on her face. "Okay, well, the best place to start is near Lord Drager. Everyone and their pet selkie will be there to greet him, and we can hear them speak."

Lord Drager. Like he was so fucking important. Yeah, sure, he was a god and all that, but… Okay, there was no *but* in this situation. Being a god kind of trumped everything, and yet I was still annoyed by his existence.

Stupid sexy god with his stupid sexy voice.

"Morgan," Lexie snapped, sounding more like her old self. "Are you listening to me?"

I hadn't been. Not even a little. "Sorry, what did you say?"

She shook her head. "I said that there are a lot of dangerous creatures in this room. Don't be fooled by the beauty and glamour. Most of it is literal glamour, hiding their true natures. Even Drager. His other form would terrify you. You should hope it doesn't come out to play."

I didn't reply, because what the hell could I say? I was just the prey in the midst of predators; the best thing to do was stay silent and get this job over with. Though I'd be a liar if I didn't admit to a tiny, *tiny, tiny* sliver of curiosity about Drager's other form.

I mean, he was a beast of a man, and my favorite hero in the magical movie realm might have been a bit of a beast… so, this was just normal human curiosity, right?

In truth, the sun god in his *humanoid* form was too much for my poor human hormones, let alone if he turned into something more…beastly.

As we got farther into the room, I noticed there was a large dance floor filled with fae. There was no awkward prom-style swaying here though. These magical folk moved in synchronized and stylized dances that were apparently universally known. I blinked as I noticed that a few of them weren't even touching the ground, small, shimmery and translucent wings lifting them to drift a few feet above the marble.

There were many signs of magic, and as sparkles of energy flashed over the dance floor, my skin tingled like when I'd been in Lancourt.

"Come on," Lexie said, jerking me from my daze, moving us away from the largest crowd. "The djinn won't let us through the dance floor; they trap you in the music. It's best if we go around."

Djinn. I'd only ever read about them in books, of course, and I found my gaze swinging back to examine that dance floor once more. I had no idea which dancers in particular were the djinn, but I found myself pausing on a large group of mostly males, shirtless with black fitted pants, who were right in the center of the dancing. Their skin was a shimmery red, and they all had the same short black hair and slitted dark eyes. One on the edge caught my eye and flashed pointed teeth at me, while crooking an extra-long finger as if to say *Come a little closer*. Fucking hell.

With shivers racing down my spine, I hurried to keep up with Lexie, averting my eyes so I wouldn't accidentally catch the attention of someone who wanted to eat me. We ended up near a platform off the left of the dance floor. Here sat a large chair, black and red, with a high back and lots of sparkling stones embedded in the carved frame. Upon this chair was the sun god, holding vigil with his people.

Since he'd walked away from me, I'd been mentally downgrading Drager, convincing myself I'd imagined how gorgeous and powerful he really was.

Wishful thinking.

As he sat up there, filling that huge chair, legs slightly spread as he sprawled back and observed the scene before him, my body reacted in a way that was definitely not appropriate for a public space. Why did he have to be so enticingly attractive? *Why?*

He was every book boyfriend I'd ever dreamed of wrapped up in one package, and he'd probably be the reason I died today.

If there was a walking red flag in a book, that was my man.

Apparently, the same went for real life.

Typical.

CHAPTER
ELEVEN

Drager didn't seem to notice Lexie and me as his bored gaze spanned out across the top of the crowd. A crowd that was pressing as close as they dared to get to him, all of them dancing and preening before the sexy god.

A small group near the base of his platform were dressed in what looked like cream linen wrapped strategically across their breasts and butt. Each piece was extravagantly adorned with jewels and glittery objects. Their complexions were pale pink, like a new rose, and they all had very long green hair, thick and coarse, almost like seaweed, that danced with their movements.

"Nymphs," Lexie whispered. "They feed off sexual energy and will stay near Drager because he's essentially sex on legs."

Okay, then. Apparently, I wasn't the only one who'd noticed that about him.

"He's about to start the greeting," she said, pushing me a few steps closer to the gyrating nymphs. "I don't really understand why he didn't just bring you up there with him in the first place."

Probably because he didn't want to be near me any longer than was necessary.

Drager straightened, some of the "bored" in his expression clearing, and that was all the nymphs needed to know their time for basking in his glow was done. They faded away like they'd never been there, and then a line started to form for this official greeting event.

"Why does he appear at these parties," I asked, keeping my voice low, "when he clearly hates this more than my existence?"

I might have thought he'd missed our presence in the crowd, but as I said that his sharp gaze snapped to me. My ability to freely breathe ended as he coldly examined me. *Yep.* No doubt about it, he hated me with a passion.

"Gods that forget their people fade from existence," she whispered back. "Drager is one of the most powerful, and he won't ever let that go. This also cements our loyalty to him, and he's huge on loyalty."

The first in the line moved up to the platform toward Drager, stopping a respectful three feet away. I couldn't see much of the fae before him, but I did note a small set of curved onyx horns poking up from a mass of dark curls.

"Chaple," Lexie said. "He's a satyr. He's actually pretty good friends with Drager. He's not one you need to worry about."

I pushed in closer this time, hovering on the edge of the stage so no one would mistake me for cutting in line. Unfortunately, I was still too far away to make out the conversation clearly, and there was no way I could identify a voice from here. From this angle though, I noticed that Chaple's legs were definitely curved and hooved in a way that told me he might be exactly like the satyrs of human mythology.

I kept edging forward while Drager conversed with Chaple, the two seemingly happy to chat, even as everyone waited in the forming line. It was apparent that faerie folk were much more patient than humans. None of them fidgeted or looked toward the stage with annoyance. They either stood still and silent or spoke quietly together.

Others remained back on the dance floor, maybe waiting for the line to grow shorter, or maybe they didn't care for Drager.

Or more likely they feared him.

Edging even closer, I was starting to draw attention from those in the line, and I felt Lexie latch on to my arm as if to draw me away, when there was a rumble from the stage.

I tilted my head back and looked up in time to see a monster god above me. Drager reached down and wrapped huge hands around my biceps, lifting me right up onto the stage. "What part of stay out of fucking sight don't you understand?" he muttered. For a moment, I wished to hear those words in his native tongue, wondering what fae curses sounded like. Lexie made my life easier by embedding their language into my mind, but it also humanized these beings.

There was nothing human about Drager, and I wanted to experience it all.

My skin burned under his touch, but not as extreme as before. I wouldn't say I was getting used to his energy—*impossible*—but it wasn't taking me by complete surprise now. My body was learning to anticipate the rush of power that being near Drager brought.

"You dragging me onto the stage is hardly going to help," I muttered back, making sure to keep my words low. "I couldn't hear what was being said, and it's kind of important that I do. Right?"

This was his brilliant fucking plan.

"Hence why you're on the stage," he snapped back. "Now sit down and stay quiet."

Somehow a small padded stool appeared at his side, by his feet. Like I was his goddamn pet. Whatever. I just had to get through this one task for him, hope he didn't decide to kill me in the end to hide this secret, and then I'd never have to deal with him again.

"Next," Drager called, that bored look returning to his face as he sank into his massive throne chair. If that bastard patted me on the head I was going to bite him on the hand. I'd show him *pet*.

And if he called me a good girl...

My body froze up, and I had to breathe through my hot flush then, because *damn*...

"Lord..."

I was distracted by a bowing fae. She bent so low before Drager that her nose almost touched the ground. She wore a full-skirted gown in teal green that contrasted nicely to her auburn hair which reached to her toes, braided back from her face in an intricate pattern, littered with flowers and what looked like vines. She had olive skin, large green eyes, and a neutral expression on her face as she rose to her full height and regarded Drager.

"Approach," Drager drawled.

She took a few steps forward.

"Place your honor," Drager added in that same rumble of annoyance he did so well.

"Of course, Lord," she went on quickly. "I am Lady Florentine of the House of Green Hollow. We have bestowed fifty new ravens upon your land for protection and observation. We hope you are pleased and honored." She dropped a single raven feather at his feet, all of us staring at it before Drager turned his gaze and caught my eye, his expression questioning.

I gave a very subtle shake of my head. She wasn't the one from the room.

Lady Florentine had a light and airy tone, without that unique huskiness that had been in the other voice.

"I accept your honor," he said, waving his hand to dismiss her. She smiled brightly and bowed once more before turning and leaving the stage. Just as she left, she shot one brief, confused glance my way before she disappeared into the crowd.

This continued on and on, with everyone announcing their offering and *honor* to Drager, and he would give me a brief glance before dismissing them when I shook my head.

Exhaustion pressed in on me as I shifted in the chair, the lines of fae continuing into the early morning hours. I was just despairing of ever finding who had spoken in the library and stolen his book, when there was a commotion near the back of the room. It sounded as if a hundred windchimes had been struck at once.

Drager lifted his head briefly, as if it was unexpected.

Unexpected for the god who created and controlled this place made me uncomfortable.

From my position *at his feet,* I couldn't see through the crowd, and when Drager stood, I desperately wanted to follow but decided it was better just to remain where I was.

"Lexie," Drager snapped, and my friend was on the stage in a heartbeat. I hadn't seen her nearby during this meet and greet, but she must have been there.

"Lord?" she said quickly.

"Is that the call for fertility?"

Lexie paused for a brief second, before she went deathly pale, her eyes meeting mine. "It is," she whispered. "It's early this year."

I found myself rising because this didn't feel like information I should hear while seated.

"What does this mean?" I whispered.

"Is it too late to get her out of here?" Lexie whispered back, ignoring my question.

"Yes," Drager said gruffly. "Seal the entrances. The dance of fertility must begin."

With that, there was a slamming of doors around the ballroom, and the lights dimmed low.

"Lexie," I whimpered, and she shook her head at me.

"Sorry, Morgan. I'd suggest finding someone appealing and see if you can ride out the next few weeks. Literally."

Literally? What the fuck had I gotten myself into?

CHAPTER
TWELVE

Drager growled, his chest shaking, and I briefly thought I saw midnight-purple scales ripple across his hands, but when I looked again it was just the same smooth dusky skin as always. "I'll take care of Morgan. She's a human, and this is a dangerous situation for her. I don't particularly care if she's torn apart *after* she identifies the traitor, but for now she's important. Whoever stole that book is part of the bigger picture. You know that."

Lexie nodded. "I know. I'll leave you to it, Lord."

Wow, I was feeling all the warm fuzzies from these two psychopaths this evening. Bastards continued to treat me like I was a dumb animal that had stumbled into their midst, and I was fairly sure I'd proven that I was more intelligent than a fucking animal. Well, most animals—

"Follow me, human," Drager said bluntly, and I realized I'd gone off on a rant in my own head and missed Lexie leaving. As I took in the rest of the room, it was clear I'd missed a little more than my traitorous former best friend's departure.

The chiming that had indicated the start of this *fertility call* must have been what set everything into motion.

"What's happening?"

I choked on my words, reaching out and touching Drager of my own volition, an action I'd been avoiding up until now. As our skin connected, there was a rush of energy between us so strong that I felt as if I should have been blasted back by the impact. Instead, my hand was bound to his forearm, and no matter how hard I tugged, there was no way to release the hold.

"What the fuck?" I cried, fear trickling like ants across my skin.

Only, it wasn't just fear. My skin was coming alive, burning and tearing, even as no visible signs of damage were present.

"Morgan," Drager growled. "You need to listen to me. We don't have much time before part two commences. Now that you've touched me, we're committed to being part of the ritual. There's no fucking choice. I might be a god, but I'm not beyond the natural order. It's the time of fertility, and it only happens once a year. To our misfortune, this is the day."

"Just one day?" I choked out.

He looked grave. "It runs for the next thirty Earth days." His eyes and expression darkened. "During that time, you belong to me, human. Mine to own, control, and destroy. You should start praying that your body can contain the force of mine, because there's no other choice. It is time."

The confusion and panic were too much for me to bear, and I wished that I could just pass out and wake up when this was all over. Because if I was reading this situation correctly, I was about to take part in a thirty-day faerie *fertility event*. Fertility made me think of only one thing, and when combined with Drager's warning, I knew I was in big trouble.

Another chime echoed through the room, louder this time,

sending literal vibrations inside my body, and with that my legs grew weaker as heat unfurled through my belly.

"You feel it now," Drager said softly. He'd pulled me to stand beside him, our limbs still touching, energy racing between us. "When you connected with me, I became your chosen partner in this mating dance. But we are human and god, which is not ideal. Usually, I leave before this event, but my distraction over the traitor has now left me to deal with the ritual."

He was talking faster, as if our time for coherent conversation was running out. The panic I'd been feeling was fading under the heat in my body. My breath came out in quick pants, and I hated how restrictive the dress felt on my sensitive skin.

"Everyone in this room will fuck." That blunt statement jolted me from my current obsession with how hot and bothered I felt. "They will fuck every which way with their chosen partner. They will stop to eat and drink and refuel with sleep, before they start again. The magic of this fertility ritual cannot be circumvented, and if you resist, you will be punished with enough pain to destroy your mind in less than a day. Do you understand?"

I nodded, swallowing roughly as my chest and throat tightened. At this point I had no idea if my reaction was fear or excitement, because the magic in the air was pushing me into wanting what Drager offered.

"This ritual fuels our people for the next full cycle of seasons," he told me softly, stepping even closer until my body was trembling. "Without it, there would be no new fae born, and we would weaken and eventually die out. Do you understand?"

I understood the basic concept of what he was saying, but there were so many questions in my head, so much confusion, that I'd be a liar to say I completely understood what was happening.

Not that it seemed to matter. Whether I understood it or not, I was part of this ritual now, and since the alternative was death, I was hoping that Drager didn't have a ten-foot god cock. Because one month of sex might actually be the death of me in that case. Or at least my vagina.

But fuck, what a way to go.

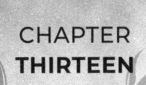

CHAPTER
THIRTEEN

T he third gong was where absolute chaos reigned across the room. The final beat of this ritual slid into place, and as clothes vanished from all the fae I could see in my peripheral vision, the need in my body grew. Small moans escaped from me, and now with both hands free I desperately tried to claw my dress off, the restriction too much to bear.

This fertility power was going to render me helpless to resist Drager, and while that might have felt somewhat rapey, in truth I'd been attracted to the sun god long before that first gong. Who the hell wouldn't be? It was a comfort, too, that he'd taken the time to explain everything as best he could, holding himself back and fighting the magic that was near driving me insane with need.

He wanted to make this as easy for me as he could under the circumstances, and that made it a tiny bit more bearable. I mean, sex with a god wasn't the worst way to spend a month. He'd also mentioned sleep, food, and drink, which were among my favorite activities.

Maybe I could just look at this as an all-expenses-paid sex holiday. I'd been meaning to do one of those.

"Human," Drager snapped. "You need to try and focus. For this to work—"

"You need to stop calling me *human*," I snapped back as my body arched and I moaned again, hands pressed to my tits as my nipples throbbed against the heavy material of the dress. The need in my body almost drew me to my knees. I wasn't surprised that resisting this for hours led to the sort of pain that would kill you.

Drager regarded me closely for a beat, and under his scorching gaze I burned hotter. "Okay," he nodded. "I won't call you human while we're together. We'll never be equals, but for this month it's as close as a human will ever get to a god. Especially since I need to infuse some of my power into you to ensure you survive."

My panting grew louder, and around us the room filled with the sound of pleasure. Desire was slick—deliberate use of that descriptor—in the air, and it heightened my own desperate need to get naked.

"Do you accept my offer, *Morgan*?" Drager rumbled, and there was a deep burning glow in his eyes, and this time I was much more certain I saw scales ripple over his skin. Those marks I'd seen earlier and assumed was a tattoo was actually in fact... scales. The need was getting to him too, and as I sank to the ground, unable to hold my legs up any longer, I could only sob and nod. Words were beyond me.

"The accord is accepted," he said, and then I almost screamed in relief when he reached down and sliced straight through the bodice of my dress. How he did so, I had no idea, I was too far gone to look for claws or anything of the like. Maybe he used his power. Maybe he had a knife. Whatever the means, I was just glad it was gone.

As my dress fell away, there was a beat of relief across my skin.

I never even knew that I could be this sensitive. Did the human body usually have enough receptors for this level of stimulation? The magic in this room had me feeling as if I was about to explode out of my skin.

I arched again, naked breasts bouncing in front of me as I lost control of myself. Drager growled once more, before he reached down and pressed a hand to my center, pushing me to the ground.

"You need to breathe," he told me, his voice rumbly but gentler than I'd heard from him before. "Breathe through this need and breathe through what is about to happen next."

In normal circumstances, I'd be panicking at those words. But hey, let's be real, in normal circumstances I wouldn't be in a room filled with naked *fucking* fae, and feel okay about it. These were not normal circumstances, and the way to get through this was to pretend it was all a weird sex dream, and that I'd wake up soon. In thirty days' time.

The hand pressing me to the ground did help with calming myself. His hold was an anchor, comforting when it felt like my body was out of control. Out of control in a way I'd never experienced before.

Drager's palm started to heat. A warm glow at first, but all too soon it was a searing, branding sensation against my bare skin. I arched again, whimpering, and the bastard almost looked as if he was enjoying this moment of domination over me. I couldn't move. I couldn't resist. Despite the pain, I needed what he was offering, and I pressed up into him.

"More," I gritted. "I need more, dragon."

His golden eyes turned dark, until they were stormy clouds. "What did you call me?" he rumbled.

I swallowed roughly. "Your name. It reminds me of 'dragon.' And you're so huge, and the scales…" I cried out as the heat burned me once more, and this time his power slithered under my skin. Insidious and foreign, it didn't mesh with my energy at all, until Drager muttered something I didn't catch, a language not English or Fae apparently, and with that his power fused to my soul.

The pain faded and suddenly that heat was everywhere. It felt so damn good, and without him even needing to move his palm from the space between my breasts, the swirling of energy in my center erupted and I arched as I cried out through my first orgasm.

Holy fucking fuck.

He'd done that without fully *removing my clothes.*

The next thirty days were going to be beyond all reality.

CHAPTER
FOURTEEN

Drager tilted his head to regard me, like he wasn't quite sure what he'd just tied himself to for a month. "You're responsive," he rumbled. "And your energy accepted mine easily. Interesting."

Was it interesting? Or was it really unimportant in the scheme of shit we were dealing with?

My panting increased as the swirls of desire built within me once more; the energy of this room and the spell were just too strong to fight. The rumbles in Drager's chest amplified as he continued to observe me like I was some enigma that had landed in his lap.

Guess that was the truth, though I knew there was nothing mysterious or particularly interesting about me.

Drager leaned down and scooped me up from the platform, pressing my naked breasts to his armored chest as he strode from the room. His firm hand against the back of my head stopped me from really seeing the mass orgy going on around us, but I could hear it perfectly well.

"I don't share," he growled as we left the main ballroom. "For thirty days you are mine, and there's no way they get to see your pleasure. Or take from our energy. We will participate only as much as we're forced to under the circumstances.

Forced. The word every woman wants to hear when they're about to be fucked senseless by a god.

Whatever. I knew what I was getting into, and I'd already made my peace with it.

Drager took us up the stairs, into the shelves, deep in the section with the oldest books. My favorite part of this building. I had no idea if he knew that somehow, or if maybe… this was his favorite part as well.

There was no bed here, but there was a table, and that's where he dropped my ass. Not that gently, but I welcomed the bite of pain against all the swirls of need inside me. It helped me deal with it.

"Are you feeling the desire at all?" I breathed, my voice a husky mess. I stared up into the dark clouds on his irises, and I loved that in this state his eyes weren't pure black orbs but a multi-faceted series of gray and navy.

"I'm feeling it," he reluctantly admitted. "No one escapes the most ancient of magicks. Not without a lot of prior planning."

The energy picked up, so intense that it sent me crashing back onto the table. Or it would have if Drager didn't reach out with super speed and catch me before I ended up with another concussion on top of everything else.

He gently sprawled me onto the huge, thankfully solid, wood table and stared down for a few unbearable moments. Then, in torturously slow movements, he started to unbuckle his armor. Piece by piece, he peeled it away, until I could see all of his smoky skin, with rippling muscles and so many abs that I'd never doubt him for a god. The scales sprinkled across his body in increments, usually with each swell of fertility magic.

A moan escaped me. I was clawing the table, my nails chipping against the grain. "Please."

There was no pride. There was only begging at this point.

When he ditched the rest of his thigh armor and pants, I sobbed. "Thank fucking god."

His smile was feral. "No need to thank me, hum— little one."

Arrogant bastard.

He stepped to the side of the table, and I finally saw… everything. *Fuck me dead.*

No, like literally, he was about to fuck me dead, because he had that god cock I'd been so worried about. Long, thick, and straight, it jutted out before him, and there were… scales… on it too, or were they ridges? God help me.

Was I ready for this? I mean, I *was for sure ready*, but could my body handle that size without real injury?

"The need will ease after the first fuck," he said as I writhed on the table like a lunatic. "I'm going to hurt you, but I will heal it after, so relax for me."

"Just break me, dragon."

Despite my fears, those words rang with truth, and it was official—I had lost my mind, and there was no going back.

Maybe I didn't want to go back.

Drager stepped to the side of the table, right between my open legs. He grabbed the tattered remains of the dress and tore it free, before his hands settled on my thighs, tight and firm, pressing them to the table, almost past the point of my flexibility, but I didn't care. Once again, the pain helped deal with the energy permeating me.

Heat flowed under his touch, slithering deep into the place

he'd already infused with his energy. I tried to jerk up against his hold, but I couldn't move. He was unmovable, and I was under his complete control.

The heat swirled harder and hotter in my gut, and my head spun as I cried out, waves of an orgasm taking me under with the touch of his energy once more. During this orgasm, he thrust that impressive cock forward. But despite me being wet, and so needy, already in the midst of orgasming, it took a long minute for him to work the head inside.

I was just too small for his size.

"Fuck," he muttered, before he released a long breath with a distinct fire scent to it.

Dragon was fitting more and more, even if I had no idea what he truly was.

"I'm going to have to help you adjust," he said swiftly, and I cried out as he withdrew the thick head.

"No," I said. "Please fuck me. I can take it."

He paused for a second, watching me closely, before he shook his head. "The spell is clouding your mind. Breaking you a little is fine, but I need you functioning for the next thirty days."

As I went to protest once more, he shocked the hell out of me by dropping to his knees between my legs. I tried to sit up to see what he was doing, but his hands left my thighs, shifting farther along my body to keep me locked down on the table.

"No." A growling command.

Then his mouth was on my pussy, swiping through the pooling moisture there, until he found my clit and circled it with hot strokes, all the while keeping me firmly pressed to the table.

The heat of his mouth was intense, and weirdly, I was starting to crave the burn.

The next orgasm built as he slowly circled my clit, tongue

sliding faster and faster as I mewled and cried out, desperately clawing the table once more.

I'd have no damn nails left by the end of this.

No doubt the least of my worries.

CHAPTER
FIFTEEN

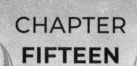

I t was becoming abundantly clear that when Drager set his mind to a task, he was *all* the way in. Total focus. He ate my pussy like it was his fucking reason for existence, spreading me wider and wider with his power, stretching me so I'd be able to fit that massive dick.

He didn't stop until I'd come so many times my head was spinning and I'd forgotten my name. He made the most delicious rumbles whenever I arched and came hard against his mouth like he was just as into this as I was.

It was very overwhelming to be under his sole focus, especially for a human who was used to being overlooked by men.

I wasn't the prettiest. Or the skinniest. I wasn't the most successful. Or super full of confidence. I didn't draw men in with my sexiness—I was the mousy bookworm relegated to the background. No matter how much Lexie touted my sex appeal.

But as I lay there, legs spread so wide that anyone in close proximity could have given me a pelvic examination, I didn't feel mousy. I felt alive, not to mention desirable and perfect for the god before me.

His power filled up parts of me that had been empty, shriveled and ignored. Parts that I'd neglected, or maybe didn't even know existed.

"I think you're ready now," he rumbled.

My ears weren't functioning very well, as my entire body had gone into orgasm overdrive. Maybe he'd said I was ready, or maybe he said that the world was ending. Who the fuck cared? As long as he didn't stop what he was doing.

When he got to his feet, he released me from his hold, and I was finally able to lift myself up. In a blind daze, I reached out and grabbed onto the closest thing to help me up, because this chick's stomach muscles were not made for sit-ups. No sir.

The hot, velvety hardness under my hand should have been my first indicator that I'd just used a very inappropriate handle to get up into a sitting position, and as I felt the thick ridges on either side of the long shaft, I let out a quick gasp and released him.

"Shit. Fuck. Oh my god."

I went to bury my head in my now cock-free hands, mortified by what I'd just done, when he let out a laugh. It was so weirdly unexpected, since I was fairly sure I'd only seen him smirk up to this point, and only when he was plotting my death.

"It's there to touch," he said when I lifted my head from my hands. "In fact, if you take your hands off me again, you'll be punished."

I blinked up at him, no doubt looking like a lamb in the face of a wolf. *Or dragon.*

"As fun as *being punished* sounds," I breathed, "I'll just go back to what I was doing."

Reaching out, I wrapped my fingers as far around his thick cock as I could, which was only a bit more than halfway. The shaft was a few shades darker than his body, and felt like steel under my grip. I spent a few seconds exploring the ridges that ran up and down the sides, almost from the base to the thick tip.

He was leaking pre-cum, and a sudden desperate need to taste him had me leaning forward and swiping my tongue across the slit there.

Damn.

I had no idea what possessed me. Me, a chick who had never even given a handjob, let alone a blowjob.

"Do that again," he ordered.

I didn't argue, leaning forward once more and swiping across the clear liquid. He tasted different than I expected, fresh and smoky, like droplets of pure water landing on a fire, letting off a sizzling smoky scent.

It was actually delicious, and I wondered if human males tasted like this too. Had I been missing out all these years?

I opened my mouth as wide as I could, but there was really no way to take more than just the very tip inside. So much teeth went along with that, and I soon gave up and went back to stroking and licking.

"Enough," he rumbled. "We need to keep working on your ability to fit me."

In the next heartbeat I was back on the table, legs spread wide before I could catch my breath. The taste of him remained on my tongue as he pushed that thick cock into me once more, and to my surprise, this time the pain was far more manageable.

Whatever he'd done with his mouth and power allowed my body to adjust enough to take his size. Inch by deliciously ridged inch, he pushed into me until I was so full I wouldn't have been surprised to see an indent of his cock pressing up from my stomach.

I mean, health class taught me that couldn't actually happen, but it was how it felt.

"You will take all of me by the end of this, and then you'll be ruined for all others."

Bastard sounded way too happy about that, and I had to hope that I wouldn't only be satisfied with a monster cock for the rest of my life. Because something told me there weren't many human men who were going to compare to Drager.

He thrust in further, his ridged length scraping over sensitive nerves, and once again this feeling was too much to handle. Gasping, I cried out as I reached up and gripped his forearms where he braced himself on either side of my body. He thrust again, slowly at first, before one of his hands slid under my ass and lifted me higher for better access. That left me holding on to one of his arms and trying not to lose what remained of my sanity.

With each thrust I cried out, and he rumbled, that smoky scent of his filling the room: "That's it, little one," he rasped. "Open up for me."

I couldn't deny him anything. I screamed as he thrust deeper and harder, feeling like he was rearranging my insides. He truly was going to ensure that I would never be satisfied with another. My pussy formed around his cock as if I'd been made for this god all along.

The heat of his power flowed through his dick and into me, each thrust burning with such intense pleasure-pain that I blacked out for a minute.

His power heated my clit as well, until the nub was engorged and desperate for release. The hand under my ass shifted, but somehow I stayed in the same position. His power was at work there. He brushed his thumb across my aching clit, swirling it in time to the thrusts, and I screamed and clawed at him, the pleasure too much to handle.

I never understood that saying—too much pleasure to handle —until this moment, when a god filled me with his power, fucking me so hard I was unable to control the reaction of my body.

"Again," he commanded.

My hips jerked, and he sank deeper. At least eighty percent of his cock was inside now, and I tried not to think about what he was crushing in there. All I felt was pleasure, but no doubt when this was done the other sensations would grow stronger.

"Little one," he growled, and I exploded once more, jerking so hard against him that I ended up smashing my head anyway. Not that any pain could make itself known with so much sparking pleasure.

What the hell was my orgasm count up to now? Ten? A million?

Drager leaned over farther, his thrusts harder and faster, and when his lips closed around my right nipple I dug my hands into his lush hair and held on for life. "Please," I begged. "Please never stop what you're doing. Please."

Yeah, there was no pride left in this needy bitch. I just required him to keep fucking me.

His teeth sank into my nipple, and I cried out and arched once more. I'd be an acrobat contortionist by the end of this. When Drager lifted his head, thrusting harder now that I'd adjusted, he shot me that wicked smile. "Oh, *little hum—one*, we're only just getting started."

My pussy tightened around him at those words and I exploded once more. The world went hazy around the edges. My voice was hoarse from all the cries and screams I'd released.

This time he exploded with me, his eyes darker than ever as his chest rumbled deep and very animalistically. The scales flitted across his skin, and it felt as if his cock was swelling. Not just swelling but also heating inside me.

"What…" I rasped, barely audible, "…is happening?"

Drager lifted his head and roared to the skies, and panic threaded through all the pleasure.

"What's happening?" I asked again.

His gaze slammed into mine. "This is the *sljorina*. The connection."

I had no idea what that meant, and if the fury was any indication, maybe it was best I didn't know. At least for a few seconds, I could exist in peaceful bliss.

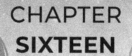

CHAPTER
SIXTEEN

"What is this connection?" I eventually asked in a huff, as he slowed the final thrusts of his orgasm, still buried inside me. His scales were gone, the darkness in his eyes receding back to golden-green, but the thick, burning swell of his cock hadn't abated. If anything, it continued to swell. And pulse.

With each pulse, I found myself arching and jerking against him in a continuous, slow-burn orgasm—a never-ending orgasm.

"We're compatible for breeding," Drager said with a deep growl. "My cock will knot inside you until I release all my seed for the best possible chance to conceive."

Fucking fuck! The spell had clouded my head to the point that I hadn't even thought to ask about pregnancy or disease. I mean, who would expect that a human could breed with a god anyway? "This is a fae connection?" I gasped, choking on my next breath.

Drager shook his head at what was no doubt a very panicked expression on my face. "Don't stress. It's only a side-effect of the spell, which will make the sex more intense."

Relief had me collapsing back against the table, before I arched into another swirling spiral of pleasure. "S-so… no chance of pregnancy?" I choked out.

He shook his head. "No. We cannot be compatible in that way. We are not the same."

Isn't that the fucking truth.

More heat burned inside me, and now that I didn't have to worry about pregnancy I could relax and enjoy the orgasms rolling through me in one continuous line. Drager groaned with each pulse of his knotted cock, and I could feel the combined release seeping out of me, so much cum from both of us that my poor human body couldn't contain it all.

It was the best fucking sex I could ever imagine having, and by the time all of his release was complete, I was near passed out. Enough consciousness remained that I felt Drager lift me from the table—like I weighed nothing, when that was absolutely not the case—and take me to a bathroom. I thought I heard him murmur words that sounded like *la moyar* as we walked but I was too out of it to know for sure.

When he stepped under the small shower, I whimpered as the water hit my heated, sensitive flesh. A moment later it burned hotter, which was the perfect temperature.

Apparently, when Drager's power was inside me, I enjoyed the heat even more.

He cleaned us, and I napped for a few seconds before he fucked me again, this time against the wall of the shower until I was once again screaming and crying his name. He slammed in so deep that when I orgasmed from it, I could taste him on my tongue. There was no knotting this time though, and I wasn't sure if that was a relief or disappointment.

The next thirty days passed in a blur of fucking, food, and more orgasms than most people probably experienced in a lifetime. Drager had made that throwaway comment on the first night about ruining me for other males, and I had no doubt at all that he'd succeeded.

The spell kept us hostage. Whenever he was near me, my body whimpered like a needy bitch. *I needed him*, the same as food, air, water. He was now a necessity to life, and I had no idea what I was going to do when the spell wore off.

"It's starting to ease," Drager said one morning near the end of our time. We were sprawled out on a bed he'd set up for us in the shelves, naked and breathing heavy. He traced fingers down my body, igniting nerve endings under the burn of his touch. "It's time to release the library and let it return to life as normal."

I jerked against his hold, my nipples screaming to be touched. "They'll all return to your world?" I whispered. "To Risest?"

It had taken thirty days, but I'd finally learned its name.

"Yes," he said simply. "And I will return to finding the traitor in my midst."

His fingers slipped down the front of my stomach, sliding over my clit and then pushing through my folds. He thrust inside of me slowly, and as I rode his hand, I forced myself to focus on every moment. On every touch. If this was my last day with him, then I would take every second of it in so I could keep these memories.

Something told me I'd need them to get through the many lonely years after this.

———

"We will reconvene here next month," Drager announced to the fae in his midst. "Return home with the knowledge that we have ensured the next generation of fae will be born—that the power of our world will be stronger than ever."

I stood off to the side, dressed for what felt like the first time in years. The clothes itched, foreign against my skin. It was just a random shirt and pair of soft shorts Drager had found for me, but the material chafed, and I tried not to mourn that this was the last moment I'd be here under the command of a god.

Those thirty days went by so fast, and having woken this morning without his cock inside me had me irrationally pissed.

"The doors have opened. Return home now," Drager said, and everyone in the room bowed to him and then left. Most of them had really enjoyed themselves too—from what I'd heard even secluded away in our little sex cave, or sex library as was the case.

When the room was empty, only one person remained there: Lexie.

I had no idea who she had ended up with during fertility month, but she had a very rosy glow to her cheeks now, looking satisfied in a way I'd never seen before. "Lord," she said as she moved over to Drager. "Are you leaving too?"

His eyes were on me, and I tried not to squirm under that burning gaze.

"I am," he replied gruffly. "I need to ferret out the traitor. I have a good idea where to start now."

Lexie's worried stare turned my way. "What about Morgan? What's going to happen to her?"

Scales briefly rippled over his skin. "She stays with me. I need her to confirm the traitor."

The heat burned deep in my center. A heat that was supposed to fade with the fertility spell, but it weirdly felt deeper and stronger than ever.

Lexie's eyes were wide, and she was blinking slowly like she couldn't quite understand. "Stay with you?"

Drager nodded slowly, and I took a step forward, needing to be closer to him.

Why did I still feel this way? The fertility energy was no longer holding my body hostage to its own desire and need. But some-how… Drager still did.

"How will she survive the energy of Risest?" Lexie asked, gaze darting between both of us. "Or even worse, Lancourt."

Drager moved so fast he was a blur as he reached my side. Towering over me, his stare was unwavering. "I have my ways."

I needed to breathe, but the air wouldn't escape my lungs. "I'm going to stay in Risest?" I gasped.

"You're going with me to Lancourt," he confirmed. "Until we find the traitor."

My pussy fluttered. *Legit.* As if it was shedding a cocoon and turning into a butterfly.

Drager hadn't made one mention of anything other than using me to find the traitor, but it didn't matter. My time with the god wasn't done, and that meant anything could happen.

I was ready for this adventure, even if it killed me in the end.

After being part of this magical world, my human life held no appeal.

"Let's go to Risest," I said, attempting to keep my voice even. "I'm ready."

His smile was darkly sinister, and I wondered what I'd just gotten myself into.

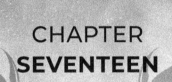

CHAPTER
SEVENTEEN

It was a silent journey back through the doorway. Even Lexie kept her thoughts and feelings to herself, and I hated the distance that had settled into our previously comfortable friendship.

The other fae must have already returned, since no one else joined us. The passing between worlds was seamless, and this time we ended up in a different room. "Not the cloak room?" I said with surprise, looking around.

Drager shook his head. "No, I can control where the final pathway leads, as long as it's in Lancourt."

He wasn't called a god for no reason.

The new room we stepped into was a large, white-tiled space, with pillars lining the edges. It was empty though, as if a thoroughfare between destinations. "This is one of the courtyards," Drager said shortly. "I'll send someone to show you to your room."

Before I could reply, he walked off, and I was left staring at broad shoulders moving rapidly out of sight—as if he couldn't get away from me fast enough.

And just like that, all my excitement at being here with Drager shattered in my chest, leaving a deep ache behind. Sucking in a deep breath, I reminded myself that this wasn't a romantasy story; there was no happy ending here for me with a god-dragon. My focus needed to be on finishing this job and eventually returning to my normal life.

Even if it took me a lifetime to forget about Risest and Drager, it'd be better than getting my heart broken.

"How are you feeling?" Lexie said, eyeing me hesitantly. She was dressed in her regular jeans and a black band tee, but even without Drager's energy amplifying hers, I could still see the flickers of magic around her—see the little *extra something*.

"The magical force of Lancourt isn't as bad as last time," I admitted. No doubt due to the swirling heat of Drager's power that remained deep inside me. Whatever he'd done to allow me to accommodate his energy and *er, size*, hadn't faded yet.

"How is this my life?" The muttered whisper escaped before I could stop it. A part of me had been in shock for the past month. The fertility energy—and Drager himself—was a massive distraction, but without both it really hit home.

Everything that had just happened... the last thirty days of my life...

"Morgs?" Lexie eyed me.

"This can't be real," I choked out. "None of it. Not the magic doorways, or the sun god, or his magic cock. I swear to fuck, I have to be in some sort of coma living out my best life."

Lexie's smile was sad, and she reached out to touch me, before clearly remembering that we weren't there yet. As she withdrew her hand, that sad smile faded into nothing. "This isn't your best life, friend. I wouldn't have written your story like this. You have so much love to give and you deserve the same in return. You deserve someone capable of unwavering loyalty, and unconditional, world changing love…"

What she hadn't said there told me everything. She was warning me not to fall for Drager, warning me that he wasn't capable of more than what he'd given at the library—facts I already knew, but it still bothered me. Swallowing hard to clear the lump in my throat, I shook my head and set my face so she wouldn't know the turmoil inside. "I'm under no delusion of a happily-ever-after with dragon man. This was just an itch to scratch."

And damn did he scratch it.

"You're going to be both hated and feared for what happened in Dragerfield House," Lexie said. "Everyone wants a piece of the gods, but very few ever get close enough to bathe in their presence, let alone touch them. You had Lord Drager for an entire month. That's virtually unheard of."

I was hit with an urge to close my eyes and relive the days when I'd belonged to the sun god. I could still feel the brand of his hands against my skin and taste him on my tongue, but I couldn't let myself go there. I had to keep my last threads of sanity by distancing myself from the fertility ritual. Drager clearly had already.

"There's no need to hate me for it," I managed to say, forcing images and memories out of my head, working desperately to keep my face blank. "I was just an available hole for him to plunge his massive di—"

My eloquent sentence was interrupted by the arrival of a familiar fae. Not that I knew him personally, but I remembered him all too well.

"Chaple!" Lexie said with a spark in her voice. A spark that told me she had a friendly and comfortable friendship with the satyr. "Are you in Lancourt for the next season?"

He gave her most of his attention, but I felt his curiosity as he side-eyed me as well.

"Yep," he rumbled, his deep voice had vibrational undercurrents that sent shivers down my spine. It was almost as if he bore magic in that voice. For all I knew he did. "Drager wants me to stay close until the end of the year, especially in light of the recent betrayals."

A thirst for information about this world reared its head inside me. If I spent my time here inhaling this fantasy world like it was my next life-changing book series, then it wouldn't be a wasted experience. Even if there was no future with the sun god.

Lexie nodded. "Yeah, once he figures out where the betrayal originated from, then life can go back to normal. At least until the Annual Academy Event."

Of course they had an academy. Was it even a fantasy story without one? And why the hell did my twenty-five-year-old self really hope I got a letter of admission to the academy? Was that too much to ask?

Chaple and Lexie continued to chat politely for a few seconds, talking about events and gatherings happening across Ocheran. Most of which meant nothing to me, so I spent my time observing the satyr as unobtrusively as possible.

When I'd seen him on the dais back in the library, the dim and moody lighting hadn't given me the clearest of pictures. I hadn't noticed the depth of animalistic quality to his features. His eyes were large and very dark, with ridiculously long lashes. His jaw was slightly elongated with sharp cheekbones. There was also hair —*fur?*—along his cheeks and up the sides of his nose. It wasn't super obvious, being short and only a shade darker than his brown skin. Those horns were shinier and more pigmented than I'd expected, buried in the mass of dark curls.

He was about Lexie's height, and wore a regular white button-up shirt, but his pants had clearly been designed to fit his curved legs.

He was utterly fascinating, and also completely adorable at the same time.

"…ready to go to your room?"

I caught the end of that rumbly sentence as their gazes focused on me. I cleared my throat instantly, and nodded, hoping Chaple hadn't noticed me gawking. "Yes, that would be great. It's been a long month." A really long month.

Chaple nodded, and it felt like there was a spark of under-standing in his gaze. Or maybe I was imagining it. "Don't worry, Drager is going to make sure you have everything you need. You're important to—"

For a split second I thought he was going to say him. *You're important to him*. But then he finished the sentence.

"—to this court. We appreciate your help in ferreting out the diseased flesh from the whole. Once it's cut free, then the rest of us will heal."

Nodding to cover up my stupid heartache, I forced a smile across my face. "Happy to do whatever I can to help—before I return to Earth of course. But in the meantime, I'd love to rest, shower, and change into clean clothes."

"Of course," Chaple said, and he moved closer to me, his thin lips spreading into a smile that was more wolfish than I'd have expected. Satyr was part goat, right? Or was I mixing up my mythical creatures?

Not that it really mattered. I got why I was trying to mesh this new fantastical world with familiar myths from home, but the truth was that Chaple was his own self. Which was none of my business.

He held his arm out toward me, and I linked mine through his, unsurprised by the strength of his limb under my light touch. Chaple might not be the tallest man I'd ever seen, but he was clearly muscular. I had a sneaky suspicion that he could probably lift a car over his head without much effort.

He led me from the white, empty courtyard, and we went in the opposite direction to where Drager had exited. Lexie tagged along with us.

"You can return to your post, Lightsbringer," Chaple said to her, tilting his head in a confused manner. "I've got Morgan Starrer from here."

I didn't even bother to ask how he knew my full name. It had been on my application form for the Dragerfield job, so no doubt it was easily obtained information for Drager.

"Morgan is my best friend," Lexie said firmly. "She's in this situation because of me. She's my responsibility, and you know how seriously I take that. I'll ensure her safety first before I do anything else."

I wanted to tell her that *I didn't need her fake friendship kind of help, thank you very much*, but in truth I needed all the allies I could wrangle in this foreign world. Lexie's comment before about being hated for my brief time with Drager hadn't completely gone over my head. I could trust her enough to keep me alive, I was fairly certain. She'd never physically hurt me in our many years together, and she'd had ample opportunities.

As a fae, born here in Risest, Lexie was my best chance at staying alive, the only person I could give even a remote sliver of trust.

Just because I wasn't in danger this very second didn't mean this world wasn't dangerous. If books about fae had taught me anything, it was that they didn't consider humans their equals.

And they weren't to be trusted.

CHAPTER
EIGHTEEN

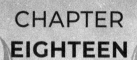

Lancourt turned out to be what felt like miles of winding white halls with white tiles underfoot. There were doorways at various intervals that I assumed led to different rooms, but since none of them were open, I was only guessing.

"How many fae live here?" I asked when we'd been walking in silence for about ten minutes.

"I'd say about four hundred," Chaple replied without hesitation. "On and off. Drager rotates out those who visit Dragerfield Library."

"Energy is easier to absorb from Dragerfield when you're not there all the time," Lexie added. "Gives everyone a chance to reap the benefits, borrow books to expand their knowledge, and in the end, Lord Drager and all of us benefit from time near our god."

"Does Drager take the energy that all of you build here, and in Dragerfield, to power himself?"

They took a second to answer, and it was Chaple who finally replied. "It's not so much 'take' as in we freely give him small slivers of our power. We still retain most of it because a powerful whole is stronger than a powerful one. But in the end, Drager is the protector of this land, and without his influence and control, it would be chaos. We *were* chaos before the Fallen."

Before the Fallen…

He said it as if I should know what he was talking about, but I had no clue, having never heard them use that particular phrasing before. I was about to ask for clarification, when we reached another closed doorway, only this one was apparently mine. As soon as we paused before it, the door slid into the frame and the room lay open before us.

"Holy shit," I muttered, blinking at the magical opening.

"That door will respond to you now," Chaple explained as we entered the room. "When you want to enter, just stop before it, and when you're ready to leave, you do the same from inside."

"Okay, then," I said faintly, shaking my head. "I mean, we have automatic doors back home, so I'll just think of it like that. Even though there's clearly no sensor above it. But whatever. It's just a really advanced automatic door." I wiped a hand across my brow, unsurprised to find a few beads of sweat decorating it.

A small laugh escaped Lexie. "You'll get used to it."

There was literally zero chance I'd get used to it, but I admired her confidence.

Chaple released his hold on me, and I marveled at how warm my arm was where he'd been touching. Made even more obvious by the icy air in my room. A room that felt as if no one had entered it in a really long time.

In the midst of those thoughts, the air literally warmed around us.

"Were you cold?" Chaple asked with a smile.

The eerie feeling that my mind was being read was very uncomfortable. My extended silence must have said just as much.

"The room is tuned to your energy now, and should respond

to your wants," Lexie explained quickly. "Drager runs hot so most of Lancourt is colder than if you're in Ocheran, which is more temperate like back home. Within this room, you control the thermostat."

There was no appropriate response, so I changed the subject. "How is Lancourt *above* Ocheran?"

Lexie's smile was a brief glimpse of the familiar, even when everything else was so damn weird. "I'll show you."

She led me farther into the room, which looked a lot like a fancy apartment. The living area was sparsely furnished with white leather couches and a small glass table. Glass-like, anyway. Its appearance was similar to a diamond, filled with glitter and faceted fragments. Off to the side, we passed a bedroom with a large white bed, and I found it surprising that the god-dragon who burned so hot for me in Dragerfield decorated his home in such a sterile and frankly disturbing white extravaganza.

But hell, what did I really know about him, outside of his impressive appendage, and skilled use of his tongue? In truth, he'd been fairly reticent with shared knowledge.

Lexie led me to a large window, and when she parted the sheer —*you guessed it*—white drapes, it was to reveal a spectacular view. This was my first true look at Risest. My first moment of existing in a magical fairytale world, and I honestly forgot how to breathe for a second.

"It's…" *Stunning, incredible, breathtaking, beyond words…* The adjectives fell hard and fast through my head as I tried to take it all in.

"It is," Lexie agreed.

The sky was a dusky rose, almost as if the sun were setting on a perfect winter day, but it was clearly bright and not night at all.

"Our days are a little longer than Earth's," Lexie explained, Chapel silent at her side. "Probably about sixteen hours of sunshine, and then nine of darkness. Our weather is also more stable. There are five lands in the Eastern Realm of Risest, and each of them have their own unique weather. Drager's is the land of Ocheran, as we said before."

I repeated the name in my head, wondering at the beauty of his name. "So Risest is the world, and this is the Eastern Realm, which has five lands and five gods?"

I was arranging the information in my head, needing a clearer view of how everything worked here.

"Correct," Lexie said, beaming in a familiar way. She'd always been proud of my achievements, even if they were as simple as putting information together in a logical manner. "The Eastern is probably about the size of America, Canada, and Mexico. It's a giant parcel of land divided by our gods. Then there are the Western, Southern, and regional realms of Risest, but they're so far away, through treacherous waters, that we all rarely interact. Especially since the Fallen took over the Eastern Realm."

The Fallen was a subject I had a lot of interest in, now that they were dropping little pieces of information about their place here in this world. But for now I decided to stick with learning about the lands.

"Is this pink sky through all the lands of the Eastern Realm?" I asked, mesmerized by the sheer beauty of it. Drager's court was high above Ocheran, which was visible below and way off into the distance.

"We live under one sky, but mostly everything else is different," Chaple said. "Our courts don't interact much except at the academy. It's neutral grounds, located center of the five lands. It's here that our young fae are trained before they return home to one of the lands."

"Can they choose a different land?" I asked.

Lexie sucked in a rapid inhalation. "Never," she breathed. "Oh no. We're born to our courts and it's here we stay until we die. How else would you be loyal if you were able to just pick and choose where to go?"

I blinked at them, looking between their shocked faces. "It's my belief that loyalty is stronger when it's freely given versus forced. Taking away someone's freedom to choose is kind of terrible."

Their shocked expressions were replaced with the sort of quiet anger that told me to shut up. "Best to keep your thoughts to yourself in that regard," Lexie said shortly. "Drager values loyalty, whether forced or not, and speaking ill of the rules that govern this world and keep us from chaos is considered treason of the highest form."

Okay, then. "Sure, but you know how I feel about this. Questioning authority is not treason. Unless, of course, you're all prisoners of the gods."

Chaple cleared his throat. "I'm going to take my leave now. I'll inform Drager that you're safely in your room. Food and clothing will be delivered."

He spun on his hooves and took off, and I kind of wished I'd kept my mouth shut. I was in another world, one with customs I didn't understand, and I had to go and shoot off with my opinions like they were worth shit.

"Sorry, Lexie," I said before she could say another word. "Whether I agree or not, it's not my place to judge."

Her face relaxed, and this time she didn't hesitate before pulling me into a hug. "It's all good. It's going to take time for you to learn our customs, and you know I encourage independent thought and actions. I'm mainly worried that you'll say the wrong thing to the wrong fae. Some of them take their loyalty to Drager very seriously and will strike you down for a simple opinion." With that terrifying warning, she released me from her hug. "Just promise you'll be extra careful. If you don't know what to say, say nothing at all."

I nodded, but part of me knew that the odds of me not screwing up and pissing someone off was slim. "I'll do my best."

The twitch in her lips said it all. We both knew I was a ticking time bomb. Having a curious nature and strong opinions was both a blessing and a curse.

"Okay, well, I have to report to my lieutenant now that I'm back in Lancourt," Lexie told me. "Technically I'm still part of our military."

Trying to wrap my head around her *other* life was harder than I expected. I couldn't quite mesh my side of Lexie with the fae side, and it left me feeling alone and confused. The Lexie who did body shots with me in college and held me as I sobbed over my family and other heartbreaks was familiar, but Lexical Lightsbringer was completely foreign.

"How old are you?" I asked, before wondering if knowing would freak me out.

She flashed a full set of perfect teeth as she threw back her head and laughed. "Of all the questions you could ask, it's my age. I should have known. I'm about a hundred years old, but we live near an eternity. So still a baby if you ask some of the older generation."

I blinked. And then blinked again. "You're twenty-five," I said firmly. "Twenty. Five."

Her laughter continued, and with it some of the tension that had been wound tightly around my chest eased. "You're correct, Morgs. I'm twenty-five. Now go and have a shower before your food and clothes arrive. Everything here works similarly to Earth. Our worlds aren't as different as you might imagine."

My gaze flicked back to the endless expanse of pink outside the window, to the edge of the land clearly floating on nothingness, and I nodded as sarcastically as I could. "So similar, Lex. Like looking into a mirror."

Of insanity.

The odds of me making it through all of this intact, whether physically or mentally, grew slimmer with each passing minute and new revelation, but at least I wasn't bored.

Ugh, I really needed a drink.

CHAPTER
NINETEEN

L exie left and the door closed behind her without a thought from me. If this room was under someone's control, it wasn't mine.

I remained at that window for a long time, just taking it all in. I couldn't tell if this land moved in the sky or was stationary, since there wasn't a landmark for me to judge against. From my window I couldn't see the sun, but the light remained strong and bright.

Finally, I left the stunning view and made my way through the room, checking out the very sparse details. There was no kitchen, or anything that resembled a place to cook or store food. It was just the two rooms, the living room and the bedroom.

Oh, and a bathroom, thankfully. It had white floor-to-ceiling tiles, large and glossy. There was a basin to the left of the entrance, unusual in that it looked like a large piece of stone extending from the floor, growing wider and wider until it became a sink. The color was amber, with lines of gold threading through the stone.

and maybe it was all the white backdrop, but the vibrancy of those colors were almost as breathtaking as the sky outside.

The tiles behind the sink were quite reflective, and when I stepped closer I saw myself as clear as if I were staring into a mirror. I hadn't seen my reflection in a month; there were no mirrors in Dragerfield, not even in the bathroom. Stepping closer, I wondered if it was the reflective tiles distorting my image or if Drager's power had changed me.

My hair was messy, but attractively so. Like I'd had it styled and then took a nap, so it wasn't perfect but also not the bird's nest I expected. My curls were more defined, falling down past my collarbone, and the gold seemed brighter in the brown lengths as well.

Leaning over the stone basin, I found myself staring harder, as if the image before me would change the longer I examined it. Why was my skin so clear? My eyes were brighter blue than I'd ever seen, and they'd already been bright.

Was this what a month of mind-blowing sex did to a human? Or was it a month of sex with Drager?

Tearing my gaze away, I had to shake my head. Morgan Starrer was ordinary, book in hand and head in the clouds. At best, my usual role was the quirky sidekick position. Maybe a secondary love interest. But never the female main character. Of all the changes I expected from being here, a glow-up didn't even make the list. It was a nice bonus, though, even if it only lasted as long as the swirl of Drager's energy in my gut.

Pulling myself from the mirror before my obsession got embarrassing, I approached the shower, hoping it was going to be easy to figure out. Eyeing the plain white stall, hidden behind the same sort of crystalized diamond glass as the table out in the living area, I slowly opened the door, surprised by how light it was.

Inside there was no sign of lever or shower head, and I wanted to strangle Lexie again. *Everything is similar to Earth.* Explain this then, former best friend.

Raging at her made me sad, so I quickly shelved that train of thought and focused on the shower once more. Now that I was standing here, I had a desperate urge to be clean.

Reaching out, I touched the wall, feeling along the panels, wondering if maybe a tile hid the control for the water. But every-thing was solid, even as I stepped further into the large area, pressing and prodding tiles as I went.

"For fuck's sake," I spat as frustration took hold, "is it too much to ask for a little water."

An immediate stream of water tumbled from the ceiling and walls, drenching me. Spluttering, I straightened and arched my back to remove myself from the direct line of spray. I choked on water for a moment, before I swiped a hand across my face and cleared my vision.

"A little less water." I choked once more, and the water eased, allowing me to stand without drowning under the warm stream.

Since my clothes were soaked through, I hurried out of them, kicking them into the corner of the stall. I'd wring and hang them out later, since that was all I currently had to wear. Running a hand through my hair, I closed my eyes and really enjoyed this moment of peace.

The water pressure here was clearly a million times better than our crappy apartment, and more than that, the water itself felt so much... *lighter... cleaner... pure.* Yeah, that was it. This water felt pure and fresh, like it had never been tainted by chemicals and pollution. Despite my better instincts, I couldn't stop myself from opening my mouth and swallowing down large gulps.

Fae lore said that if you ate or drank in Faerie aka Risest, you would have to stay there forever. Of course, in the high fantasy books I read, most of the women didn't care if that was their fate. They inevitably ended up banging the hot winter prince anyway, before finding out they were his true or chosen mate.

Clearly not my fate, and yet, I was drinking the water anyway.

Living on the edge.

Or more accurately, accepting the reality that I couldn't stay here much longer without eating or drinking.

Testing out the limits of the hot water, I remained in the shower stall for longer than I'd ever remembered taking a shower for. With my parents, my mother's guilt-trip over power usage, and her missing out on hot water, had always cut my showers short, and then with Lexie, we had about twelve minutes of hot water total between us.

But Lancourt was apparently blessed with endless hot water. Drager's will, I was sure. Bastard didn't look like one who'd suffered or struggled in his life, and since he insisted I stay here in Lancourt, I was going to take full advantage.

When I was finally finished, a new problem arose.

How did one dry themselves in this world?

"I'm done showering," I announced to the room, feeling like a complete moron.

The water stopped and all steam and moisture disappeared, as if it had been vacuumed up immediately, faster than any exhaust fan on Earth could manage. Even my clothes looked less soaked, though they were still too wet to wear.

Stepping out, naked, I looked around for material to dry myself with. Like the shower, there was nothing marring the white stone walls, and no sign of shelf or towel rack, just that sink and reflective tiles.

"Do you have a towel or cloth?" I asked the room.

It was disturbing how quickly I'd adapted to this place, unbothered by this sentient room that apparently worked for me. Not that I had much choice. This was an *adapt or die* kind of situation.

I barely blinked as a white towel fell from thin air and landed in my hands. Hugging it closer, I was instantly warmer, and I marveled at the unnatural softness of whatever this was made of. Just like with the water, it held subtle signs of not being from Earth.

Once I was dry, I wrapped the material around myself a few times and tucked it in at my chest, wandering back out into the living area. A gasp escaped me as I rushed to the window and pressed my hand against the glass. The sky was no longer pink, but now a brilliant bronze steaked in gold.

"Nightfall," I breathed.

The sun must have set during my marathon of a shower, and the beauty was beyond anything I'd ever seen. There had to be a billion stars, still brightly visible even in the bronze and gilded night.

It was pretty enough to hurt here, but from my ex-beauty queen of a mother I'd learned early on that "pretty" hid rotten cores. I couldn't grow complacent with Risest and forget that I was a human in a world of fae. I didn't belong here, and if I wasn't careful, I could lose myself to this place.

To this place and those who called it home.

Speaking of... the door to my room slid open and I spun, clutching at my towel. Drager strolled in like he owned the place.

Fucker.

"Get dressed, human," he said gruffly. "Your work is about to begin."

Blinking at him, I managed to gather some wits and not lose

myself in his green-gold eyes. "Dressed in what?" I shot back bluntly, unable to be afraid of him when I was this annoyed.

Drager lifted his head, and I followed that line of sight but couldn't see anything to have drawn his attention. That was until a crack echoed to my right, and I tore my gaze from the ceiling toward the wall, where a new door had just formed. "You should find something there," he said without inflection. "Meet me in the courtyard."

He left and the room grew colder. My limbs trembled as I stumbled toward the new door, which opened to reveal a large closet, similar to the one Drager had taken me to the first time here. Rows of clothes led to drawers at the back with underwear, and everything was my size. It wasn't my style, if I was being honest, more fancy than I'd normally wear, but I tried not to worry about that and just be grateful that I wasn't going to be wandering naked.

Apparently, his rule about dressing me had changed now that I was stuck here. Stuck here and filled up with his energy. That had to be the reason I could remain here longer than his previous *thirty minutes* of time. He hadn't said as much, but it was the clear change in our circumstances.

Searching hard, I found what was one of the more casual outfits—a white pants suit. Drager clearly wanted me to blend right into his world. The shoe situation was even worse, until I eventually grabbed a pair of black Mary Janes with only a few inch heels. The shortest heels I could see.

Once dressed, I tried my best to power march from the room, but without my usual runners and jeans, I was a fish out of water. Drager's work was going to be the death of me, and with that morbid thought, I swallowed roughly and sent out a small hope it'd be over soon.

There was a life waiting for me on Earth. A lame one, but now that I was distanced from the power and influence of Drager, I was scared by what would happen to me here. Lame or not, I was suddenly determined to make it back to Earth and reclaim what was mine.

CHAPTER
TWENTY

By the time I made it out into the hallway, Drager was nowhere to be seen. I wasn't surprised. No part of Drager was designed to stand around and wait for others. He issued the orders, controlled the pace and way of life, and everyone else followed.

It niggled at me deep inside to just jump at his command, but I had to acknowledge that I was outpowered here. Probably outbrained too, so the current gameplan was to remain quiet, observe everything I could, do the job for him, and escape with my life.

Leaving here with my life *and heart* intact was definitely on my to-do list.

Starting off at a wobbly pace, I tried to remember what direction Chaple had taken when he led me along these corridors. There had been what felt like a million twists and turns to reach my room, along a multitude of white hallways, which turned out to be a series of eerie mazes.

Possibly the entire reason this section of Lancourt looked like something from a mental hospital. Keep the prisoners from knowing how to escape.

I was under no delusion that I was a free human here in a faerie world.

With a deep breath, I pushed on in what I hoped was the right direction, stumbling often as I attempted to get the hang of heels. After a few more corridors and turns, I ended up in a hall that was a darker cream color, and that was when I knew I was very lost.

I hadn't seen cream walls in Lancourt before.

Cursing, I reached down and yanked the stupid heels from my feet and pitched them across the vast hallway. There was a clatter as they hit the wall, and then they were gone, vanished into this creepily alive building.

Whatever, as long as they weren't on my feet, I didn't give a shit.

Reversing my direction, I walked faster, the slightly long cuff on my suit pants sliding across the smooth tile. Smooth and apparently super clean. There wasn't a single mark on my white pants.

Despite having reversed my direction almost as soon as I saw the cream, the white walls didn't return. "What the fuck?" I breathed, looking around. There weren't even doorways in this section, for me to try and open to see if they led somewhere.

A very clear magical switcheroo was going on.

"I need to find Drager," I said quietly, waiting for my fairy-god-house to grant my wish.

But nothing happened.

Waiting a few seconds, I tried again, asking for the courtyard this time.

Again, nothing changed.

The cream appeared to be mocking me as it remained motionless, its actions informing me that I had no control out here. Drager was the lord and master, and I was only a lowly prisoner.

"Fine," I snapped. "Tell the lord that I'll be sitting right here until he bothers to come find me."

Sliding down against the wall, exhausted and homesick, I curled my arms around my legs, and even though it pissed me off, a few tears escaped. The last month had been like a waking dream, keeping me enthralled in the presence of a god, and I'd had no real time to dwell on the massive upheaval of my life.

An upheaval that was so much more than just mind-blowing sex with a fae god, though that was a nice bonus. It was about the removal of the veil hiding this secret supernatural world from me.

I mean, I'd always believed in aliens, and expected that there was unexplained magic around the universe. I believed in gods, plural, but before this last month my beliefs had all been formed around faith and the logic that humans couldn't be the only sentient beings in the multiverses.

I'd never had evidence. I'd never even had a ghostly encounter like some people.

To find this all out in the way I had, with no gentle easing into this world, was a lot. I'd been thrown in the deep end from the second I crossed paths with Drager.

The reality of my *new reality* crashed into me hard, and I stifled the next sob, scared to show deeper emotions here, in the house of who could very well be my enemy.

In the house of a self-proclaimed god, with power beyond anything I'd ever experienced.

The hot swell of Drager's power gave a sudden jolt inside me, reacting to my emotions—I assumed. It knocked me out of my melancholy, and my tears faded under the heat. As I lifted my head, there was a swipe of something warm and wet across my cheek, as if an invisible tongue had tasted my sadness.

I gasped and surged to my feet, every vestige of fatigue gone as I frantically searched the hallway. "That's assault, buddy," I said tersely, wishing for those damn heels back so I at least had a weapon.

There was no visible sign of anyone else, but I heard a small rumble, followed by a hot breeze against my skin, before the wash of energy faded. My heart slammed hard in my chest as I pressed back to the smooth walls, wondering if that had been the house again, or another entity hidden within these walls.

Before the panic attack could take me over completely, Lexie burst into view about fifty feet down the cream hallway. "Morgs!" she shouted, her voice echoing toward me as she sprinted in my direction. "We've been looking everywhere for you." She skidded to a halt in front of me, her eyes wide, and a darker brown than usual as they examined me.

"I've been lost in this lovely hallway," I said sharply. "Having a right cracking time."

Lexie's face relaxed a touch. "When your British accent emerges you're either drunk or mega pissed off. Understandably so, but there's no time now to rage. Drager is waiting for you." She gulped. "He doesn't like to be kept waiting."

Oh, she was very much mistaken. I had plenty of time to rage. *"Then he shouldn't have fucking taken off and left me to wander his stupid piece of shi—"*

Lexie reacted in a flash, one hand wrapping around my arm and yanking me closer, while the other covered my mouth. "Don't insult him here," she said roughly and with urgency. "Everything in Lancourt is loyal to him and him alone. The very walls can strike you down, Morgan."

She held me long enough for a fraction of my anger to ease into a simmering burn. "I know you're upset," she continued in that same low voice, "and you have every right to be. But I also need you to table it until you're safe. You're going to have to swallow it down, file it away, and when this task is done, we can figure out how you find your peace again."

When this task was done, as she'd put it, I was going to make some big changes in my existence. Lexie was right, though, I needed to be smart about it. Smart enough not to get myself killed before I had a chance to live my new life.

"I'm calm," I mumbled, moistening my lips. "Take me to Drager. I have work to do."

Our gazes met and held for what could have been an uncomfortably long moment, but instead it felt like comaraderie. And while I knew it would take time to fully trust her again, it was a relief to feel our friendship still simmering there. Ready to be rekindled.

This time when we walked together, comfort fell between us. "The halls are changing and shifting here, aren't they?" I asked as she took a right and then a left, around corners I hadn't even seen on my way here.

The halls were designed to hide everything until you were right at them, which explained how I ended up taking so many wrong turns.

"Lord Drager designed parts of Lancourt to be impenetrable and unescapable." Lexie shrugged.

"Like a prison?" I'd already guessed as much, but it was nice to have the confirmation.

Lexie shot me a side-eye. "Yes and no. When only those who have the right to traverse have the knowledge, it keeps us safe." And I was apparently without the right. "Drager is the only Fallen who prefers to exist above his territory," Lexie continued. "He's always been focused on Lancourt and the Library. Focused on building his power. He's never told me of course, but I feel that he—"

She broke off, clearing her throat, and when she spoke again her voice was much lower. "He's building enough power to take over more of the Eastern Realm of Risest. He wasn't initially assigned the largest territory, and it has always bothered him."

"Who has the largest territory?" I asked.

Lexie's warm brown skin paled. "Zahak. Elemental god from the Isle of Denille."

There was a note of fear and reverence in her tone, and now my curiosity was really piqued. But when I attempted to ask more, she cut me off and shook her head, so I decided to leave that line of questioning. Apparently this Zahak was scarier to talk about than Drager's quest for more power and land.

"How would he go about taking more territory?" I whispered as she made another right turn, and we were back to the white walls.

"He only has two options," she said immediately, since we were apparently back on the allowable conversations. "The first is obvious: war. But we haven't had any fae wars for centuries. We all signed the Peace Covenant of Eastern Risest when the Fallen appeared and brought us back to some semblance of normalcy. To start a war now without provocation would bring all the lands down on Drager, and even with his power, he'd crumble under that might."

"So, the second would be…"

Her lips thinned as she said gruffly: "Betrayal. Find a powerful fae in one of the other lands, preferably a land that borders his, and have them betray their god. It's what he thinks is happening in his land with this thief and the missing book. Which equals to missing power. Now Drager is more determined than ever to amass enough power and territory that no one can ever challenge him."

"Shouldn't he be forming alliances, then? Not isolating himself away up here in his ivory tower?"

They called these men the *gods of Risest*, but their strength still came from the blind worship of others. Alone, they would fall.

Lexie lowered her voice: "None of the Fallen are big on alliances; despite the fact that they're all brothers. With each weird occurrence here, Drager grows more paranoid and secretive. He trusts very few, and I don't see that changing any time soon."

"What other weird occurrence?" I asked. "There's more than the missing book?"

Our conversation had to end then as the courtyard came into view, and for the life of me I'd never have found my way here on my own. Chaple was waiting for us, standing with a fae that I'd never seen before. He was a head taller than me, with dark skin and vibrant green eyes that were unnervingly piercing. Add in broad shoulders, heavily muscled arms, and black hair shaved close to his skull, and this was one dangerous—though intriguingly handsome—fae.

He regarded me without expression, but I felt judgment oozing from him. "This is Jords," Lexie said stiffly, and *was there tension between them or was I imagining it?* "He's a lieutenant in Drager's military."

Jords nodded stiffly, just the slightest of head tilts, and then dismissed me by locking his piercing gaze on Lexie. "You're late," he said, in a voice that reminded me of a mini avalanche. It was deep and rumbly, with an accent that I'd never be able to place because there was none like it on Earth.

"No I'm not," she shot back, showing more than a little defiance toward ol' Jordo.

Leaving them to glare sexy glares at each other, I turned my attention to Chaple. "Where's Drager?" I asked, since me racing here had been to not upset the *almighty god* waiting for me.

Chaple's smile was easy again. "He got called away, so we're here to escort you."

Called away? That seemed highly unlikely considering he was top of the food chain around here. But whatever. As Lexie said, the less time I spent annoying Drager, the more chance I had of surviving my time here.

"Let's do it." I was ready to get this over and done with.

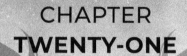

CHAPTER
TWENTY-ONE

The animosity between Lexie and Jords didn't fade, but they tabled it to get Drager's work done. Work which turned out to be me sitting in a glass paneled room behind a glass desk. One fae after another was brought in to meet me, most of them introducing themselves and nothing else.

Drager was giving me a chance to listen to those in Lancourt, so he could rule them out as suspects. So I did, one by one, with Lexie at my side and Chaple and Jords standing behind us like our own personal security.

"Well, nothing like a crash course in meeting fae," I said when a tall, blond female harpy left. She had clawed hands, a beaky nose, and sharp dark eyes that had focused on me for a lot longer than I was comfortable with. This might be the quickest and easiest way of eliminating suspects, but Drager was definitely putting a target on my back.

If only because they were curious about this powerless human sitting at the table with high-ranking fae of this land.

The next group to enter were sirens, according to Lexie's introduction, and I marveled at the tall, voluptuous women with long legs, and thick hair of various colors falling down their backs. They had an unusual structure to their facial features: huge round eyes, extra pronounced cheekbones, and teal skin that appeared to be dusted with silver glitter. When they first spoke to me, it wasn't in the regular fae language that I'd been implanted with, but they switched as soon as Lexie uttered a sharp word.

"Why have you brought this human creature into our midst?" the first one said, and I had to grip the side of the glass table to keep from falling out of my chair. Her voice was warm honey dripping across my nerve endings. My insides tightened and I expected Drager's power to react to the clear sexuality of these fae, but it remained stable.

No one answered her. Lexie just turned to me and I shook my head. "You're dismissed," she told them. "You can return to the land of Ocheran below and resume your cyclic power build. Just stay out of trouble."

"Always, Lightsbringer," that same siren said again, though her focus remained disconcertingly on me. They left without issue though, and I let out a long breath of relief.

"That was uncomfortable," I said quickly.

Lexie chuckled. "Yeah, they have that effect if you're not prepared for the voice. It's one of their weapons."

One of many, if what I'd seen was any indication. "What's a cyclic power build?" I asked.

"They gather power by hunting fae across the lands," she said simply. "They're a fairly bloodthirsty race, hunting, mating, and then eating their prey. It's nasty business, but we allow fae to be themselves here. Those who fall prey to the siren Voice are weak, and that's on them."

"So, technically, they can't force you, but you have to be strong enough to resist?" I confirmed.

Lexie nodded. "Pretty much. You must give yourself freely to them or their power build will fail. It's not the worst way to weed out the weak."

Right. Nothing like getting a little action only to find your partner ready to eat you after. *Literally.*

"Well, thankfully, the voice I heard in the library sounded nothing like the siren. And if the other sirens have a similar quality and energy to their voices, it wasn't any of them."

"They do," Lexie confirmed. "They all sound so similar that when they talk as one it's like a hurricane of energy and music. It's very disconcerting."

I vowed to never find myself alone in the room with them, because I wasn't sure I'd survive that "hurricane."

The next few hours were filled with one fae after another, and I managed to meet a few more of their unique races. A lot looked like Lexie and Drager, amped up humans, but many were incredibly unique. It took immense control to keep myself from visibly reacting, especially with the kitsune, who were covered in red, orange, and brown fur. The fur spanned across their delicate faces, which were humanoid despite the other foxlike features. On top of that, they had tails, seven or more in total, depending on their power levels.

"Their tails are sacred and powerful," Lexie told me when they left. "If you touch them without permission, they will strike you down."

"So no petting of the kitsune?" I joked. *Sort of.* Because they were adorably cute. Too cute to think of as dangerous, and yet I had similar feelings about tigers and lions, so I wasn't the best judge.

Chaple snorted from behind us, and Lexie shook her head, but they didn't continue the lecture.

After what felt like days of meeting fae, I slumped forward

and groaned into the glass desk.

"Are you okay, human?" Jords asked, the first time he'd spoken to me in… well, ever.

An angry hiss emerged from me. I sounded like a furious kitten, but I was too tired to be embarrassed.

"She doesn't like to be called human," Lexie snapped at him. "She has a name, and you know how to use it."

I couldn't see Jords, since I was still face down, but his reply sounded confused. "She is human, right? What's the insult in calling her what she is?"

"Does everyone here call you *that Giant Asshole with an Attitude Problem*?" I mumbled, too tired to care about death at this point.

"Not to his face," Lexie deadpanned.

"Not if they want to survive," Jords added with soft menace.

I gulped and picked myself up. "Oh good. Well, I won't call you that either, Jordo."

My secret nickname for him slipped out and there was no doubt it made him even madder. "It's Jords. Just Jords."

"Right!" I nodded hard, meeting the glare of his green gaze. "I'll ensure that I never exchange a single letter of your name if you ensure not to call me *human*." See how annoying it is, *Jordo*.

It was growing clearer that my odds of surviving here were slim, so I might as well be as annoying as possible to these arrogant fae while I had the chance. Maybe next time they'd think twice about bringing a human captive into their land.

"Are we done for the night?" Lexie asked. "It's nearing morning and Morgan hasn't had food since we arrived. If you want her to remain healthy enough to help us, then you need to ensure she's taken care of."

"How often does she need to eat?" Jords asked.

"*She* is right here," I muttered, but no one cared.

"Every four or five hours is best or they start to get hangry,"

Lexie said seriously, like we were deep in a documentary on humans.

Turned out the fae were quite literal, and even having no idea what hangry meant, they took Lexie's warning seriously, and food was soon in front of me—five platters of various fruit, breads, and dried meats. "These are the closest we have to food from Earth," Lexie said, pushing everything my way. "You're safe to eat everything here, but I wouldn't advise randomly eating if you find yourself in the wild. Some of our plants bite back."

Now my head was filled with imagery of apples with sharp teeth, and that was too creepy to think about.

Starving, I reached for the first platter, ending up with a dense bread covered in seeds. It was smothered in a delicious spread that tasted like a mix of garlic, herbs, and salt. "Oh my God," I groaned after the first bite, chewing fast and near choking as I shoved bite after bite in my mouth. Thankfully, despite the dense feel, it dissipated in my mouth easily.

"Please don't choke on my watch," Chaple said, voice wavering.

"I'm an expert eater," I replied when my mouth was empty once more. "It's my number one skill on my CV."

He chuckled politely, no doubt with zero idea what a CV was.

No one spoke after that, and I spent my time sampling the food. A lot was like Earth, with apples, oranges, melon balls, along with cheese and those cured meats. Of course, while recognizable, nothing looked or tasted exactly the same. The apples were pink on the inside, the oranges had blood-red streaks through the flesh. The meat and cheese weren't from a cow, that much was clear, but despite the differences, there was one universal truth. Food in Risest was delicious.

When my stomach was full to bursting, I drank some of the

water and groaned. "Can I sleep now?" I mumbled, my eyes fluttering closed, my head heavy.

As I grew closer to sleep, Drager's face appeared in my mind's eye, and like a shot of adrenaline I was suddenly wide awake once more. I'd managed not to think about him for hours, keeping busy, learning about this world. But this would be my first night in weeks without rough hands stroking my body to bring it to life. We'd been completely wrapped up in each other for a month and he hadn't even bothered to see me for more than a few minutes since returning to Lancourt.

Drager was making his position perfectly clear. He'd told me not to get attached, that our time together was only due to the fertility ritual. Now I just had to make myself believe it.

"Come on, Morgs," Lexie said gently, wedging a hand under my arm and hauling me up from the chair. "Let's get you to bed."

I really was exhausted, and since I couldn't control my dreams, if Drager crept in, then I'd just have to deal with it. Jords and Chaple followed us down the endless white hallways, and we didn't see any other fae on our journey. There was no way for me to know how huge Lancourt was, having only seen a small section of it, but clearly it was large enough that all the hundreds of fae here could wander around and never be seen by another.

When we reached my door, it opened automatically for me, but I didn't step straight inside. "Why is there no sign of anybody else in any of the rooms along here?" I asked.

"This isn't an area where the general population lives," Lexie explained. "They're in the west and east wings. This is the south section. No one lives here."

A spike of panic at being so utterly alone hit my chest, and it must have reflected on my face, because Lexie reached out and patted my arm. "I'm here now, and so is Chaple and Jordo. We're assigned to keep you safe."

"It's Jords," the military fae replied roughly.

She didn't even acknowledge that statement. "You can rest easy, Morgan. Drager is keeping you safe, in his own way."

I tried not to let that affect me. Keeping me safe because I was an asset wasn't the same as keeping me safe because he cared. If he cared, he'd be the one protecting me.

Assigning three guardians was nothing more than assuring his only means of identifying the threat in his midst remained alive long enough to do her job. In truth, Jordo's presence appeared more to keep me in line than anything else. Not that I was any sort of threat, but this way Drager knew exactly where I was and what I was doing every single moment of the day.

"Okay, well thank you," I said softly. "I'll see you all in the morning."

Lexie chuckled. "It's nearing morning now. We'll see you at lunch."

"Sounds like a plan."

I stepped into my white prison, and they remained at the door until it slid closed, leaving me alone with only a gilded sky for comfort.

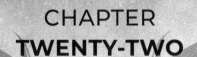

CHAPTER
TWENTY-TWO

S leep came easy, and there were no dreams, much to my surprise. I woke on my cloud-like mattress feeling refreshed and ready to deal with this new day in Risest. *Risest!*

A freaking faerie world. As scary as being here was, there was a buzz of excitement in my body. My routine, mundane existence was gone, replaced with a complete unknown. A good night's sleep made all the difference, because I was ready to see what this day would bring.

Padding from the bedroom naked, since I hadn't bothered with pjs, I paused at the sight of the dusty pink sky. That view would never get old, and the urge to walk outside and breathe in the air grew stronger within me. I'd seen nothing but white walls and this view since arriving, and I wanted to go a little farther. Maybe Lexie would be allowed to take me exploring today.

Drager's power stirred slowly in my gut, weaker than yesterday, and as it faded from my being I felt more like myself.

During my shower, the room provided me with a hairbrush. It had very soft bristles that felt almost like fur, and I didn't expect it to work on my tangle of thick curls, but it somehow smoothed and shined the length in seconds.

No toothbrush appeared, and instead I received a small handful of what looked like dark mint leaves. Giving them the sniff test quickly, the mint scent was confirmed, so I tentatively put them into my mouth and chewed. After about a minute, the mint flavor faded and the leaves vanished completely in my mouth, leaving behind clean teeth and fresh breath.

A glance in the mirror-tile reflected shiny white teeth.

Earth needed to investigate these leaves; they were far superior to what we used.

When I was dressed in another pants suit, this one black, I reluctantly perused the heels selection once more. The ones I'd thrown at the wall last night were back in their place. I bypassed those and chose a different style with an even chunkier heel.

Drager seemed determined to get me into heels, and while it was annoying to cater to his needs, at this stage I had little choice. When I stepped out of the room, Lexie, Chaple, and Jords appeared, like ghosts who had been lying in wait for me.

I ground to a halt as I blinked at the three of them. "Whoa, where did you all come from?"

Lexie was the first to approach, her smile warm as she ignored my question. "How did you sleep?"

"Great actually," I said. "Whatever that mattress is made of, we need to get some for Earth."

Her smile grew. "They're made from the fleece of a *gorangi* mule. It's the softest material in our world."

My world too, as far as I was concerned.

"Are you ready to start work again?" Jordo drawled, sounding annoyed.

No. "Sure, lead the way."

He did, and all of us remained silent as we traversed the white maze. At least when we arrived in the glass-tabled room, there were multiple trays of food already waiting for me.

Taking the same seat as yesterday, I reached for the delicious bread. "Are you guys going to eat with me?" I asked them.

Lexie was the only one who didn't look confused. "We don't eat while we're working," she told me. "When we're with you, we're on duty."

Letting out a breath of exasperation, I leaned back and crossed my arms. "If you don't eat, I won't eat. It's rude and awkward, and it's impacting my enjoyment of this meal."

Drager had better not starve his people, or I was going to lose my shit.

None of them moved for a hot minute, and I was about to panic at actually having to follow through on my threat of not eating, when finally Jordo broke: "Fine, we'll eat with you, but then work must begin," he said stiffly.

He folded his huge frame into the chair across from mine, and with methodic precision ate his way through one of the platters. One piece at a time, three large bites and it was gone. Chaple sat also, but his method was different. He was pickier, clearly, searching through all the fruit until he found a piece that must have been perfect. He polished it on one of the cloth napkins, and then took a slow bite, chewing that piece just as slowly.

Lexie I'd eaten with a million times, and I already knew that she would start on fruit, and then pick up meat, and then by the time she was done she'd have ten half-eaten food items in front of her.

We all had our quirks, but at least they were eating, and that meant I could eat as well.

Between the four of us, we finished the platters, which were then removed by Jordo. He returned about thirty seconds later, leaving the glass door open for the first group of fae to enter.

This day was a carbon copy of the previous, only this time I met nymphs, who I remembered well from Dragerfield Library, gargoyles—their voices were far too gravelly to match our thief's —and various clans from the land of Ocheran.

Including one familiar woman.

Florentine, Lady of the House of Green Hollow, arrived with a dozen or more of her clan. She met my gaze, and that same curiosity was in her stare as the first time she'd observed me on the stage at Drager's feet. "You're human," she said as a way of greeting.

"I am," I replied, already knowing she wasn't the one who betrayed Drager.

"Why have we been called here?" she asked softly.

She was the first face that I'd met in this room to question Drager's order. It made me like her just a bit.

"That's none of your business," Jords said without inflection. "Do as instructed and introduce your clan to Morgan."

Her expression didn't shift; she was clearly an expert at masking her thoughts. "I'm Florentine." She waved her hand to the others in her clan, and one by one they introduced themselves, allowing me to eliminate all of them as suspects.

The fact that I'd met so many fae and not one of them sparked a memory of that voice had me second-guessing how well I was remembering that odd tone I'd heard. I'd been so sure that I'd immediately know it when I heard it again, but it was becoming abundantly obvious that most fae had unique lilts to their voices. I was starting to worry I'd oversold my usefulness in discovering the traitor.

Not that I was about to admit any such thing to Drager. A quick death wasn't on my to-do list for this week.

"You're dismissed," Lexie said, after waiting for me to shake my head. It was our subtle communication, but Florentine noticed. This fae was observant and curious, and the vibe she threw off as she left was annoyance at this forced meeting today. Not that she said a word, ushering her clan from the room without bothering to look back.

"I think we're almost through everyone in court," Lexie said with a sigh. "And still no sign of the traitor. Drager's going to be… annoyed."

Some of the tendrils of his heat in my gut swirled in response —agreement?—and I wondered what the next move to track this traitor would be.

Pushing my chair away from the table to stand, my back groaned at me, and I tried to guess at how many hours I'd been sitting stagnant. "I need to go outside," I said firmly. "I need fresh air and to walk so I can stretch out my limbs."

"No!" Jords said abruptly.

Cute that he thought I gave a fuck what he thought. "I'm not a prisoner, Jordo," I reminded him. "And I will be going outside, with or without your permission."

"I'll lock you in your room," he shot back.

Not so subtle a way of countering my "I'm not a prisoner" statement. "Then I won't tell you who the traitor is," I choked out, panicked at this new element of being trapped. "You-you need me. Remember that."

Jords opened his mouth but I didn't wait to hear what he had to say. I strode right out the door and exited into a white hall, turning to go in the opposite direction to my room. Lexie was the first to catch up with me as I teetered along on stupid heels. She linked her arm with mine, and was able to keep me steady, since she was dressed in flat black boots, and dark leathers with armored panels across the chest and down her thighs. She looked like a sexy cat-woman-warrior, and I looked like a frazzled bank manager who couldn't find her car in the parking lot.

"I really enjoy Jordo being put in his place," she said with a chuckle. "Everyone except Drager is terrified of him, so he rarely ever gets questioned."

That didn't surprise me. He had *intimidating and scary* down to a fine art. "You don't seem terrified," I observed, still curious about their history.

"Don't mistake my defiance for anything other than fear," she said flatly. "It's just built around different reasons."

And now I was more curious than ever, but with the footsteps of Chaple and Jords approaching behind us, we didn't speak about it any further.

"This is the way outside, right?" I whispered to Lexie.

"I'll get you there," she promised.

Warmth settled in my gut, and this time it had nothing to do with Drager. This time it was the bond I'd shared with Lexie from almost the first moment we crashed into each other at a college pep rally, both of us trying to avoid the crowds. We'd laughed as we apologized, before we realized we were clutching the same fantasy novel that was currently taking the world by storm, filled with dragons and vampires, and a series of islands that trapped souls.

From there the rest was history. A love of books started our friendship, but it was the unconditional love and acceptance she offered me that strengthened it. Lexie was the first person I'd truly trusted, the first to help me break the chains that bound me at home.

The irony of her not actually being a person at all wasn't lost on me. It made sense in hindsight, since I'd never related well to any other humans in my life.

Maybe I was a touch fae?
Wishful thinking at its finest.

CHAPTER
TWENTY-THREE

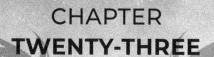

The landscape of Drager's home changed as we got farther along the white maze. The white darkened until it became an earthy tone, and eventually we reached an atrium. It was the only way to describe the area, which spanned at least fifty feet high and double that wide. The ceiling was made of glass panels, without the crystalline nature of those back in my room.

There were plants everywhere.

Growing in small rows along the ground, some were just starting to bloom, while others appeared ancient, with thick trunks, and branches that sprouted well up into the cavernous ceilings above.

For the first time since arriving here, I found myself taking a deep breath, tension easing inside. "This room is incredible," I said.

As I spoke, the flora awoke. The buds I'd thought unbloomed burst to life, revealing brightly colored flowers in a myriad of shapes and sizes. I'd never been much of a gardener, so I had no idea if there were beauties like these on Earth, but I sensed that these plants were unique to Risest.

"Are the flowers following my voice?" I asked, feeling my brow crinkle.

Lexie frowned. "Looks like it…"

Drager's power swirled stronger in my gut than I'd felt for many hours, and then it all made sense. This was his garden, and it was responding to me because I carried some of his energy.

"They're not posing a danger, so you're free to wander," Jords said, on alert as he observed the room closely.

Now that I knew the reason for the plant interest, I felt comfortable moving through the brightly colored landscape. "I'm guessing we're close to the outside?" I said in a low voice. "I'd like to breathe some fresh air."

"Just through here," Lexie said, waving me along the path.

As we continued, I tried not to flinch as the flowers nearest to us brushed their foliage against my arms and face. Likening it to a playful puppy wanting affection, I went with it, and by the end found it almost comforting.

"Why did Drager shove me into the starkest, most lifeless part of his home?" I asked, wishing that waver in my voice would go away. "The part that's basically the prison. I've never given him any reason to treat me like this."

There was no need for him to relegate me to being a threat or annoyance to hide away.

"Drager isn't in the habit of informing us of his reasons for anything," Chaple said with a chuckle. "But if I had to guess—"

"Don't guess," Jords snapped. "It's not our place to guess or question Lord Drager."

"Not your place to freely think either by the looks of it" I added. His glare this time was all for me, but I didn't let it bother me. "You should never give up your ability to question and create your own truth. Trust me, nothing good ever came from an unquestioned supreme leader."

The full force of Jords' anger was directed at me, but I'd grown somewhat used to his brand of intimidation and barely even flinched. "The Fallen saved us from ourselves," he informed me stiffly. "Fae cannot go ungoverned. Fae cannot rely on individual races to keep ourselves safe and capable of long-term survival. Fae needed the Fallen, and we owe them complete fealty."

Fanboy down.

In truth, there was still so much about this world that I didn't understand, especially those years before the Fallen, and the changes that had occurred since. Hell, I knew next to nothing about the Fallen in general.

I'd reserve judgment on Jordo's views until after I'd learned more about this world.

Once we cleared the atrium, there was another short, glass-lined walkway, and then the glorious final doors that opened for me to step out into the warmth. The temperature rose at least ten degrees and I did a little dance as happiness filled me. "You have a sun!" I lifted my face toward the glorious ball of pink energy burning above us. I hadn't seen it from my window, so I'd had to assume that was what created the light. Now I had proof.

It wasn't as bright as Earth's sun, and the color was just a darker pink than the sky, but I felt energized standing beneath it, which led me to believe it held similar life-giving properties.

Fresh air filled my lungs as a light breeze buffeted us, reminding me that we were floating high above the realm of Eastern Risest. I felt a sudden urge to rush to the side and peer over the edge—dangerous as it would be—to experience the sensation of floating like this.

"Morgs," Lexie said warningly. She'd read me like a damn book.

I shot her a reassuring smile, but the suspicion did not die on her face.

"I just need to see what the edge looks like," I said in a rush. "I'll be safe." Kicking my shoes off, I ran before she could reply, knowing all the while they were more than fast enough to catch me.

Oddly, no one stopped me as I raced across the land, the hard surface under my feet feeling like terracotta tiles—it looked like them too, no dust or debris kicking up. My pulse thrummed as the edge came into sight, the breeze growing even stronger. This had me slowing as I wondered if this little act of defiance was riskier than I'd thought.

Slowing again, about eight feet from the end of the terracotta, it grew harder to stay balanced. "Be careful, Morgan," Chaple said from nearby. "It's a long way down."

He wasn't kidding. As the land below came into view, it looked like a blob of green, with patches of brown and lighter greens mingled throughout. Wild and undeveloped, I couldn't make out any cities from this vantage point.

Dropping to the tiles, I inched closer, until I was a second from hanging my nose off the edge. Just as I was about to pop my head over the side, a whooshing sound broke through the silence, louder than the breezes still rushing around me.

"Holy frogs!" Lexie cursed from behind me.

On instinct, I scrambled to my feet, all the while forgetting how close to the edge I'd been. It wasn't until I stood that I noticed my precarious position, especially as a heavy wind slammed against me. At the same time, there was a rumble from nearby that broke through my fear, sending a tingle of energy from the tip of my skull down my spine.

Another blast of wind hit me, and I overbalanced, toppling forward in a dramatic, slow-motion movement. I had enough time to acknowledge that I was going to fall, with no hope of saving myself, even as my hands waved in the air, searching for a hold.

Lexie screamed behind me, a high-pitched shriek that chilled my blood, but I knew she was too far away to save me.

Sending out a prayer that this would be quick, I closed my eyes and let myself go into the abyss. As I toppled forward, there was a near-deafening roar, and another gust of hot wind, only this time it was in front of me, and so unnaturally strong that my forward momentum was halted.

My eyes shot open as I hung there suspended over nothing, my feet the only part of me still on land as air buffeted against me and held me in place. My breaths were short and shallow, my lungs barely getting enough oxygen to keep me functioning, as my gaze remained on the miles of land below.

Why am I not falling?

"What's happening?" Lexie shouted, much closer as her hand wrapped around my shirt. She yanked me back onto the land, both of us tumbling down together. "How did you not fall?"

Her question was answered a beat later when that hot air grew stronger around us, chapping my cheeks and lips. A huge creature rose to hover before us, and I was strangely calm as I stared up at what was unmistakably a dragon. It was matte black, with just the tips of its thick and heavy scales gilded, like the ends had been dipped in pure gold. That gold spanned out farther as it reached the massive wings, until those appendages were almost purely gold. Shimmery and powerful, they were spread at least twenty feet on either side of the beast, flapping occasionally as it hovered there, sending hot wind across us.

Wind that had saved my life.

I was unable to tear my eyes from the creature which looked *exactly* as I'd always imagined a dragon, with four strong, muscled legs, each ending in lethal golden claws. The body was massive—

the size of my living room back home—and it had a long, powerful neck and a huge head. The dark orb-like eyes that observed me were clearly filled with intelligence, and it was hard to miss the row after row of lethal teeth crowding its long jaws.

A snarl escaped the beast, and I found myself locked once more in those depthless eyes. It roared, which broke my trance, and I scrambled to my feet with Lexie right beside me. "Do we run?" I murmured.

It felt like the dragon had saved my life, but maybe that was all a coincidence. It certainly wasn't acting particularly friendly as it roared in our direction.

"He's just warning us," Lexie replied stiffly, not sounding completely convinced of her own words.

"Don't make any sudden moves though," Chaple added from close behind.

Lexie started easing back, one small step and then another, grabbing my arm to pull me along. As I retreated, the beast growled louder than ever, and the temperature must have risen another five or ten degrees.

"It's going to blast us," I whispered.

The urge to try to defuse the situation that was growing more volatile filled me, and shaking Lexie off I lifted both hands in the air in front of me. "I'm sorry," I shouted, and the others grew silent around me. "I misjudged the wind and almost landed on you. Thank you for saving me."

The dragon tilted its head to the side, wings slowing even as it remained somewhat stationary. It drifted closer, until it was almost over the edge of the land, and another rumble filled the air. Only this time it didn't come from the dragon.

At least not the one in the sky.

The energy in my center started to roil slowly, and I turned to see Drager striding across the terracotta toward us, his face wreathed in fury. In truth, a part of me had wondered if this massive beast was Drager.

It would explain why it had saved me. And I'd always thought of him as a dragon.

But clearly, I'd been massively mistaken.

The black beast was something—*someone*—else, and it looked like Drager was none too pleased that he was here.

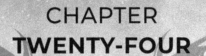

CHAPTER
TWENTY-FOUR

"You bring war, brother." Drager sounded calm, but his expression told another story.

The dragon's chest puffed and there was no denying the increase in heat this time.

Lexie dragged me further from the edge, leaving Drager to stand between us and the dragon. Jords and Chaple followed us, remaining protectively at our sides.

"Is that a *dragon* dragon or a person dragon?" I asked, my words both confusing and strangled, but I knew Lexie would understand.

"Person dragon," she breathed. "One of the Fallen." I could feel the tension in her body. "Stay here, Morgan. We must assist Drager."

Yeah, I didn't need to be told twice not to get in the middle of a dragon battle. She said it was one of the Fallen. That meant Drager's other form was just like this stunning but terrifying beast.

When I nodded, she took off, pulling a flaming blade as long as my torso from *somewhere*. There was zero chance that had been stashed in her clothing, so it had to have been magically yanked from another realm or an invisible backpack. As she raced forward, Chaple and Jords with her, I really saw Lexical Lightsbringer for the first time.

Lexie would always be my best friend, but she was clearly also a warrior.

They reached Drager's side, and now the dragon was outnumbered, but it didn't feel like they had the upper hand.

Feeling no urge to move closer, and not wanting to be any further trouble today, I remained exactly where I'd been left, my gaze locked on the dragon. Despite having been in a mythical world for two days already, seeing a creature so fantastical had my limbs shaking and my temperature zooming from hot and then back to cold over and over. Shock, it had to be shock.

Those dark eyes met mine and I jerked my focus away fast enough to jar my neck. It roared, and the winds picked up once more, before there was a whoosh and it dove out of sight, below the lands of Lancourt.

Holy dragon drama. I might not know for sure what just happened, but it was intense enough for trickles of sweat to bead my forehead.

Lexie was the first to come back for me, her magical sword once more in a magical pocket. I must have said as much in my dazed state because she laughed. "It's an invisible sheath tied to my energy, but you were close, friend."

Of course I was. Two decades of hardcore fantasy reading hadn't been for nothing. *Told you, mother!*

"I think it's time you provide me with information about this world now," I said as Drager, Chaple, and Jords reached us. "So I don't accidentally get everyone killed."

Drager snarled, and before Lexie could answer, he wrapped

his hands around my biceps, firm enough to bite into my skin, but it wasn't unbearable. Leaning closer, he breathed deeply near my exposed throat. "Who the hell are you?" he rumbled, sounding exactly as he had that very first night when he called me.

My legs went a little weak as a hint of beast filtered across his face, scales sliding over his skin. "Who are you?" he roared louder this time. "Why do you bring them to my door?"

I gulped before answering. "Human," I choked out, and thankfully he lessened his dragonhandling of me. "I'm just a human. No one important."

He stared down at me, an unbreaking, unblinking stare, and I couldn't look away. "I'm just a human who was in the wrong place at the wrong time, and now I'm stuck helping you."

His expression grew grimmer, if that was possible. "I'm starting to think your help might be our undoing," he finally muttered.

When he released me, I landed heavily, and would have fallen if Lexie hadn't steadied me. Blood pulsed back into my arms, the pain sudden after his strong grip. "Return her to her room," Drager said shortly, "and don't let her leave until I figure out our next move."

A new fear made itself known then. My room, that stark white sterile environment, was to be a literal prison. "No," I said with force. "You can't leave me locked in there, with nothing and no one. I'll lose my mind! I'm not your prisoner."

His power locked around me, holding me in place. Drager didn't need to touch me to enforce his will. "Little human, we both know you've been my prisoner for the past month. Just because there was pleasure doesn't mean the flipside to the coin didn't exist. Everything in life is a balance, and you're about to find yours."

The silence was heavy as I stared at him, but on the inside I was raging at myself for being so fucking stupid. I'd never fought him, not for one second of it. Not when he'd claimed my body in the library, or when he'd told me I was returning to Risest with him, and not even now as he stared at me with an unreadable gaze.

I'd allowed him to freely take from me, to control me, and here in a faerie world I was powerless and alone. I could feel my body shutting down as my mind screamed against what was happening to me.

"Come on, Morgan," Lexie said with urgency.

Fear and panic held me immobile, but her voice reminded me that I wasn't as alone as I'd thought. I still had an ally here. While a sliver of distrust remained between us, Lexie remained my best and only chance of escaping.

I needed to discuss my options with her. Which meant getting away from Drager.

I allowed her to pull me along, and no one stopped us as we hurried back into the main building of Lancourt. Chaple and Jords remained with Drager, so finally something was going right for me.

"Fuck," Lexie choked out, and I gasped loud enough to snap her out of her panic.

"You swore," I whispered, and my hope that she might be my savior faded.

Lexie never dropped the f-bomb, and the fact that she had today told me this was not going to have a happy ending. Lexie had no idea how to get me out of this situation.

She gripped my arm harder, pulling me along faster than I could comfortably keep up with. "Morgan, we're in so much trouble. Drager has supreme control here, and he's an energy manipulator. He can legitimately take anything that contains energy and bend it to his will. If you don't know how to shield against him, he could snuff your life out with a mere squeeze of his hands."

"Drager could snuff my life out with one punch," I snorted. "He doesn't need fancy powers."

Lexie's expression remained sober as she slowed a touch, leading us through the atrium. "I know, and that's what has me panicked. I don't have the power to get you out of here. There's nowhere we can run, not even on Earth. Not to mention you've now, somehow, drawn the attention of another Fallen." She shook her head. "It makes no sense. You're human."

"So Drager turns into a dragon like that one?" I asked.

She nodded. "Yes, the same with slightly different colors. All five of them are uniquely colored in their beast form."

"Five raging beasts?" I breathed.

No wonder the fae all bowed down and called them gods.

"Yes," Lexie said as we entered the white halls. "They fell to Risest a couple of hundred years ago. Fell, took control, and divided up our world. They hold tightly to their territories, and with all of them able to manipulate energy like Drager, they're formidable."

"Their dragon forms look formidable," I agreed, that black dragon so clear in my mind it was as if it still flew before me.

"They're beyond anything we know here," Lexie admitted. "They're also invulnerable to most fae magic. Their greatest threat is from each other."

We were silent then as we weaved through the maze toward my room, until eventually my curiosity wouldn't remain at bay. "This is what has Drager so worried about the traitor," I said quickly. "He's assuming it's one of his brothers behind it all, since no other fae would risk the dragon's wrath."

Lexie nodded. "Exactly, only he doesn't know which one, and

he wouldn't want to target the wrong one. That would cause the others to move against him."

I lowered my voice. "Will he release me when I figure out who this thief and traitor is?"

Lexie didn't say anything for a moment, before letting out an extended sigh. "I don't know. I want to say yes, but he's acting even more irrationally than usual. We should let him calm down for a few days. Then I'll approach for more information."

"Don't put yourself in any danger to help me," I said in a rush. "I can hang out in a soulless room for a few weeks if that's what's needed."

She squeezed my hand tightly. "We are going to figure this out together."

I appreciated that more than I could articulate to her, but I also wasn't prepared to just sit back and let her deal with everything. I was done being in the dark.

"I need to learn more about this world," I said. "I don't know a damn thing. I don't even know what powers fae have. It's my life on the line, and it's stupid for me to just keeping wandering around without a clue."

We reached my door and it slid open to allow us entry. Lexie followed me in, and I sank into the couch, exhausted. All of that unspent adrenaline had me crashing.

"Every race of fae is different," Lexie said, and I was ecstatic that she appeared to agree with my need to know more. "But truth be told, most of us are a lot like humans. Stronger, faster, and with more animalistic-like reflexes, but we don't have power like the Fallen. Or like most supernaturals you read about in your books."

My eyes narrowed on her. "You pulled a flaming sword from a magical sheath."

She laughed with actual amusement, and for some reason I found myself relaxing. "I'm from a warrior clan in the North

Sandingshire province," she said as she calmed. "The upper quadrant of Ocheran. We're known for our skills with a blade, and our ability to manipulate energy. Nothing like Lord Drager, of course, but enough for me to conceal my weapons and heal mild injuries. The sword itself was handcrafted by goblins in the Trainker Mountains. They have learned how to infuse their steel with a touch of the natural energy of Risest. It gives each blade its own unique strengths and—" Her smile grew wistful. "…personalities, if you will."

In just a two-minute conversation with Lexie, my mental image of Risest was clearer, and it eased the panicked swirl in my chest just a fraction. I might be a temporary prisoner, but Drager still needed me to find his traitor, so he'd eventually have to let me go free. Then he'd be busy with a dragon war, and I'd escape back to Earth.

As plans go, it wasn't flawless, but I'd worked with less.

CHAPTER
TWENTY-FIVE

L exie stayed with me until the food was delivered, and this time she ate without any prompting on my behalf. "It's weird to me that you say fae don't eat much," I said between large bites of what was turning into my favorite food here: the bread slathered in that herby, garlicky, delicious spread. "You out-ate me most days, and that's saying something considering I'm a chronic overeater."

She snorted. "More lies from your insane mother. You don't overeat. You're not overweight either. You have amazing curves that most humans would kill for. Fae in my clan are naturally thin, and let me tell you, I've wished many a time I could eat myself into curves."

Lexie had told me before she wanted to eat herself into curves, but I'd never seen her gain a pound, which made perfect sense now.

She was quiet for a few seconds as she played with a piece of fruit in her hands. "I've changed, Morgs," she finally said. "My time on Earth affected me in a way that a few decades in Risest could never. From fae to a hybrid human-fae—maybe not in genetics but definitely in fundamental personality traits."

I couldn't argue with her, and I loved the duality of her personality.

"I've noticed a lot of fae don't have pointed ears," I said, hoping that wasn't offensive.

Lexie flashed me a cheeky grin. "You're not looking close enough," she said. "Despite your vast fantasy knowledge, the human eye still sees what it expects to be there. Try again."

Lifting her hair from her face, she revealed perfectly human shaped ears. The same ears I'd seen a hundred or thousand times before. Leaning in closer, I narrowed my eyes, and as I tilted my head, the slight point became obvious right at the tip of her ear.

"That's it?" I burst out. "It's only noticeable if you're eyeballing the ear like it stole your man."

More laughter spilled from her. "That's true, but as you've no doubt noticed, more than a few of the races have more prominent points. You'll see that clearer if you ever get out of Lancourt and down to the mainland."

Flopping back onto the couch, I let out a sigh. "Doesn't look like it's going to happen anytime soon. Drager is all ragey about the interloper. Speaking of, who the heck was that? Like, which specific Fallen?"

Her amusement disappeared in an instant. "Zahak."

That was all I got. One name, and it was clear that she wasn't about to expand.

You bring war, brother. "He called the dragon brother. Are they actually related?"

Brother held multiple meanings on Earth, and I wondered if it was the same here.

She nodded. "As far as we know, they are all blood-related

brothers, born of another world, and when their race was on the brink of extinction, their family sent them here to escape."

Leaning into her, I gasped in a few deep breaths. "Are you telling me they're literal aliens? Dragon aliens who Superman'd their way into a faerie world?"

What in the tripped-out-author storyline was happening here?

Lexie shook her head. "We've got to get you out of books and into the real world. You look like the next twelve Christmases have come at once."

It was no secret that I was obsessed with Christmas. We never had much money, but I always found a crafty way to add to the over-decoration of our tiny apartment.

"But this is the real world," I reminded her. "And I've officially been training for twenty plus years to survive here."

She gripped my hand, yanking me up from my supine position, her expression deadly serious. "That's just the thing, Morgan. This isn't an actual story where someone controls the outcome. Risest is terrifying, with many creatures beyond your knowledge. You don't have my training. You don't have Drager's power. You are weak and vulnerable, and the fae love that. Not in any way you might expect, but in the way a predator loves prey."

Having almost landed on a dragon today did a lot to back up her point. But I couldn't think too deeply about her warnings. My panic at being a prisoner continued to simmer low, even as I kept it locked down. For now I'd focus on being safe, fed, and with my best friend in a fantasy world.

Worry and fear were tomorrow's problem. Tonight, we were hanging out, and I was going to enjoy every second of it.

———

Turned out they weren't tomorrow's problem. I remained trapped in my room, the door no longer responding to my command to open. All pretense of me not being a prisoner was gone. At least Lexie could still visit, eat meals with me, and basically keep me sane.

My joy at having my best friend back was strong, even if the rest of me felt weak and lost.

"I have a few questions," I said the first afternoon of my prison stay, and she chuckled.

"Not even remotely surprised, Morgs."

We both knew my mind wouldn't let me rest until I had my answers. "The fertility ritual went for thirty days, so how is it that we've never been trapped in the library before?"

Lexie's smile was slow. "Remember that forced vacation I made you take two years ago?"

I remembered it all too well. It had been a month in California, where we drained our meagre savings to visit theme parks and other tourist locations. I'd loved it, but I'd also been missing the books like crazy. "So, you usually know when it's coming and ensure that we're not at the library? But that's the only long vacation we've taken."

She nodded. "Most years Drager keeps the fae from the library during the ritual. We stay in Risest. This year for some reason, the ritual snuck up on us. Drager believes that it's connected to the missing tome, and other strange happenings. The balance is being disturbed by some fae."

As concerning as that was, the rest made perfect sense. "That's why there's weeks where almost no books get borrowed."

I loved those weeks because all we did was dust and read.

"Exactly," Lexie confirmed.

"Okay, that answers question one." I moved on to my next

pressing thought. "You were trapped in the library for the fertility ceremony, right? Who were you with?"

It was a testament to how much damage had been between us and how long it took to rebuild our trust and communication, that I didn't already know every single detail of her time during the ritual.

Her face was shadowed as she swallowed roughly, and I wondered what she was about to tell me. "Jordo."

It was a whisper, but I heard the name as loud as if she was screaming it. I gasped. "Shut the fuck up!"

Finally, a smile cracked the stoic expression on her face. "I wish I could. As one of my commanding officers, we have worked in close proximity many times before I left for Earth, but we never had anything other than a platonic relationship. That bastard is so dominant that even under the spell we battled. Battled and screwed, in that order. Which leaves us now in a weird spot of professionalism but with more simmering between us."

Having met Jords a couple of times now, it was nearly impossible to imagine him in a sexual situation. "Drager is dominant too," I said. "But the difference is, in the bedroom, I'm not dominant at all." I pressed my lips together before shrugging. "I actually enjoyed him bossing me around in that way."

Lexie's lips twitched. "Why does that not surprise me." She settled back against the couch cushions. "Tell me what it was like with Drager," she added. "How did you survive?"

I pressed my hand to my stomach, missing the slow roil of heat within; his power had faded almost completely now. "It was his energy. He infused it inside of me and that allowed me to accept not just his size but his strength."

She nodded like that made complete sense to her. "How was the sex?"

I didn't even have to think twice. "It was incredible," I told her.

"Life changing and mind shattering. The sort of sex you read about in fantasy books—and I get it now."

Lexie side-eyed me. "You get what?"

"Why female protagonists lose their brains the moment the dick appears on the page. It's hard to keep your head straight with so much energy and male magnetism. You get kind of—"

"Spelled," Lexie snorted. "That's what we call it when the sirens use their song. Spelled. You fall under their control and your will becomes theirs."

I nodded. "Yep, that's what it was like with Drager, but he didn't abuse the power. He actually took really good care of me." A memory rolled through me. "Have you heard of knotting?" I asked her.

That got all her attention as she shot up into a rigid position. "Knotting? Why are you asking about knotting, Morgan?"

Her reaction intrigued me. "The very first time we had sex, when his energy infused into me, he knotted inside. Drager said that it usually means the Fallen have found a compatible woman for breeding, but this time it happened because of the fertility ritual. It was just the one time, so that makes sense."

Lexie was wide-eyed, staring like she'd never seen me before. "The Fallen don't remember the exact events that caused their fall," she said in a hushed whisper. "Their memories were stripped from them, but they did retain a few customs of their world. It's rumored that they only have one true mate, one who can absorb their energy and carry their child. Knotting is the way they confirm it, even if they already feel the connection."

I'd had my period just before we came to Risest, when Drager and I had already slept together many times, so I was certain there was no chance of pregnancy. Side note, dragons did not give a shit about human blood when they wanted to have sex. Not squeamish at all. Also, orgasms were most definitely the best cramp-pain relievers.

"It had to be the spell," I repeated. "I'm not pregnant, and it only happened the very first time we were together."

Lexie didn't comment again, but I recognized her expression. She'd ponder this for days until she'd come back with a different angle to discuss again.

I looked forward to hearing her new perspective.

After that conversation, she left for another war-strategy meeting with Drager—the visit from the black dragon had not gone over well with her lord and leader, and he was determined never to be taken by surprise again. My anger toward Drager had burned hot on my first day in here, simmered moderately on the second day, but as I opened my eyes on the third, there was nothing but a dull rise of any emotion inside.

Lying there, more exhausted than when I went to bed, I wondered what the point of even getting up was. Sure, I could shower in the best shower that ever existed, and eat delicious food prepared by fae who cooked like a dream, but then I'd just pace up and down in front of the windows staring at the gorgeous dusky pink sky that was well beyond my reach.

As I remained a huddled lump in bed, my fatigue allowed me to doze for a few more hours, and the next time I woke up I felt even worse. I'd experienced mild depression before, when my mother had been on one of her rampages, but it had never felt like this.

Here, there was a sense that my existence was seeping out of me, as I faded into the mattress.

Even if I'd wanted to move, I wouldn't have had the strength to do so.

But I didn't want to move.

I didn't care to even try.

"Morgan!"

I heard Lexie shout, and hands roughly lifted me from the bed.

"You're freezing," a deep voice said.

Drager's fire was finally quenched, and with it I'd become an icy, brittle shell.

Lexie spoke again. "Drager will kill us, but we have no other option. I won't let her fade."

"—off… the land… might save her," the male answered, but I missed a lot of it as my eyes grew heavy once more and darkness danced on the edge of my vision.

Sweet darkness.

"Morgan," Lexie snapped, and I felt a jolt to my chest as she hit me with a bite of her power. Liar-liar was nothing like humans.

"Fu… off," I muttered.

"Okay, good, she's cursing," Lexie said in a rapid exhale. "We still have time. Move fast, Chaple."

Chaple carried me as they ran, and even in my shattered state I knew we were moving fast. My first attempt at opening my eyes and lifting my head was a failure, as panic threaded through the darkness. This wasn't normal depression.

Was I dying?

"Most of the transports are out on patrol," Chaple said, and thanks to Lexie's little zap before, I had enough mental cognition to catch every word.

"I'm going to call *Calendul*," she replied.

Chaple's reply was hard. "Are you sure that's wise?"

"It's our only option," she snapped back.

The satyr wisely shut up after that, and when we made it outside, the gentle breezes caressing my cheeks saw more of my energy returning. I even managed to pry one eyelid open in time to see that the sky was at its brightest pink, and there was a huge bird waiting for us on the edge of Lancourt.

The bird, standing a good six feet taller than me, wasn't like any animal I'd seen before. It reminded me of a giant stork, with long legs—thick and powerful looking—topped off by a midnight blue body. Its wings were flat against its side, and when Lexie moved toward the creature, it craned a long neck, its beady eyes peering down at us along the length of its lethal beak.

"I'm sorry to call you out like this," she said in a rush. "But we have an emergency. Morgan needs to get out of Lancourt and back down to the mainland. Would you please take her? I'd owe you a very large favor."

The bird opened its sharp, orange beak and made a low humming noise.

Lexie released a loud breath. "Thank you, friend. I promise I won't forget this."

Another humming sound, and then Chaple placed me on the ground. Lexie dropped down beside me just as the bird spread huge wings, displaying a hue of orange that contrasted to the blue of its body.

"Morgan, I need you to listen to me," Lexie said with urgency, and I managed to focus on her. "Calendul is a *yonter*, which is a very powerful bird of prey. She's an old friend of my family, and as such, is granting me this favor. Calendul will not hurt you, but others down there will, so I need you to stay alive until we find you. Okay?"

That one eye I'd managed to open was wavering, exhaustion pulling me down once more.

"Morgan!" She zapped me again.

"Okay," I mumbled. "No petting the birdies."

Another zap, and I wasn't surprised that this one had more voltage behind it.

"We'll be down to Ocheran as soon as we find transport,"

Chaple said from above Lexie, his voice farther away. "Just stay where you are and touch nothing."

"No petting the faerie," I mumbled again.

"For the love of French fries," Lexie muttered. "She's going to get herself killed in the ten minutes she's alone down there. I can already see it."

Calendul let out a long humming sound, and then I was jerked up into her powerful clawed feet, and we were setting off over the side of the land.

As the scream ripped from me, I wondered if this was better or worse than fading into nothingness. Here was hoping I didn't feel it when I hit the ground.

CHAPTER
TWENTY-SIX

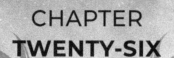

After that first terrifying drop, Calendul must have caught a draft, as her downward trajectory leveled off. From there it was a much gentler ride down to Ocheran, that wild land of green that I'd only glimpsed a few times.

By the time she placed me gently on the grassy ground, I was able to open both eyes, and breathed deeply. The sickly, icy feeling from deep in my chest continue to fade until I could push myself up to a sitting position and look around.

Calendul had brought us to a hollow of grass with small hills on either side, keeping our presence somewhat hidden. As I got to my feet, the bird made her humming noise, and I shook my head.

"I'm sorry, I don't understand what you're saying. But thank you for bringing me here. You saved my life."

She hummed louder, jerking her long beak toward me, and as Lexie's instructions returned to my now functioning brain, I remembered that there might be dangers here that Calendul was warning me about. In a rush, I scanned the landscape, fear trickling through my veins.

It was too dangerous to remain in the base of this hollow.

If a fae creature appeared at the edge of that ridge above, I'd be at a massive disadvantage.

Without another thought, I scrambled up the side, the yonter's humming following me, but I didn't look back. When I reached the crest of the hill, I paused and assessed the situation. Calendul had clearly dropped me in the middle of nowhere. I saw green rolling hills, the dusty pink sky, and forests in the distance.

Yet, that feeling of foreboding didn't abate.

Was it because Drager had expressly warned them not to let me leave Lancourt? Or was it just the urgency in Lexie's voice as she panicked about sending me down here alone?

There were no obvious signs of danger, despite the consistent humming from Calendul, and still the fear persisted. Remaining motionless, I tried to expand my senses into the land, hoping to ascertain what had me spooked. Of course, I'd conveniently forgotten that I was a human with the dullest senses of any animal on Earth. Here, I was akin to a slug.

Or slugs were probably more advanced—who knew.

Lexie might think fae were just slightly advanced versions of humans, but since I'd seen her move faster than I could think, while pulling a magical blade from its magical sheath, it was clear she was wrong. Completely freaking wrong.

Calendul's humming grew louder and closer, and I almost tumbled down the damn hill I'd just climbed up. Apparently, my less-than-a-slug senses were *so strong* I didn't even detect her moving up behind me. Tilting my head back, I met her gaze, and realized how giant she was.

Giant and dangerous, if Lexie's last warning was any indication.

Dark eyes locked on me, unblinking. Swallowing roughly, I slowly raised both hands and held them before me in a placating motion. "I'm sorry. Forgive my human ignorance, Cal. Just think of me as a silk-pajamas-clad baby. I have no idea what I'm doing out here, and I only moved from the very safe place you dropped me because of these damn tingles down my spine. It's my danger warning, you know?"

She tilted her head to the side, and I couldn't read her bird face well enough to know if she was confused, annoyed, or trying to figure out the quickest way to stab me to death. She didn't attack though, and I decided that since she wasn't murdering me yet, I should continue to check out the scenery.

Turning in the direction of the closest forest, I expected to see the same empty expanse of green. Only we were no longer alone.

I gasped before I could stop myself, examining the small creature which sat about three feet away. "Uh, good bunny?" I said quickly.

It wasn't a bunny by any means, but it had the look of a hare, covered in gray fur, with short, pointed ears. Dark red eyes examined me, and its nose twitched, as if my scent was so foreign it didn't know what to make of me.

Cal moved even closer, her humming a vibration in the air. The creature's ears were twitching now too. It didn't stick around, disappearing down what had to be a hole in the ground, because one second it was there, and the next gone.

Thank God for Cal, because clearly it wasn't my confused stare that scared it away. Lexie might have been right about me getting myself killed in the ten minutes it took for them to make it down here.

Glancing up, I saw floating Lancourt, seemingly miles away. It was odd to see it from this angle, and I was surprised at the sheer size of Drager's home base. "Where are you, Lexie?" I whispered.

She'd made the right call in sending me down here. My energy had returned, and it was clear that Lancourt had been draining me almost to death—a fact Drager knew, and yet that fucking rat bastard kept me prisoner without infusing his own power into me so I could survive.

Fear pulsed within me once again as I stopped staring at Lancourt and stared around Ocheran once more. "I can't stay here," I said to Cal. "There's danger here."

She hummed—and no lie, it sounded a little like a snort.

That was the moment my dumbass finally clicked on what she'd been trying to tell me all along. "It's you," I deadpanned, shaking my head at my own stupidity. "You're the danger I'm sensing?"

Cal hummed louder and bobbed her head closer to me so that our gazes could meet. As she moved farther into my personal space, the tingles down my spine and swirls of dread in my gut increased, to the point I was barely able to stop myself from running and screaming. Every instinct I possessed, even as dull as they were, warned me to escape her.

Thankfully, she pulled away and took a few steps back, allowing the raging river of fear to calm into nice summer rapids. That was some weapon she possessed. Not only was she lethal to look at, she could also drive a human out of their mind with those waves of fear she induced.

Thankfully, understanding the fear allowed me to calm down and return to the hollow of the hill, Calendul right behind me. Hoping there were no bitey insects in the ground, I dropped down in my tiny silk shorts and let myself fall back against the soft grass.

It didn't feel like grass back home, more velvety, as it cushioned my skin without irritation. Considering my shorts weren't the only skimpy part of my pjs—the shirt was a bare slip of silk, and only yesterday I'd woken with one of my tits in the bathroom and the other out in the kitchen making coffee—there was a decent chance I'd have another nip slip here at some point.

Hopefully Lexie had noticed my state of undress, even in her panic over me dying, and would bring a change of clothing with her.

I didn't close my eyes. I wasn't sure I trusted Cal that much, but I was able to relax and stare into the pink sky, watching Drager's home drift aimlessly. It was during these moments of reflection that I missed the huge dark shadow appearing at the top of the hollow. It was only when Cal started humming in a harsher tone than before did I realize that help had finally found us.

Only it wasn't really help.

The shadow belonged to a being far more dangerous than that bunny from before, or even Cal with her fear factor.

It was Drager.

A pissed-off Drager.

He raged forward. The grass beneath him withered and became dust as he cut a path along the beautiful green hill to reach me. On my feet, I backed up, wondering if he was about to murder me with his bare hands. As he moved closer, I noticed that his skin was darker, scales visible across his neck, hands, and face.

"How dare you disobey my orders!" he seethed as he closed in, his dark as sin eyes spitting at me. "You were ordered not to leave Lancourt."

Calendul's humming grew louder, and that was when his attention snapped to the bird. She stepped in front of me, and it was clear that she was willing to stand between me and this scary-ass dragon guy out of her loyalty to Lexie. But I'd never allow any creature to be hurt protecting me, not while I had the strength to prevent it.

Drager's roar was animalistic, and as Cal spread her wings wider, clearly preparing to battle the dragon, I threw myself between them. "No!" I screamed. "Don't hurt her. She saved my damn life."

He was all puffed up as the dragon pushed beneath his skin as if about to break through. Cal's fear factor was nothing compared to Drager's when he turned it up, but I'd spent a month under, on top of, and entwined with this dragon, giving me a layer of resistance against him.

"Drager!" I snapped, drawing his gaze away from Cal, who was trying to edge around me. "I was dying in Lancourt. I could barely open my eyes this morning, and they took the only action they had to save my life."

His lips thinned, and more grass wilted around him. The green hollow was almost completely dead now. "Why didn't they come to me?"

Shaking my head, a snort of laughter escaped. "Everyone is terrified of you," I told him without inflection. "You control with fear and power, and that means your subjects are loyal, but they're never going to approach you first. Especially not when it comes to me, since apparently I make you even more unreasonable than usual."

The humming grew louder from behind me. "Can you tell me what Cal is saying?" I asked Drager, relieved to see him starting to calm.

He took his time, chest heaving with rumbles. "She said that you're the weirdest creature she's ever come across, and she doesn't understand why you protect her when you're weak and useless."

I shrugged, unoffended by the truth. "I won't let others get hurt to protect me. Your fight is with me, your anger is with me, and Cal would have just been the bird who saved my life getting killed for no reason."

Cal hummed louder and harder, and Drager shook his head.

"You inspire the oddest loyalty in what should rightfully destroy you with its presence." He waved his hand at Cal. "You can leave now. Your services here will be rewarded."

He was still calming, scales all but gone, even as the grass around him remained in a ring of death. Turning my head, I found Cal close enough to stir that fear, but I welcomed it this time. She was alive, and that was all that mattered. "Thanks, friend," I said brightly. "Don't be a stranger."

Her eyes narrowed as she shook her head, then spread her wings widely again, and took off into the sky.

Returning my gaze to Drager, I let out a small scream. He was right in front of me, leaving us barely two inches away. There was no chance I could escape him if he decided it was time to kill me and get rid of his stress, but as he reached for me I sensed that killing wasn't the action on his mind.

I recognized that look on his face, and it was clear he had a completely different plan to punish me this time.

CHAPTER
TWENTY-SEVEN

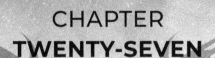

The heat of his touch seeped through the thin silk, his hands firm on my hips. "You disobeyed me," he said, voice smooth and hypnotic. Those deep rumbly tones had been my undoing since the night I answered my phone. A call that had changed everything.

"I-I was dying," I managed to reply, sounding calmer than I felt. My traitorous body was already back under his spell.

He leaned down, and the scent of fresh air and sunshine followed. Most of the time the *sun god* smelled of a perfect summer day, except when he was pissed, then he smelled of fire and ash.

"No one is allowed to disobey me without punishment," he continued. "Dying or not. The circumstances only change the punishment."

His grip tightened further and I moaned, letting him know exactly what I thought about his punishments. As much as I wanted to resist him, he drew me in like no other. I assumed this pull I felt was due to his godlike power here, but a small part of me feared it was because of this odd connection between us.

A human and a dragon-shifting-god. A more unlikely pairing had never existed.

As he released my hips, the smooth graze of his palms brushed up under my shirt and across bare skin. He grazed the underside of my boobs, and another surge of heat rocked my core.

Pressing my thighs together in an attempt to ease the ache there, my head fell back, giving Drager access to my throat. He pressed his mouth to the bare skin there, tracing along my pulse points, scraping his teeth so I felt each bite. He never broke the skin, but he enjoyed marking me.

His hands clutched my shirt, and in a single rapid move, he tore through the silk, leaving me completely topless. The warmth of the sun and his touch felt so good on my skin, filling me with life and energy, the sensation even more delicious after experiencing the cold iciness of almost dying in Lancourt.

He was too tall to keep bending down to me, and it wasn't his style anyway, so I felt no surprise when he cupped his hands under my ass and lifted. I wrapped my legs around his waist, and he wasted no time devouring my body. His mouth was hot and hard as it closed over my right nipple, sucking and gently biting until the peak was hard and throbbing. The left got the same treatment, and I was rocking against him, desperately needing some relief from the ache in my center.

Drager slipped a hand along the side of my shorts and found me bare beneath, thoroughly soaking the silk. "Fuck," he groaned. I waited for him to tear the pants from me too, but instead he gripped the edge and pulled them tighter until the seam of the shorts were pressed right along my pussy, rubbing the clit with each yank of his hand.

"God damn," I moaned, riding hard as he used my own shorts to get me off.

Drager's laugh was dark and sensual. "So responsive. It's unexplainable."

It wasn't really. He clearly didn't see himself as women did, because he was completely desirable. I must have moaned out words to that degree, because he shook his head, his fingers pushing my shorts inside me now, as he fucked me with the silk material.

"Humans are weak. Every instinct you possess should warn you to run from me, and yet you open like a newly bloomed flower in the light of its god."

Arrogant fucker. He'd chosen those words deliberately, and we both knew it.

Not that I cared right now, on the edge of an orgasm, with Drager's fingers and my shorts buried inside me. When the heat in my gut exploded, and I cried out, he let out a satisfied rumble from deep in his chest.

His strong hold kept me stable as my body shook and shuddered through an orgasm. It hadn't been that long since I'd been with Drager, but still it felt like a lifetime as I cried out and dug my nails into his shoulders. The buzz of his power seeped into me again, even without him infusing it as he had at the library.

Without dropping me, he removed his fingers, my shorts still inside me. His free hand gripped the waistband and slid it down slowly, until my ass was completely exposed to the world. Lifting me away from his body, he kept sliding the pants down my legs until the material dragged from inside me, and with each tug another shudder of pleasure slid along my spine until I was arching once more.

I'd liken this to a slow, pleasurable torture, and if this was the style of punishment Drager doled out, there wasn't a whole lot of incentive to obey him. Though, he did say the circumstances dictated the punishment…

No, Morgan. No risking your life for a good orgasm.

When my shorts went the same way as the scraps of silk top, fluttering to the ground, I pulled back to stare into his eyes. "Is that it, dragon?"

My name for him was even more accurate than I'd expected, and while in the library I'd though he might have a form that was part dragon and part man, I found it even more impressive that he became a literal massive beast.

All coherent thought disappeared as the thick head of his cock pushed at my entrance. It was fast, and while I'd had plenty of prep, there was no amount of prep that would allow Drager to fit inside me without literal manipulation of my body. He was just too large.

Pain was all I felt at first, and I wondered if he was going to tear me apart in punishment. A small cry escaped even as I tried not to let him know he was hurting me, and almost instantly his hands under my ass heated as his power seeped inside.

The pain instantly morphed into pleasure, and this time when I cried out it was due to an impending orgasm. Drager continued to slowly thrust inside, and it felt so… damn… good. The ribbed edges of his cock scraped over what had to be one billion nerve endings, filling me so completely that by the time he was seated as far inside as possible, I was breathless.

Lifting me, he slid out, before thrusting hard inside, and I could do nothing but cling on and hope to survive the fallout. The build was fast, the sort of orgasm you had no chance but to ride out, because it was barreling through you at rapid speed and you either went with it or got destroyed in the process.

My cries filled the air, and for once in my life I had no cares about the voyeuristic aspect of being out here, exposed to the fae world. All thought of other fae faded from thought as Drager increased his speed, moving faster and harder, his powerful body driving into mine. The spirals of pleasure skyrocketed and I lost control, small screams escaping me even as I sobbed his name.

He all but induced one continuous orgasm with no end in sight.

This was our first time together outside of the influence of a faerie ritual, and I was surprised that it was just as intense, the sensations heightened in the same way. That told me maybe the ritual had less to do with our sexual compatibility than I'd initially thought.

Drager's pace increased, and at this point it was too much. Everything shattered, and my mind went fuzzy. Drager's groan drew me back as he thrust one last time, his cock swelling as he came.

We both lost our minds for a time, as the swirls of intense pleasure held us immobile, but eventually, my senses returned and I was able to breathe normally.

Breathe and think.

Our sex had definitely held the same compatibility, but there were differences too. In Dragerfield I'd been his sole focus, while here he'd ignored me for days until I almost died. He'd fucked me as a punishment, and that truth left a heavy weight on my chest, and a bad taste in my mouth.

He untangled our bodies and set me on my feet. My legs wobbled briefly, but I managed to catch myself, and stand without issue. "Are you okay?" he asked, watching me closely. "I lost control when you vanished from Lancourt, and while I wanted to punish you, the aim wasn't to break you."

His concern had a tiny fraction of that weight on my chest easing.

"I'm perfectly fine," I told him, hoping the feeling would hurry back into my legs so I wasn't a complete liar. "Your power ensures that there's no lasting damage." Even if I would be hobbling for a few hours after this.

A slow smile slid across his face, and it was such a rare sight that the world felt a little lighter just for that reason.

"So... what happens now?" I asked, noting he was dressed once again, while I was still naked and standing in Ocheran. Not the most comfortable of situations, but hopefully he had a solution, one that didn't involve his obsession with pants suits.

"You will return with me to Lancourt," he said without preamble.

The fuck...? "I won't," I said stiffly, crossing my arms over my tits. "I'm not going to be a prisoner up there in my room until I die."

He growled, scales briefly appearing across his cheeks before they faded once more. "I won't let that happen, Morgan. I underestimated how long my energy would remain within, strengthening you. I won't let it go so long between now. There will be regular infusions of my energy."

While a part of me was excited by the prospect of Drager *infusing his energy* inside me, another part knew that it was a bad idea for me to get more attached to the sun god—more attached to this world.

I just had no idea how to tell him that without incurring his wrath once more.

"Look, it's not—"

"Morgan!"

Spinning on the spot, Lexie was sprinting toward us. And bless her heart, she had a stack of clothes in her hands.

"Looks like I was correct in assuming you'd need a change of clothing," she said when she reached me.

I laughed. "You are an angel. Thank you so much."

Drager remained a silent, scary shadow as I quickly pulled on clean underwear, jeans, and a plain white shirt. Lexie's outfit was the most casual clothing I'd worn in this world so far, and I felt so much more like myself.

"Lexical, I told you I would take care of this," Drager rumbled from behind me.

"I know," she replied quickly, stepping between the dragon and me. "But I'm here for more reasons than to bring Morgan clothes. Jords said that there's been a call from the Fallen. A meeting request. It appears that their lands have also had some issues, and they want to discuss it."

Drager's attention on me faded as he stepped closer to Lexie, expression blank even as his eyes blazed. "A request from the Fallen? All of them?"

She nodded. "It appears that way. It might be a trap, but Jords suggested we use this opportunity to expand our search for your traitor. Figure out which of your brothers is behind it all. We haven't had a meeting request in decades."

Drager pondered that for a beat, before nodding slowly. "He might be right."

Lexie smiled broadly. "Of course, and with your absence in mind... I was thinking I could take Morgan to Fae Academy while you're away. She can't stay on Lancourt, but it appears she's fine here on Ocheran."

Drager's eyes narrowed, focused on me for a beat like I'd somehow orchestrated this idea. "Why would I let her attend the academy?" he growled.

Lexie, clearly well versed in dealing with this dragon, didn't bite back. "It's neutral grounds, safe as any place in Risest, and if she enrolls in classes she can start to learn how to survive here. It's looking more and more likely that Morgan will have to stay here long-term, and she's woefully uneducated in all things fae. Cal said she almost approached a dunedin, imagining it was a bunny from Earth. It would have torn her to pieces. She doesn't know what is a threat, and I need her to survive."

"I didn't *almost approach it*," I muttered, but they weren't listening to me.

Drager pondered on it for about a second, before he nodded. "That makes sense. Let's get her enrolled so I can focus on this meeting."

No one bothered to ask me, but I wasn't about to argue. This plan appealed more than going back to my white-walled prison. "Lexie will be with me, right?"

"Yes," Drager growled. "You're as weak and vulnerable as a pixie right now. I need you strong enough to survive."

Both of them had conveniently forgotten I was still a human, and there was only so much "strength" I was capable of, but it couldn't hurt to learn as much as I could about this world. I was excited by the prospect, actually. After all, how many times did a human find themselves in another world? Never, right? The answer had to be never.

Before me that was.

Wait…

"Are there other humans in Risest?" I asked suddenly.

Lexie and Drager both gave me their full attention, which was unnerving to say the very least.

"Yes."

That was it. That was my entire answer.

"I don't want to know what they do here, do I?"

No response this time, and I tried not to panic.

"Only a few, and none in Ocheran," Lexie assured me. Like that was really a reassurance.

Part of me knew that nothing good came from humans in a world of fantasy, but it was too late to stress about it now. I was here, and as Lexie pointed out, would be for the foreseeable future.

CHAPTER
TWENTY-EIGHT

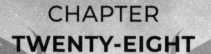

Walking after being railed by a dragon man was interesting, and when a small, pained sound slipped from between my tightly pressed lips, Lexie smirked at me. "Need a little healing?" she whispered. "It's a long walk to the academy."

"Leave her," Drager drawled. "You'll not remove my mark."

Lexie's head snapped around as she blinked at him. "You marked her?"

Drager's tone didn't change, but there was a tightness around his eyes. "Not as a mate. Why speak of impossibilities? But she's dripping with my seed right now, and the others will scent the mark on her. They'll not touch my property."

What in the…? "Your seed?"

I mean, he wasn't wrong. The lovely clean underwear was already soaked with our combined pleasure; I could feel that as we walked, but he didn't have to be so animalistic about it.

Okay, yeah, he was a dragon, so placing human values on him was plain stupid. I had to be less stupid to survive here.

"Exactly what I said, little human," he drawled. "I won't have your safety compromised while I have need of you. Whatever it takes."

Time for a subject change. "Why do you live above your land and fae?" I asked quickly. "Surely you can keep a closer eye on everything from down here."

He stared, brow furrowed as if my question was confusing. "I prefer to look upon my land from above. It's the dragon way."

"Do all of the Fallen look down on their land like you, then?"

"They don't have the power," Drager replied with an edge.

"What about Zahak?" Lexie piped up, before she clamped her lips shut. Apparently, she'd forgotten this wasn't just a casual conversation between friends.

Drager snorted. "If he has the power, then why the hell is he flying around in my territory?"

An image of that huge and terrifying black dragon entered my mind.

Zahak.

I wondered what the man looked like, because the beast was more intimidating than anything I could imagine. "He saved my life," I said softly. "Why would he do that?"

Drager's energy pulsed inside me, hot and angry.

"Zahak does nothing without an ulterior motive," Drager snarled. "Don't paint him with a savior complex, for there is not one within him. That was a dominance play aimed at me, and you just happened to be in the wrong place at the wrong time."

Drager was no doubt correct—he knew this world and his brothers far better than me. But it irked me nonetheless. Not everything was about him just because he assumed it was.

Tension remained between us as we finished crossing the green plains of the area Cal had dropped me. When we reached the trees, there was a sparse canopy above, so slivers of pinkish light spilled in around us.

I focused my attention on the foliage, examining the many flowers and plants I didn't recognize. Closest to us were low shrubby bushes, covered in a six-point lavender flower. "Angener flowers," Lexie said as I leaned down to examine them closer. "They're good for healing. You crush them up and place the oil on wounds."

She brushed her hand across a particularly bushy one to her right, and the flowers appeared to swell and grow larger under her touch. I did the same, warmth following the path of my hand as I caressed the petals. I turned wide eyes on my best friend, and she let out a soft laugh.

"They're not sentient," she told me. "I know you're panicking about crushing them now, but trust me, they don't have pain or feelings. They're seeking your energy to power themselves, the same way flowers back ho—" She cleared her throat and side-eyed Drager briefly. "—flowers back on Earth follow the sun. It's just about energy."

It made sense, but a part of me knew I'd never crush these flowers unless it was a desperate situation.

Drager, to my surprise, didn't hurry us along as I took my time examining everything. There hadn't been any creatures at first, but over time they made themselves known to us. The first was a sleek cat, about four feet long and the same high. It reminded me of a panther, but with a glossy red coat, more elongated nose, and whiskers that were thick and long, like mini tentacles moving about its face.

"*Sabre*," Lexie told me. "They're non-lethal."

Her point was proved when it prowled forward and rubbed its head along my side, in the universal cat sign for wanting to be pet. "Oh wow, aren't you adorable," I said with a smile. It wasn't as soft as it looked, the fur dense and I'd guess waterproof.

"They're plant eaters and free spirits," Lexie said, and even Drager, who was standing to the side all silent and deadly, gave the sabre a pat. It was brief, but I saw it.

When it left, a different fae creature appeared. It was small, glittering as it fluttered above an angener flower bush, one, and then another, until a dozen glittering lights shone in front of us. Even within the well-lit forest, they were bright and beautiful. I made a move to go closer, but Drager stopped me. "Don't ever follow the light, human. They draw you in with their beauty but it's death that awaits."

I squinted into their lights, shuddering when I finally saw past the dazzle. "Shit," I breathed. It looked like a mini piranha. Fish-shaped but with tiny wings holding it afloat, its jagged teeth were the largest part of its body. As more of them arrived, I imagined they could work together and strip the flesh from my body in seconds.

"Clearly, size is no indication of what is deadly here." I'd have run from the sabre and went right up to these balls of light.

"Concors," Lexie said, revulsion in her expression. "They're terrifying. But they don't attack unless you touch them first. They have to draw you in, and many a fae has lost their life to the light."

"If you can catch them in a jar," Drager added, "they do provide an excellent and eternal source of illumination. They don't die from entrapment or lack of food."

Good to know.

We continued on, and as I glanced back the concors had already disappeared—lying in wait for their next victim.

The forest continued on and we walked for many hours, meeting a range of creatures along the way. The most terrifying was a *fantine*: a carnivorous deer-like animal with tan leathery skin, sweet brown eyes, but a mean, *mean* temperament. "They're pack animals," Lexie told me, after Drager shooed it away. "One scouts and then the rest will arrive so they can hunt together."

"Should we move faster?" I said, panicking at the thought of a pack of carnivorous fantine arriving. Drager's laughter was my answer, since I'd dumbly forgotten we had the scariest predator with us, and nothing was going to attack.

"How far is the academy exactly?" I asked when we'd been walking for what felt like half the day. "The human needs water, food, and indoor plumbing. Not necessarily in that order."

Drager's determination to keep his "mark" inside me was great in theory, but in truth I hadn't peed since we'd been together, so there was no doubt a lovely UTI in my future. More than keeping Drager happy, there were too many bitey creatures in this forest for me to feel comfortable hanging my bare ass out in the woods. Though, if a bathroom didn't present itself very soon, I'd have no choice. At least I had Lexie to watch over me, and I wouldn't have to rely on Drager.

We weren't at the *peeing in front of each other* part in our relationship yet. Mostly because we didn't have a relationship yet. Or probably ever.

"We're still some distance away," Drager told me. "Ocheran is vast, and the academy sits in the center of the five lands. Neutral grounds, as you know."

"Let's call the *crion*," Lexie added with a bright smile. "They live to please you."

Drager grumbled under his breath. "I'd rather not. They grow clingy when called on. I'll just carry her."

Her was still standing right here, and *her* didn't like the concept of being carried like a damn helpless baby. They already thought of humans as less than fae, and I couldn't really argue, but I'd keep representing us best I could.

"I'd rather walk and pee in the bus—"

Drager knocked me off balance with one hand under my ass as he lifted me up in his arms, and before I could make my distaste known, we were moving so fast that my head spun, and I had to take deep breaths to stop from vomiting all over the dragon lord.

Not that he didn't deserve it.

During the journey, I could only open my eyes for brief moments, and each time I saw Lexie running at his side, looking like she was loving every second of this speed. Her face was lit up, eyes sparkling, and though I couldn't hear her, I knew she was singing as she ran.

Just like humans my ass. She was so full of it. She ran at the speed of a damn bullet train.

Drager's hold on me was firm enough that I had no fear of falling, and as we continued I stopped trying to open my eyes.

Even at their speed, it took another couple of hours to reach the academy. I'd had to ask for a bathroom break just before we left the forest, and thankfully, my butt remained unattacked.

Once we exited the forests, we ended up near the largest lake I'd ever seen in my life. Drager had slowed as soon as the emerald-green and crystal-clear water came into view. As he set me back on my feet, I drifted toward the lake. It looked so inviting, especially after our long journey and the heat of the afternoon sun beating down on us.

"Is the lake safe to swim in?" I asked as I wobbled on legs that hadn't quite found their balance again yet. "Or to drink from." My parched mouth screamed at me to dive headfirst into that water.

"Safe to drink," Lexie confirmed. "This water is filtered through millions of underground tunnels as it races between all five lands. I wouldn't swim in it alone though. There are many fae that call it home, including merpeople."

I widened my eyes. "Merpeople?"

She nodded. "Oh yeah. They're pretty much as you imagine them, but a little more fish-like than that redhead one from the movie you like."

On shaky legs, I made my way down to the bank, scanning the calm unbroken surface of the lake. There was no sign of any life, and unsure if I was disappointed or relieved, I knelt on the edge and cupped up a clear handful of water. Drinking slowly, I barely repressed my moans at how good it tasted. Sweet, quenching my thirst immediately, I grabbed as many handfuls as I could before my stomach groaned.

"Come, it'll be dark soon, and I need you settled before that," Drager ordered from the bank.

As I got to my feet, the muscles in my body protested. Not only was I sore from the sex, but I'd also walked for hours, and then got hauled along at warp speed. My poor bookworm body was not used to this sort of activity, and was making those pains well known.

My legs warmed up as we made our way along the path around the lake, and within a few minutes, in the darkening of the pink sky, the academy came into view.

Oh… my… sun gods.

CHAPTER
TWENTY-NINE

The Academy was incredibly impressive, spanning out across at least a mile of land. In my mind I'd been expecting it to be dark and imposing, a gothic style academy, akin to those exclusive and well-established schools I'd always admired in England and Europe. But Fae Academy was nothing like that.

It was mostly white, with pops of gold on the windows, doors, and arches. It was more modern than I expected as well, with three or four levels, no turrets or towers, looking like a beach-mansion cross Hamptons billionaire's playground. Windows and balconies spanned the left and right sides, and I was going to guess they were the dorm rooms. In the center, half a dozen steps led up to massive double doors that were almost purely gold, with swirls of words and images moving across them.

Despite Lexie's assurances that Risest wasn't hugely different to Earth, the faes' ability to manipulate energy was obvious to me. "How many children or students go here?" I asked quietly. I felt out of place and uncomfortable already.

"There are no children or young here," Lexie said quickly. "This is more like college, where you choose a specialty and get advanced training before returning to your land and commencing work."

"But I need basic training," I reminded them. "I can't take part in any sort of advanced classes."

Drager didn't appear to be worried. "You won't be in classes that are above your abilities. Most of it will be observational only. That way, you will learn what our world is about without having to participate. We can add in private tutors as well."

"Is this really necessary?" I asked. "I mean, I'm not planning on living in Risest forever. Maybe it makes more sense to stick with Lexie until we find the traitor, and then I can go home."

Drager's expression was hard to read, but he didn't look happy with my suggestion. "The fae world moves much slower than the human one," he said slowly, as if to prove his point. "It might take years or decades to track and deal with the traitor. Besides, no education is a waste of time. You should feel grateful for this opportunity. Humans are not generally welcome into such a space."

"Ohhh, right! You should have said so earlier." My reply was all false cheer. "I'm ready to charge into those golden doors and give myself over to this experience I don't deserve."

His expression darkened, and Lexie jumped in suddenly. "It'll be fun," she chirped. "I enjoyed my time here, and it'll be good to get in some training since I've grown a little rusty during my time on Earth."

Breathing deeply and counting to ten, I decided that as long as Lexie was with me, I'd be just fine. "Okay, I'm ready," I said. "Speaking of, where are all the students?" It appeared deserted, with no fae in sight.

A gong rang out around us, like a bell tower had just tolled in one long, deep note, and with it the quiet stasis of the academy was broken. Windows opened as students appeared on the balconies, and just like that, any sense of the academy being deserted vanished.

The fae had simply been in their classes.

"There are a few hundred students here at all times," Drager told me. "We don't have a lot of young in Risest in general, so even though the academy can house many more, it usually remains around that number. They stay a two-year cycle, which is about four hundred days."

Shorter than most college degrees back home. "The Fallen created the academy?" I asked.

"We created everything," he said shortly. "The five lands were in disarray, with no direction or purpose. Fae warred and did not interact as one world."

"What's it like in the other lands of Risest? Outside of the Eastern Realm?" I asked. "I'm assuming they don't have their own Fallen, so are they still chaotic and war-driven?"

Lexie answered me: "We know very little about them. We're separated by vast, treacherous seas. We've only met a few inhabitants over the centuries, and at that time they didn't have the same issues we have here in the Eastern Realm. It was assumed that due to our pathways to Earth, we have more chaotic energy, and it impacts our races."

This connection between Earth and Risest fascinated me the most. "How do these pathways work exactly? How did they even come into existence?"

"We have no idea," Lexie said with a shrug, dispelling any hope I had of learning more. "It's theorized that Earth might be a product of the energy of our world, millions of years ago, but

173

there are none left who know the truth. Funnily enough, it was a human who discovered it first, stumbling into this pocket between our worlds. Only a select few humans have the energy to cross the path alone, and most of them are still destroyed in the process. All doorways in the Eastern realm are monitored now, so that no fae enters Earth without permission."

"Most of the doorways are in my land anyway," Drager added. "And my fae are restricted to using the library and gathering energy from there."

"You told me that the sun powers you," I reminded him of our first conversations. "And yet you all only visit at night. How does that work?"

He smiled briefly. "The building is gathering the sun energy, and then we are using it at night when we visit. It's just easier that way. Humans sleep while we use their world as we see fit."

And that right there told me that not all fae remained in the library when they crossed. Not if they were wanting to infiltrate the land while humans slept.

At this point, we were starting to draw attention, as more of the fae students appeared on their balconies, peering down at us. I heard whispers of *"One of the Fallen is here."*

Drager at the academy clearly wasn't a regular occurrence.

"Come." The dragon lord ignored the curious faces. "Let's get you settled."

He headed toward the stairs, as if ready to enter the academy, only to pause before he took the first step. In a slow turn, he looked out toward the lake and his expression darkened. Wondering what had distracted him, I also scanned the lake and horizon, and gasped embarrassingly loud when four shadows appeared.

It was the dragons. All of them.

They soared over the forests and skimmed down across the lake, four gigantic beasts, silhouetted in the last rays of the sunlight. They all had the same powerful shape as the black beast, with massive wings, a thick heavy body, and gilded wings and scales, just with different coloring as Lexie had explained to me before.

Front and center was a forest-green beast, a little smaller than the black one, sleek and fast. Beside him was a burnt orange, and on the other side a red.

Above them all, not flying in any formation, was the black-scaled beast, larger and scarier than the others combined.

"What color is your dragon?" I asked Drager, unable to tear my gaze from the approaching beasts.

His chest rumbled, which almost drew my attention, until the other four banked to the left, coming to land on the grass about fifty yards from us.

Drager's rumbles picked up in intensity, and I wondered if we were about to see a dragon battle in the flesh. A possibility that should fill me with fear, and yet some messed-up part of me wanted to experience it.

Behind us, the students were losing their brains, shrieking as they called out to others, and a quick glance over my shoulder confirmed that the balconies were absolutely packed. Every single student was out here for the show.

Hot air whooshed around me as Drager started to move. "Stay here," he snapped as he strode across the grass toward his brothers.

"I think I finally understand why you all bow down to them as gods," I whispered to Lexie. "They're impressive."

"You have no idea," she shot back. "I haven't seen all five of them together in literally years. They don't get along very well,

175

and there's always so much suspicion between them. I don't understand why the other four followed Drager to the academy."

"Maybe they decided to bring the meeting here?" I wondered.

"That, or war," Lexie replied drily. "I'd say we're about to find out which."

Drager stood before his brothers' beast forms, and it was the first time I could really judge the sheer size of them. Drager was a giant of a man, and he looked positively tiny. Even against the green one, who was the smaller of the four.

"How will we know if war is about to start?" I asked, speaking louder as the fae behind us grew more excited.

"You'll know," Lexie said with a strangled laugh. "They're not subtle. The first few years when they were establishing territories and dividing the races of fae across their lands, fires ravaged our world."

Thankfully there was no fire yet, but the atmosphere was certainly tense.

"Make sure you have the meeting room set up for them," a high-pitched voice said behind us, and I turned to find a massive fae hurrying down those front stairs. Wearing a suit with a skirt and jacket, she was clearly one of the teachers here, and she stood almost as tall as Drager.

She had broad shoulders, a craggy face, and just one single eye —an eye that was huge, in the center of her face, unblinking as she focused on the dragons.

"Troll," Lexie said softly, right beside my ear. "Rolta, the head-mistress of the academy. Trolls' skin is super strong, they're resis-tant to most energy manipulation and other fae gifts. They cannot be bribed or sold to the highest bidder. Hence, the perfect fae to keep the students under control here."

I chanced another glance at Rolta, to find that despite her unique features, she was impressive and statuesque. She had wavy blond hair to her shoulders, skin that was a deep gray color, and a square shaped body, giving her the appearance of a weightlifter. I tried not to stare at the single blue eye above her small nose and thin lips.

Recognizing that my observations could be construed as rude, I went back to watching the beasts in our midst.

"Holy shivers, they're going to shift," Lexie murmured.

The troll was forgotten as I laser focused my attention on the Fallen. I needed to know how a seven-foot man turned into a fifty-foot dragon. For science.

The green one went first.

"Kellan," Lexie told me, and I filed that name away, wondering if I'd ever need to use it. "He controls the Seas of Verdin with his strength in water manipulation."

More information to reflect on later, but for now it was all about the shifting. It started with a hot gust of wind, apparent even from here, and the light around us grew brighter. Their energy was strong, and I wondered how uncomfortable it would feel if we'd been closer.

The light engulfed him, cutting off our view of twisting and turning limbs, and the green beast was no more. In its place stood a tall male. Similar to Drager in build, Kellan had white-blond hair, and super tanned skin. He looked like a surfer who spent his daylight hours in the sun. I couldn't clearly make out the rest of his features from here, but I saw enough to know he was as gorgeous as his brother. His human form appeared fully clothed in shorts and a shirt, feet bare.

Wow. I wondered how intense it would be when all five were shifted.

Clearly dragons, and whatever world they'd fallen from, were at the peak of the genetic pool. Godlike for sure. But even though they called themselves gods, and gathered power from fae worship and adoration, in the end they were only dragons. Alien dragons at that.

I wasn't actually sure of what classified someone as a god, but it was an interesting thought all the same. One thing was for sure, on Earth they'd definitely be supreme beings, and as a human I had to acknowledge that. So... gods it was.

CHAPTER
THIRTY

"Are you freaking the freak out!" Lexie sounded breathless. She wasn't the type to get flustered, especially over men. She'd never had crushes like me, instead choosing to just sleep with who she wanted, while never desiring more. There were no dreams of marriage or a family in her ten-year plan—she was adamantly against planning in general—and I'd always wondered why. I had the answers now, of course; Lexie was very far from a typical human woman.

"I don't know what to think or feel," I rasped as the red dragon shifted into his human form.

"Tylan," Lexie informed me. "His affinity is fire based, and I've heard his flames can reach a hundred feet when he's raging. He lives in the craters of Lastoa."

Another name, another of the five lands. "I'm going to need a map at some point," I told her.

Her lips twitched. "We'll find you one during your studies here."

Studies. It'd take some time to wrap my mind around that, but for now I was focused on the dragons. The light increased in intensity, and the heat surrounded us until we had a third Fallen in humanoid form.

Tylan was slightly shorter than the other two, by maybe an inch. His hair looked to be a dark brown, but I thought there were tinges red, like his dragon's color, through the shoulder-length strands. His skin was darker than Drager and Kellan's, a deep rich brown. Again, I couldn't see his eyes, but he had a thick beard, and gave off a woodsman vibe. Especially dressed in jeans, boots, and a black fitted t-shirt.

"Gods save us all," Lexie said hoarsely. "I forgot how potent they are together. It's the reason they were able to become gods here so easily. Their energy together is amplified. If they ever stopped fighting long enough to work together, they'd easily rule the whole world of Risest."

"Siblings always fight," I said with a shrug. "It's just that most of them don't have the power to destroy lands when they do. At least these five work together enough not to break your world."

"That's a good point," she said, as she started to fan herself against the heat pouring over us. Sweat already beaded on my forehead, and I wondered how bad it would be by the time the last two made the change.

On our left, Rolta moved forward. She cast shadows across the grass, seemingly even larger than I'd first thought. After taking those initial few steps, she didn't move any closer though.

"If she's hesitating, we all should be," Lexie murmured. "She's not scared of anything."

I wasn't surprised considering how impressive she was. Maybe all trolls were like her, but I sensed that even amongst her race she was exceptional. The fact she ran the only neutral grounds academy in the Eastern Realm—with minimum blood-shed—indicated that she was one powerful being.

Another gust of hot wind hit us, drying my sweat in one blast. Orange dragon had made the change, and in his place was another spectacular male.

"Emmen," Lexie told me. "From the wilds of Santoia. His affinity is with the land, able to draw up vast minerals with his power."

Emmen was the same height as Tylan, the red dragon, though his skin was much paler, glistening a light golden in the setting sun. His hair, which was shaved on the sides and near shaved on top, looked like it was golden brown, and he had a smooth, clean-cut face.

He was dressed formally, like Drager, in dress pants and a white dress shirt. He buttoned up his cuffs as he shook off the change, standing taller and facing his brothers as they conversed.

During these dragon shifts, I'd been patiently waiting for the final beast to reveal himself, the huge black dragon, his gilded wings so much brighter against the midnight background of his scales. He'd remained slightly apart from the others as his brothers shifted one by one, until he was all that remained.

The heat picked up more intensely this time, and I struggled not to take a step back. The burst of light was blinding. "None of us have ever seen the actual change," Lexie said as she bowed her head. "But Drager and Zahak are always the most intense."

Thinking of Drager shifting, I wondered again what color his dragon was. No doubt Lexie could tell me, but a part of me wanted to discover it for myself the first time I saw his beast.

When the light faded and we were able to look upon the group again, I failed miserably at hiding my reaction to the five of them together.

No. That wasn't entirely accurate.

I failed to hide my reaction to the final of the five.

Zahak.

He was taller than Drager by a few inches, but his face... it looked just like Drager's, only harder, with perfect planes cut by harsh lines. His hair was dark to Drager's light, but their skins were similarly bronze. Zahak wasn't dressed in anything resembling a suit though, with black cargo pants, black shitkicker boots, and a fitted shirt in, you guessed it, black. He looked like he belonged in a secret government operation, the sort with no name or phone number.

"Shit," I muttered, "and I thought Drager was unapproachable. Black dragon is scary."

Lexie cleared her throat. "Yes. Zahak, from the Isle of Denille. He's what the dragon legend is born of—a scary, solitary beast that hunts and hoards treasures. Then he eats those legends so that none truly know him. I wouldn't want to meet him in a dark alley."

"Right... me too."

He was too similar to Drager for me to completely agree with her assessment. Maybe I was just into tall, dark, and scarily-psycho.

Zahak finally approached his brothers, and from here his expression looked tight and closed off. If I had to guess, he didn't want to be here at all. In fact, the only one who looked remotely happy was the green dragon, his smile as bright as his blond hair.

The five formed a circle, and the energy in the clearing between the lake and the academy picked up. The hairs on my arms stood as goosebumps danced across my skin.

When the Fallen turned as a single line of scary dragon shifters and faced us, there was a scurry of activity in the academy. I looked behind to see every fae disappear inside, leaving just Lexie, Rolta, and me out here with the five shifters.

The fae had acted on instinct, retreating, and yet I found myself wanting to move toward them. Taking a step forward, I gave into the draw that existed between Drager and me. A draw that was stronger with all of them together.

Halt.

It was a low rumble in my head, and I shrieked, before stumbling and falling to my knees. Landing hard on the ground, my breaths grew rapid, and I felt rather lightheaded as I ran my gaze over the five of them.

Did Drager just speak in my head? That single command sent a whoosh of heat through my stomach just like when his power had infused into me. But it hadn't quite sounded like him.

Maybe voices sounded different in mental speak, but if he could talk to me like that, surely he'd have done so before now.

"Morgs," Lexie gasped, bending down to haul me back to my feet. "What the hen just happened?"

"What the hen?" I breathed, attention still on the dragons to the point I barely registered her question.

"Not important right now," Lexie grumbled. "Why did you fall down? You're not usually clumsy for no reason. You tripped over thin air."

Nope. Not air. I'd tripped over a rumbly, deep and commanding voice in my head.

My breaths continued raging in and out of me with far too much force, and yet no oxygen was filling my lungs.

"You need to slow your breathing or you're going to pass out," Lexie warned, rubbing my back in rhythmic circles. "Slow and steady, Morgan. Slow and steady."

Her words eventually helped to calm me, even as that heat swirled through my body.

"Can—" I choked, and forced more slow breaths in and out

before continuing. "—can these dragons speak in your head?" I asked her. "Can they read our minds?"

Holy embarrassment. Had Drager been in my head the entire time without telling me he could do that...? I would freaking kill him.

Lexie didn't answer until I lifted my head and stared right at her. "I don't think they can," she replied thoughtfully. "At least not to my knowledge. I've heard rumors that they can communicate telepathically to each other if they lower their mental barriers, but Lord Drager's never confirmed it."

The energy inside finally eased, and I was able to breathe normally again.

"Morgan Starrer, you're starting to scare me," she snapped when I didn't speak again. "You're going to have to pull yourself together, because the Fallen are on their way."

I was still focused completely on the fact that there might have been a voice in my head. If there wasn't, then I was losing my mind, and that would explain a lot of what had happened to me over the last month and a bit.

A part of me wanted to run back to my parents, who were no doubt freaking out at not being able to contact me, and would have most definitely filed a missing person's report at this stage.

At least I knew the dangers there.

Here in Risest, I had a very bad feeling that the dangers were much more widespread and scary than even my most messed-up fears could create. As a hardcore bookworm who'd started her fantasy journey with a magical tree and its lands above, before slowly graduating to the steamiest fairytales one could imagine, this was still beyond my wildest dreams.

Beyond my wildest fears.

Five dragons were making their way slowly across the grass, and as they moved closer, Rolta ended up at my side. She hadn't said a word to us, but it didn't matter. We were joined in this moment of fear, wondering if this might be our last seconds in this world.

The Fallen were coming for us, and they looked pissed.

What the hen indeed.

CHAPTER
THIRTY-ONE

The heat and wind grew around us, until it was difficult to stand. "I really hope they don't get any closer," Lexie muttered, gripping my arm as we attempted to remain upright.

As if they'd heard, they stopped; only Drager continued. They were close enough now that I could see their expressions clearly, and like the sun god, none of them revealed much.

I did notice that Kellan's eyes were green to match his dragon, Tylan's were brown, and Emmen's looked very light, almost white. Zahak remained to the side of his brothers, and it felt like his dark gaze was focused firmly on me, no doubt wondering how the human creature he'd saved was here and alive still, when I had a penchant for falling off floating lands.

When Drager reached us, I waited for him to explain what was happening, only to find myself swept up into his arms once more —rougher than last time—as he strode away from the Fallen and up the stairs to enter the academy.

A deep rumble of laughter followed us, but there was no

opportunity to see which dragon was amused by Drager's actions. If I was a betting woman, I'd put money on it being Kellan, the more lighthearted of the five.

At least from an outside observation.

When we entered the academy, I slammed the flat of my palm against Drager's chest and let out my own growl, a pathetic attempt, but I was working with human vocal cords. "Put me down, Drager," I demanded. "I'm not a fucking doll to cart around."

"Quiet," he growled, really highlighting how pathetic my growl had been.

Ignoring him, I asked, "Why are they here?"

He ducked his head under the front entrance, and I was momentarily distracted by the high ceilings, white walls with gold wainscoting, and curious faces that disappeared almost instantly as we strode through the hall. The inside of the academy was very school-like, with hallways leading to classrooms and dorms.

"My brothers, in their infinite wisdom, decided that since our meetings always end in disaster, it was best to utilize the neutral grounds here in the hopes for peace. We won't risk breaking the rules of the Fae Academy."

Shocked to actually receive a clear answer from the sun god, the rest of my curiosity momentarily vanished. Except for one very pressing question.

"Did you speak in my mind when we were outside?"

Drager didn't stumble, but he did lift me higher so our gazes could meet. "What did you say?"

The gravel in his voice told me to be very careful with my next words. "I thought I heard a deep voice in my head outside."

There was silence, except for the rumbling in his chest, until he said, "It is impossible. You must have imagined it."

That was clearly the end of that conversation, and I remained quiet and confused as he continued through the main entrance before reaching an open door. As he stepped inside what appeared to be the front office, a slender female seated behind a white and gold desk jumped to her feet. "Lord Drager," she gasped. "Is everything okay?"

She had flaming red hair, cut pixie style around her tiny face, and while she was beautiful, her features were not like a human's. Her gray eyes were too big, nose too small, and she had almost no lips to speak of. Her ears were also pointed in the way I'd expected most fae to be—not Lexie's tiny tip that she liked to call a point.

"Celeste, I have a new student for you," he said shortly.

Celeste turned those huge eyes on me, and if her shock was any indication, she'd actually missed the fact that I was being held prisoner in Drager's arms. Her gaze grew icy as she examined me like I was an unwanted hangnail on her thumb.

"Is… that a human?"

Oh great, here it was, the fae reaction Lexie had warned me about. My humanness, teamed with Drager's new obsession with carrying me around, was setting me off on a very awkward foot here. Time to establish some independence.

"*That* has the ability to answer all on her own," I shot back, before slamming my hand on Drager's chest again. "Put me down, asshole."

Celeste's gasp was loud and dramatic. Her face went super gray, and with a whoosh she lost her footing and disappeared behind her desk. *Had she just fainted?*

Drager didn't move or place me on my feet, at least not until Rolta and Lexie entered the office, by which time Celeste was standing as well, her eyes wide as she moved her gaze between us both.

"Lord Drager, please come into my office," Rolta said, voice high and tight. His chest swelled and expression darkened before she even finished her sentence. "I mean, if it suits you. I thought it best to avoid the curious and prying eyes of students when they realize you're inside the academy."

"Let's go," he said with a nod.

I wanted to remain where I was, already annoyed by Drager's dragonhandling of me, but there was little point staying out here with Celeste and her wide-eyed look of disgust. I'd already known from Drager that to the fae we were akin to animals, but maybe he was giving us too much credit. Celeste looked at me like I was *animal shit* she'd stepped in.

If her reaction was anything to judge by, my time at the academy was going to feel a lot longer than a couple of weeks.

Drager nudged me forward to follow Lexie and Rolta, who were already moving past the front desk and toward a door with *Headmistress* printed on it in gold script. Other words were printed below it, but they weren't in the language I understood.

When we made it into the room, the door closed behind Drager without anyone touching it, and I didn't question how. Going with the flow, I'd decided, was the only way to survive whatever was about to happen to me.

The office was simple, dominated by a gigantic desk, chair to accommodate her size, and five shelves behind, all filled with books. The urge to wander over and check out her titles was strong—once a bookworm, always a bookworm—but I managed to resist the temptation.

Rolta sat and indicated we should do the same. I all but fell into one of the three padded chairs opposite her, while Lexie took the other, and to no one's surprise Drager remained standing to tower over all of us. The fact that I felt safe with this scary dragon at my back should be a concern, but going with the flow meant I didn't question these weird occurrences.

The headmistress steepled her thick fingers together, her expression near impossible to read as her single eye remained unblinking. "Lexie has informed me that you need a short-term stay for two. One... human, to learn about our ways and hopefully have a chance to do a job for you, and one guardian for the human."

Her voice was a touch deeper than before, as if some of her nerves had faded. She clearly felt more comfortable in her office.

"Morgan is important to me," Drager said without inflection, and I almost Celested myself onto the ground. Did he just say I was important to him? "I need her to remain alive and well until she finishes her job for me."

Oh, right. He needed me to find his traitor. *Calm down, you lovesick fool.*

I had to stop drawing hearts around us. This was clearly a business arrangement, with some occasional sex on the side— really amazing sex, but it wasn't a romance. I was adult enough to handle that without letting my emotions get in the way. I had to be.

"It seems that I will be at the academy with my brothers for quite a while as well," Drager said gruffly. "Which should keep the students under control. I'll let them know in no uncertain terms how displeased I'll be if anything happens to my human."

Rolta didn't look convinced of that, and she knew her students far better than Drager. But at least I'd have Lexie with me. I'd seen her sword; she was all the protection I needed.

"Well, there's no issue of course," Rolta said. Her words said one thing, but her tone indicated she was extremely put out that this was happening in her school. "We should get the pair of them settled in a room together. Luckily, I have one that has just become available. It's not shared with any other and has a private bathroom, limiting the chances of an ambush."

190

Oh wonderful. Nothing like a good ambush while washing my hair in the morning.

"I'm going to be attached to Morgan like a prickle," Lexie said with grim smile. "If anyone tries to touch her, I'll remove their hands."

Now, on Earth, if someone said that, there would be some side-eyes and comments about mental health, but here they just nodded and smiled. The Fae Academy ran under different rules, and I really hoped I was here long enough to really get the feel for this place. As hard as it was to be a human in a faerie world, I continued to look at it as an opportunity, and I didn't want to waste this chance to truly experience fantasy.

"It's settled, then," Rolta said, and she stood so quickly that I had to envy her athleticism. She was large and broad all around, but she was clearly at the peak of health for a troll. "Let's show them to their room."

"We must address the students first," Drager said, unmoving.

"Right!" Rolta clapped her hands, and a second later Celeste appeared in the doorway. She looked as perfectly put-together as before, and had even managed to get her face right, no longer shooting daggers at me.

"You needed something, Mistress?" she asked Rolta.

"Yes, can you send out an announcement for students to gather in the Grand Theatre. We need to address the…"

She paused and I couldn't help myself. "The dragons in the room?"

This was about more than a human entering the academy. All five of the Fallen were here now, and the energy they threw off was enough to disturb even the most solid of foundations. Students in the neutral zone would no doubt need to know what was happening.

Rolta looked directly at me. Her eye was hard, no kindness in her face at all, and I forced a protective layer around myself. If Rolta and Celeste were any indication, my presence here was not going to go over well, and I had to start preparing myself.

I wasn't welcome here. Not in the academy. Not in Risest.

And especially not with Drager.

Lexie had warned me, and I was now taking it much more seriously.

I could no longer be so complacent.

Not if I wanted to live.

CHAPTER
THIRTY-TWO

Rolta cleared her throat, personal feelings pushed aside as her professionalism kicked in. "Yes, the presence of the Fallen has to be addressed as well." She turned to Drager. "I'll arrange the best accommodations for you and your brothers. There's also the entire fourth floor available for meetings and to escape prying eyes. No one is allowed up there."

"Acceptable," Drager said with all the grace of a godlike dragon. His arrogance was insufferable at times, and yet everyone seemed to suffer it just fine.

Celeste made a few squeaks which might have been words. Rolta nodded and waved the redheaded fae out of the room. A few seconds later, a tinkling drifted through the air, and Celeste's smooth high voice was clear and precise. "*All students are to make their way to the Grand Theatre. No delays. This is by orders of Mistress Rolta.*"

Clearly Rolta's iron fist rule wasn't just an expression.

The sound of footsteps and chatter drifted through the open

door of Rolta's office, and within a minute it was very loud as most of the academy hurried to comply with the order.

Standing, I moved closer to the entrance, wanting a glimpse of the students. Outside, it had been hard to know where to look, between the dragons and all the fae, but I really was curious to see the fae. I'd met some from Ocheran in my time at Lancourt of course, but there were four other lands in the Eastern Realm, and I wondered if the fae were different in those lands.

I had so many questions. The fact that I didn't even know the basics frustrated me. Lexie had given me a small taste when she introduced the Fallen and their powers, but I needed so much more.

As I moved toward the doorway, Drager edged me back. "You need to stay out of sight until I address them," he told me. "These are the strongest, most cunning and ambitious fae of our lands, and they're always looking to move up in the ranks. I must ensure that you don't get caught up in that game."

Disappointed, I didn't argue with him. I was determined that one day I wouldn't live in the shadows of people larger and stronger than me. One day I'd stand in my own light and be enough.

One day, but not today.

Today I was still the weakest in the room.

A truth which terrified me.

It had been one of the hardest paths I'd taken to remove myself from the toxicity of my parents. From their control and influence, starting when I was just a small child. Years of my mother's conditioning had been hard to break, but I'd done it. Which meant I could do it again.

Having Lexie here would help, since she'd pushed me to make that break years ago. I did acknowledge the irony of finding independence with someone else's help, but having the right someone made all the difference.

My life with Lexie had been infinitely better and freer than I'd ever experienced at home. No guilt. No pain. No second-guessing myself constantly. I'd just lived my simple life and I'd loved it.

Lexie had also led me here, and while the jury was still on the final verdict, for now I wouldn't change a single minute of my new adventure.

After about ten minutes of tense silence, Drager must have decided that enough fae had passed, and he was ready to move to the Grand Theater. "Let's address the students," he said, exiting the office and allowing us to do the same.

The hallway was quiet, and I found myself entranced by its soaring ceilings and gorgeous wainscoting once more. The styling here was designed to invoke cool and peaceful vibes, and I felt calmer just walking through the halls.

We made our way in the opposite direction to the entrance, past many doors, some of which were open, allowing me to view the variety of classrooms. I glimpsed standard desks in rows, and other rooms that looked like a battle arena or dungeon. I had no idea what the rooms with the stone and darker styling were for, but hopefully during some of my classes I'd find out.

Drager led us up a large set of double stairs to the next level, where there was an open foyer ending in another large set of doors. White and shimmering, they were twenty feet tall at least, and wide open, giving us a glimpse of the students gathered inside.

The room was the size of two football fields, and there was no way this existed inside the academy without the use of magic, or as Lexie would call it, *energy* manipulation. It was so massive that the students at the farthest end were not clearly visible, at least to those of us with human eyesight.

Seats weren't in rows like most halls back home, but instead a mix of benches, padded chairs, and a few up in the air for those who had wings. For the most part, the fae I noticed looked like Lexie, and could have passed for human, but there was a definite scattering of fae who were more monster like. They had a variety of arms, legs, and other appendages, each with seating to fit their body type.

"You okay, Morgs?" Lexie asked. "Drager's been pretty careful in keeping the nightmare fae out of Lancourt while you've been there—not to mention most of them reside in Zahak's land, but there's no way for him to protect you here."

"I don't need protection from a fae just because it looks different," I shot back, annoyed. "I just need to know which ones will kill me, then I can do my best to avoid them based on my need to make it to my next birthday."

Lexie stifled a laugh. "Well, in that case, avoid the ones who look like evolved humans. They're always scheming to get ahead, and you're a nice easy target. I'm going to sleep with one hand on my sword while we're here."

"You did that even when you were a student here," Rolta murmured, clearly listening in as we followed Drager further into the room. "Which is wise. We're an academy filled with students from five competing lands. There's always someone trying to prove their worth by taking out another, and you know that we don't interfere in battles such as that. This is to prepare you for the fae world, and in our world, it's survival of the strongest."

"Isn't this neutral ground?" I asked, keeping my voice low. "I thought they weren't allowed to war with each other?"

Rolta chuckled, an odd raspy sound. "There's a huge difference between warring and general competition. One is against the rules, and the other... well, it's part of our way of life."

The distinction didn't feel super clear, especially when she was advising us to sleep with one hand on a sword.

Drager led us along an aisle between chairs, heading for a small stage. The fae were watching us now; my skin itched from the hundreds of eyes on me. I fought not to stare directly at anyone in the room, hoping not to offend or draw more attention than we were already getting. Thankfully it was mostly Drager they were interested in, and I expected that to remain the case.

The charisma of the Fallen was part of their innate power—even without any display of other strengths. The longer I spent in Drager's presence, and having seen the other Fallen as well now, the more sense their godlike status made.

When we reached the front, I edged behind Rolta, grateful for her broad shoulders. "Quiet," she called, and the chatter in the hall faded instantly. "As most of you will know by now, we are playing host to our benevolent leaders." Her voice was calm and even. "They will have full run of the fourth floor, which you all know is off-limits anyway, and also the east lands for flying and meetings. I don't need to remind any of you that this is neutral grounds, and outside of normal fae dominance, there is to be no warring here. The only exception is for the Fallen, so do not cross them without cause. That's your one and only warning."

The students didn't react, appearing quite adept at hiding their expressions. Rolta nodded. "Okay, good. Now, Lord Drager will address you."

He already had their attention, and if it was possible the room became even quieter. As if the students were holding their breath —those that had to breathe anyway.

"These two fae are mine," he said shortly, pointing toward Lexie and me. "They're enrolling for a short time in your academy while the Fallen meet. They are not to be touched, not even in dominance games. Do you all understand?"

No one said a word, and Drager didn't repeat himself, since it had clearly been a rhetorical question. He was Lord Drager, a Fallen fae god, and his word was law.

A hand went into the air, from somewhere back in the middle of the room. Rolta waved her thick arm toward the student. "Yes, what is it?"

"Why are the gods here at all? Is this what we've been preparing for? Is war coming from an outside source? Or between the five lands?"

A ripple of concerned chatter broke out, dying off just as quickly as Drager spoke. "There's nothing you need to concern yourself with. We're here for a meeting, with no deeper issues on the horizon. We stopped fae warring when we arrived, and there are no plans to let you descend back into chaos. This is just a convenient place for the five of us to meet, and it has been too long between those meetings."

Speaking of, where were the other four? Why weren't they here addressing the students too? Did they often allow Drager to be their spokesdragon? Or was he overstepping and they had no idea?

I couldn't imagine that black dragon being okay with anyone speaking for him. I based this assumption on absolutely nothing except the few terrifying seconds I'd seen his form. I couldn't forget that he'd saved my life, coincidence or not, and I wondered if I'd ever get a chance to ask him for the truth: why he'd been there that day at Lancourt.

Would Drager let me meet any of them? My instincts said *not a chance* as his dominance grew worse with each day I spent in this faerie world—and with each sexual encounter. All of which did not change the fact that my use to him was on a time limit. One day we'd find the traitor, and he'd throw me away like everything useless in his life.

My aim was to enjoy the ride for now and guard my heart best I could.

Oh, and get out of this academy alive.

No matter the warnings from Rolta and Drager toward the students, there was always going to be one who thought they could prove themselves by breaking the rules.

Lexie and I were the new shiny toys, and Drager had just challenged the entire student body.

If my vast fantasy romance collection had taught me anything, it was that this situation was not going to end well.

For me.

CHAPTER
THIRTY-THREE

"This is fine," Lexie said with a shrug, eyeing the dorm room we'd been assigned.

After the end of the meeting in the Grand Theater, Drager left to rejoin his brothers, while Lexie and I were swept away by Rolta to our room.

"Morgan?" Lexie continued when I didn't say anything.

Focusing on the very nice room we'd be living in over the next few weeks, I took in the two twin beds, dresser in the middle, small wardrobe in the corner, and the bathroom off to the right. "It's perfect," I said to Rolta, who hadn't left us yet. "Thanks for finding us a private space."

Rolta nodded, expression grim. "I suggest you remain in this room or with Lexical at all times. Lord Drager might have warned them, but I hope you've already surmised that a lot goes on here without teacher knowledge. We do our best, but these are highly skilled fae. We know they break our rules, but until we catch them in the act, we can't put a stop to it."

"I have surmised as such," I confirmed. I'd rather have an

honest and open conversation about what my odds of survival here were. Lies would only get me killed.

"I want her in fight classes immediately," Lexie added quickly. "With private tutors. She needs to learn at least the basics of defense and attack. Might give her a few seconds holding them off until I can get to her."

Rolta nodded once more. "That's the first arrangement I'll be making, once I've received word from the Fallen on their needs and requirements during their negotiations."

The headmistress of the Fae Academy had her priorities well in place, and I didn't blame her one bit. She left us then, and Lexie closed the door firmly, pressing her hand against it, whispering words I didn't understand. When she turned and I eyed her curiously, she said, "Just giving us a warning notice. I can't keep them out, but I can make it harder."

Alone with the one person I trusted most in the world, my false bravery fell. "I'm scared, Lex."

I'd said a variation of those two words to her many times before, especially when I'd faced my parents. Lexie had been the person I'd confided my fears in for so many years that she was basically *dear diary* at this point. For the first time, though, those words were weighty and about more than just regular life stress or drama. This was literal life and death.

"You should be scared."

She was always bluntly honest—except that one time she lied about her entire existence—but other than that, she was the friend I relied on for the truth.

"But you have me and Drager," she continued. "He knows more of what happens than Rolta expects, and even when he's not at your side, you shouldn't underestimate his protection."

I'd never underestimate that dragon, but I also knew he couldn't be everywhere at once. "What's the gameplan, then, to keep me alive?" I asked, making my way over to sit in one of the two white, fur-lined chairs in the corner.

"First we organize classes for us both," Lexie said, dropping into the other chair. She ran her hands through the soft fur on the armrest as she planned out loud. "Classes that will ideally get you up to scratch on how Risest and the five lands work. The rules. The politics. The wars and vendettas you must avoid, along with knowledge of what creatures never to be alone with." She smiled suddenly. "Most importantly, we teach you to fight."

"I'm not really athletic," I reminded her, resisting the urge to laugh at the idea of learning to fight. "I read for sport, you know that. Give me a fifty-yard dash to the next chapter and I'm your girl. But actual dashing is reserved for getting to the front of the line at a bookstore when the sequel to my favorite series releases."

Lexie's low laughter relaxed me, my shoulders easing away from my ears. I'd been holding them tense without even realizing. "I do know that about you," she said with humor. "But guess what, I'm also a book nerd. That's another one of the reasons I volunteered for Drager's Earth role. My happy place is surrounded by books." A darkly sinister smile lit up her face. "My next happy place is stabbing an asshole in the chest before he even sees my sword coming. You can have both, I promise."

She was scary, and yet it was an enticing idea to be able to defend myself if needed. Lexie had years of training I wouldn't have time for, but maybe I could reach the point where I at least wasn't in danger of stabbing myself.

"You know I'll give it my full effort," I promised her. "What-ever plan you come up with."

Lexie grasped my hand and squeezed briefly. "I know you will, and it'll make me happy to know that even after you return to Earth, you'll have skills to protect yourself. If I'm not there."

The cry that spilled from my lips was deep, like a wounded

creature. "Why wouldn't you be there?" I demanded, twisting my body so I was facing her fully, pulling one leg up in front of me to make it easier. "We're a team. I'm not returning to Earth without you."

It was a Morgan and Lexie world, and I'd be damned if any dragon shifter asshole took that away from me.

"It would depend on Drager," she said softly. "We are free here, but we also all have roles to fill. If I don't have a task to do on Earth, then I'll have to come back here and take up one of the positions in our military."

"So every fae has a job? None get to be rich assholes just lazing around in their mega mansions?"

Lexie shook her head. "I mean, there are fae with a lot of power and control, who work less strenuously because they have others to help, but everyone has a role to fill here. It's not in our nature to do nothing. We tend to gravitate toward our interests, so water fae generally have a role in their natural habitat, whether it be cleaning the waterways, or guiding the mating rituals of fae animals. Humans probably wouldn't classify it as *work* per se, but it's an important role to fill."

I tried to wrap my mind around a world like that, and I found it difficult. Difficult and enticing. "That must keep depression and boredom at bay," I wondered. "Knowing you're always busy, but without it being some shitty job you hate. Do they not even mind cleaning and removing trash?"

Lexie pressed her lips together to stem more laughter. "There are fae who consume trash as their nourishment. Let me tell you, they'd be very useful in the human world. If it wasn't for the fact that they also eat other fae who annoy them, I'd sneak a few across."

I'd seen more than a few of the nightmare fae in the theater, and instead of feeling grossed out by the thought of trash-eating monsters, I was intrigued to know which creature it was. Lexie wanted me to learn about this world as a means of survival, and that was absolutely important, but the strongest need I had was to fill my knowledge well.

The sun had set in the sky now, and the bronze and gold tendrils of light were filtering into the balcony in front of us. Lexie chatted for a few more minutes about her safety tips for tomorrow, including never going anywhere without her, never looking fae directly in the eye—since I had no idea which race would take offense to that—and never drawing attention to myself.

Most importantly, never go anywhere without her.

Not even the bathroom.

That one she repeated at least five times.

When we had exhausted her safety rules, the restless swirls inside my stomach pushed me to head for the doors that led to the balcony. They were glass, made up of three sections. The bottom two were clear, while the top panel held depictions of flowers and flying birds in soothing pastel colors.

Grasping the handle, the door slid open silently, and I stepped out to admire the last rays of the setting sun. In Lancourt, always locked away in my cage, I couldn't appreciate the night sky like this. Here, the cool breezes brushed my skin as I enjoyed the sounds of students finishing up classes and making their way back to their dorms around us.

Lexie joined me, leaning against the railing, watching the lake and students. There was a dozen or more out there now, paddling in what looked like long canoes, powering out into the distance.

"The merfolk can be hostile, but they're usually pretty good about sharing here, on academy grounds." Lexie said. "They've learned to live near the students, but I also wouldn't suggest you swim the lake any time soon."

"It looked inviting before," I told her, "but I have zero plans to ever swim in there."

Lexie knew I was a weak swimmer. My mother deemed it an unnecessarily risky activity—I mean, not being able to swim sounded even riskier, but what did I know? By the time I was old enough to learn by myself, I held a slightly irrational fear of water, especially deep, dark waters. The bath was as deep as I got.

"Right, right," Lexie said, nodding. "That's one worry to cross off my list, then."

If only there weren't a dozen right behind it.

As more students emerged onto their balconies, Lexie tried to usher me back inside, but her stress in this case wasn't warranted. The fae had their focus firmly locked on the gilded sky. The Fallen were terrifying, but also completely mesmerizing, and we all wanted to see them again.

At least from a distance we didn't have to worry about the intensity of their energy. I couldn't imagine what standing in front of the five would feel like. Drager had prepared me for it in small doses, but the five together…? I'd probably embarrass myself and faint or vomit. My body was sure to have a visceral reaction that I couldn't hide from anyone. Then I'd have to hope one of their dragons ate me to put me out of my misery.

"Hop out of your head, Morgs," Lexie said. "I understand why you're internalizing, but I promise we'll get through this together. I didn't graduate top of all battle classes here for nothing. I'll be a great teacher, along with my old trainers. We'll turn you into a warrior."

"That's almost as unbelievable as the existence of dragon shifters," I said softly.

Lexie's smile was gentle. "Yet here we are," she replied, and whether she'd sensed them coming, or it was the most perfectly timed moment in history, a flash of gilded wings filled the sky above the academy.

"Just call me book warrior, then," I breathed, watching the red beast soar out over the lake.

The fae sighed and tittered around us as we all got what we'd been waiting for—our second glimpse of the Fallen.

CHAPTER
THIRTY-FOUR

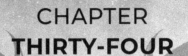

That night I slept surprisingly well. Maybe due to the miles we'd walked yesterday, or maybe it was stress exhaustion, but when I woke the next morning to the pink sky visible through the balcony doors, I felt rested. Starving, but I was grateful to feel rested.

Lexie was already up, her bed made, and I could hear the shower running. She never started her day any other way. Not even when pretending to be a human. Shower first, and then she could function in the day-to-day.

I'd slept in my underwear last night, having no other clean clothes, and I really hoped that would be rectified before classes today. As I yawned and hopped out of the comfortable bed, there was a knock on the door. Padding over, I paused on the other side and said, "Who is it?"

Lexie would be the one to murder me in my sleep if I opened the door without her being here. But I also had a feeling, thanks to a familiar swirl of heat in my gut, who was on the other side.

"Drager," he rumbled, confirming my suspicions. "I have clothes for you."

There wasn't a lock on the handle, except for whatever magical manipulation of energy Lexie had worked last night, which didn't affect me as I wrenched the door open. I completely forgot that I was wearing only a bra and underwear until I stood on the threshold, Drager's heavy gaze caressing the exposed skin of my body. Heat wrapped around me, and the remaining slivers of his energy inside roared to life, filling my veins with pure fire.

The bag he'd been carrying dropped to his feet, and he stepped into the room with a low rumble. His arm swept around me as he hauled me up against his chest, my feet leaving the ground so quickly my head spun.

"What sorcery do you weave?" he growled, leaning down to press his lips to the skin of my neck. "What power do you hold over a god that I think about you even when you're not near me?"

This sexy dragon's arrogance was a trickle of ice through my heated veins—enough for me to press my hands against his chest in an attempt to push him away. "Drager, no. If you can't figure out why you're attracted to me, then this—whatever the hell we're doing here—isn't going to work for me."

Once upon a time, my self-confidence had been so low that I'd have taken whatever scraps this god threw at me. But I'd worked hard not to be that person, at least most of the time, and I had to make a stand.

He stilled beneath me, his breathing deep, before his hold loosened and I was set back on my feet. When he stepped away, his expression was neutral once more. "You're correct, and with everything else happening, maybe we need to take a few steps back."

I blinked at him, crossing my arms over my body in a defensive pose. "What's *take a few steps back* mean exactly?"

He lifted the bag once more, and moved into the room so the door could close behind him. "Would you like to have dinner with me tonight? After your classes today?"

If he had just punched me in the face, I'd have been less stunned.

"D-dinner?" I stuttered. "Like a date?"

Dammit, Morgan! Why are you so awkward.

"Yes," Drager drawled, seemingly amused. "It feels like time I figured out who you really are, and how you managed to fall into my world."

Good luck on the first part, buddy. I didn't even have a clue who I was.

But the second part was a truth I needed to know as well.

"If I survive classes today, I'd love to have dinner with you," I managed to say, sounding almost normal.

Drager's expression darkened. "You'll survive."

That was the full extent of his confirmation of survival, before he dropped the bag on my bed. "I brought enough clothes for you and Lexie to get through a few weeks," he said, expression closed off once more. "I'll be back at your door by the eleventh hour."

I nodded, having no clue when that was, but Lexie would know.

"Stay out of trouble today," was his parting advice as he exited the room, the door closing behind him.

"Plan on it," I half-yelled back, even though he was long gone and couldn't hear me.

The shower shut off, and I managed to stumble my way toward the bathroom, desperately needing to cool off. It had been extremely difficult to stop Drager from destroying my body in all the ways, and parts of me *down low* were very unhappy with my little stance. But at some point, if I didn't demand respect from him, I'd always be the plaything he brought out when he was bored.

The bathroom door opened and a small puff of steam escaped as Lexie emerged looking refreshed, a towel around her body while another dried her hair. She paused as she stepped into the room, assessing everything in two quick glances. "Who was here?" she demanded, eyes on the bag.

"Drager," I said quickly, wanting to ease her panic. "He dropped off clothes." She opened her mouth. "And before you yell at me, I checked if it was him before I opened the door."

Her mouth closed as her eyes narrowed. "I should have guessed by the flush in your cheeks. That dragon riles you like no one I've ever seen."

He did, but he frustrated me just as hard. "We did kind of start… you know, but then he said again that he couldn't figure out why I tempted him, so I pushed him away. Told him he needed to figure it out before we hooked up again."

Lexie's eyes went super wide as she played with the edge of the towel near her hips. "He's an a-hole, but you need to be careful, Morgs. He's not used to being rejected or denied. You were totally right to do so, because you're worth so much more than that, but I need you to stay alive for me. Maybe it's best just to avoid him altogether for a while. He'll hopefully forget you exist in a few months, and I'll ferry you back to Earth in secret."

Oh man, she was going to be *really happy* with my next confession. "We actually have a date tonight at the eleventh hour. Whatever that means."

Her mouth dropped open a touch. "I did not see that coming," she finally whispered.

"You and me both," I replied with a laugh. "But until then, I have to survive my first day in the academy. Starting with a shower, clothes, and then food. In that order."

Still looking a touch stunned, she ushered me into the bathroom. "Right, right. Let's get our game faces on. I'll find some clothes while you shower, and then we can eat, after which we'll head to Rolta to get your new schedule. She should have figured out the classes by now."

"Breakfast first or I riot," I warned her, walking into the bathroom and closing the door behind me.

In the few minutes since Lexie had finished her shower, the room was already cool and cleared of condensation. On the sink, Lexie had left some toiletries for me, and I was grateful to see items to clean my hair and teeth. Having a fae friend here who knew the hygienic needs of humans was a huge bonus.

When I finished my morning routine, I stepped out to find an outfit already waiting on the bed. Lexie was still in front of the armoire, putting away clothing, and I could see the inside was already overflowing with outfits. "All of those clothes fit in that tiny bag?" I said, tone filled with disbelief.

"Drager can manipulate energy like no one else," she reminded me. "This bag would hold our entire apartment back home."

Well, okay, then.

I slipped on the plain black bra and panties set, light and silky, fitting me like it was custom made. Next was jeans and a black shirt with fitted sleeves ending mid-biceps. I finished it off with a pair of socks and black boots. The boots were calf-high and made from a soft material. Soft, but also super resistant. I caught my nail on it and it didn't even leave a mark on the side.

When I was dressed, I pulled my wavy hair back into a high ponytail, wanting it out of my face. Lexie's determination for me to learn to protect myself meant I wasn't getting through today without a fight class. I might as well prepare as best I could now.

Lexie was dressed in black leather pants, similar black boots to me, and a deep red shirt that showed off her gorgeous skin tone. It was a casual look she'd chosen for both of us, and I was relieved that Drager hadn't included his usual array of business suits.

When I mentioned that, Lexie laughed. "I shoved them to the back of the wardrobe," she said. "He's dreaming if he thinks you're going to start rocking business chic for him."

Wasn't that the truth. My look was *lazy librarian comfort*, and I wasn't changing that for no dragon.

When we left the room, Lexie insisted on going first, her hand hovering over her right shoulder. Her caution made me nervous, but at the same time I appreciated it. Better to overcompensate than under and get us both killed.

The hallway wasn't empty, as fae left for classes and breakfast too, but for the most part no one looked our way or bothered us. "We're on the floor with the high fae," Lexie said in a low voice as we hurried along. "The fae who can pass for humans reside here. Nightmare fae have their own floor of rooms in the basement."

"Good to know," I whispered back, keeping my eyes slightly lowered so I didn't accidentally challenge anyone by locking gazes.

We took two sets of stairs down until we reached one of the lower floors. I didn't know where anything was, and I doubted I'd learn my way around here in the few weeks I had. Thankfully with rule number one: *never go anywhere without Lexie*, it really didn't matter.

More fae joined us in the hall as we all headed for the dining room, but thankfully none got too close. Lexie didn't even have to pull out her sword or growl, as the masses acted cautiously all on their own. We reached a set of floor-to-ceiling double doors, already open for fae to enter the dining hall.

At least fifty tables spanned the room, in various shapes and configurations. In the center was a buffet style display of food. As we moved closer, I noticed that the buffet itself rotated, leaving the fae to remain in place, grabbing food they wanted when it moved past.

When we were only a few feet from the food itself, the area around us grew silent. My pretend bubble of anonymity burst in that second, as every gaze in the room focused my way.

And not all of them were friendly.

CHAPTER
THIRTY-FIVE

L exie didn't bat an eye, strolling in like she owned the place. I knew her well enough to recognize the show she was putting on. Not that she wasn't confident in general, but today was about shouting it to the room. Schooling my features, it took everything I had to follow her lead and *not* to gawk at the students around us.

"Let's see what they have to eat," Lexie trilled, like we didn't have a single care in the world.

We stopped by the huge rotating buffet, picking up one of the deep brown bowls housed on shelves below the food. Each bowl had unique swirls through the glaze, as if they'd been hand made. There were also similarly designed cups and utensils. The fork had more prongs and the knife a way sharper point, but their use was still clear.

Focusing on the buffet, I clutched the bowl, which was heavier than I expected. The rotation moved at a reasonably quick pace, and I noted that there were a lot of foods on here that I'd never seen before.

"This section is for the water races," Lexie said, lowering her voice. A mound of small shrimp—with two heads—drifted past, along with what resembled squid, fish eyeballs, and a very yellow pile of balls. From what, I didn't need to know.

In the next section was raw meat, mostly in chunks and on long metal spikes. A few delightful trays, though, contained meat still in its original shape—dunedin might be dangerous, but they were also dinner for some of the fae.

My mood perked up when familiar items made an appearance, and with additional help from Lexie, *"Don't touch that red fruit. It's fishy and for the lake dwellers,"* I was able to fill my plate with a variety of food.

"Don't touch that either," Lexie whispered as another section passed.

I eyed the huge pinchers of what looked like a dog-sized scorpion. "Yeah, pretty sure that's an obvious one," I said, attempting not to shudder.

Lexie shrugged. "Sometimes your curiosity places you into danger before your common sense catches up. That's a *tretle*, and its sting would kill you in three seconds."

"What do you mean my curiosity comes before my common sense?" I asked, pulling my plate closer as I narrowed my eyes at her.

Lexie stared at me without blinking, before she shook her head. "I mean, for starters, what in the hen were you thinking that night heading to the library without me? Why would you do that? Especially in response to a strange male voice calling you out of nowhere."

Two realizations hit me then. First, I'd been so mad at Lexie for lying that I hadn't given her the chance to let me know that she'd been mad at me too—fair point, it hadn't been my finest hour to drunkenly run off to the library on my own.

And second, why had Drager called *me* when Lexie was fae? Wouldn't it have made more sense to check with her first.

"Why did Drager call me and not you that night?" I decided to ask.

We were done with the buffet, so she led me toward the back of the room to find a table.

"My phone was dead," she said. "I think it was just bad timing that had you being first point of contact."

That made sense, and I felt relief that Drager hadn't targeted me that night. It was still just *wrong place wrong time*.

"It wasn't my finest hour running off without you," I admitted as we both sat at a small corner table, Lexie keeping her back to the wall so she could see the room. "I want to blame the cocktails, but Drager's voice had a lot to do with it as well."

"His voice?" Lexie wrinkled her nose as she stared my way. "What the heck did his voice have to do with it?"

Picking up some bread, I took a bite, needing food in my stomach. "His voice slithered deep inside me and wouldn't get out," I admitted, knowing it was as crazy as it sounded. "But my main motivation in going to the library was to ensure we didn't get fired. I was certain I hadn't screwed up the return of a book, and I was determined to prove it."

Lexie continued to watch me closely, her untouched plate before her. "Drager's energy pulled you there, and while I'm not angry about it, I really want to know why. Why is there a connection between you? In any other circumstance, he'd have killed a human who wandered into the midst of fae creatures."

"I have no explanation," I said as I moved on to the next item on my plate. "It's all been this crazy journey, and I can't explain one damn part of any of it."

Not from the first phone call to all the sex, and the fact I was now in a fae academy eating breakfast surrounded by creatures I could only read about in fantasy stories.

"Drager's weird obsession with you has me worried." Lexie finally picked up some fruit. "You have to be careful, Morgan. Don't blindly trust him, no matter what your feelings tell you."

Her warning bothered me, but I couldn't deny what she was saying. "You're the only person here I trust," I replied quietly. "Always."

That satisfied her enough that she focused on eating, and I did the same. No doubt we'd need the energy to survive today. We didn't speak again, aware that as more tables filled up around us, we had less privacy.

The students left us alone until we were pushing back our chairs to leave. As we stood, a group of four surrounded our table. Lexie's hand wrapped around the hilt of her invisible weapon, and I moved so I was closer to her.

The smallest of the four held both hands up. "We're not here to hurt you," she said quickly. "We want to be friends." She was a highborn fae with white-blond hair down to her waist, icy blue eyes, and the sort of pale complexion that would burn after being in Earth's sun for two minutes. Her ears were pointed, and I thought I caught a glimpse of fangs around her incisors.

"Friends?" Lexie said, her stance remaining in attack mode. "Explain yourself. You're clearly from the Emerelso clan, and I don't remember your brethren being this needy for allies."

The blonde nodded the acknowledgement of her family line and didn't appear offended by the *needy* comment. "I'm Greta Emerelso, and I'm the most recent of my clan to attend the academy from Isle of Denille. We don't usually seek out new allies, but this is a unique circumstance." She spoke matter-of-factly. "You have an in with one of the Fallen, and that's the in we all want. You're going to need allies here, even with Lord Drager's warning. It's a solid offer."

Lexie eyed her hard. "Lord Drager is not your god."

Greta shrugged. "Doesn't matter. An in with one is an in with all of them, especially while they're at the academy. I also don't agree with the constant clan battles. Powerful clans should join forces across the lands. One day there'll be an enemy stronger than all of us, and the Eastern Realm of Risest will need to be more than five divided lands."

Her offer intrigued Lexie; I could tell as she considered.

Greta's friends, a strawberry-blond female—satyr—and two brunette males—unknown race, but they were huge with a broad troll-like look to their features, though two-eyed—didn't speak. I wondered if they were all Emerelsos.

Lexie relaxed her grip on her invisible weapon, and no one in the vicinity flinched. "We'll seriously consider your offer," she told them.

Greta nodded once. "We will await your response."

The satyr, and the slightly smaller of the boys nodded as well, but the other male had his gaze locked on me, and his deep gray eyes were hard. Unwavering. I really didn't want to know what he was thinking, but if I had to guess, it had nothing to do with being my ally.

He kind of looked like the one I'd needed protecting from.

The four of them left, and I was able to breathe freely once more. Lexie's demeanor remained calm, and I worked to make sure that my expression didn't reveal a single worry filling my head. We had a lot of focus on us; everyone had been listening in on that exchange, and no doubt the second we left the room we'd be the main topic of conversation.

"Come on," Lexie murmured when we were finally clear of the dining room. "Let's find Rolta."

She set off at a rapid pace that I had to half-jog to keep up with, and all the questions I wanted to ask were going to have to wait, since she was clearly in no mood to chat. We made it down to that main entrance hall in about two minutes.

"Fuck... ing...." I sucked in a breath. "...hell, Lex. Slow... slow down for your friends."

A smile finally broke through her stoicism. "Sorry, Morgs. I fell into warrior mode and was on a mission."

Mission was an understatement. "All good," I said, breathing a touch easier. "I could use the cardio."

She pressed her hand to my right bicep. "We're going to be okay, I promise. We don't need dubious allies that will probably get us killed. We trust no one, and that keeps us alive."

I nodded rapidly, still breathless. "I'm a hundred percent following your lead here. The only thing I know about Risest is not to pet a dunedin."

Or a shifter god.

Clearly, I'd only been successful at following one of those rules.

Lexie wanted to laugh, but her worry got the best of her. "Emerelso clan is one of the strongest in Lord Zahak's land. They're like the Lightsbringers, filled with warriors and energy manipulators. They command respect *and fear* wherever they go."

"Your clan is like that in Ocheran?" I asked. "Powerful and respected?"

She shrugged. "We're their counterparts in Ocheran, yes, so while I'm a touch suspicious of her offer, I'm also not completely shocked. It has positives for both sides. With their alliance we'd be much stronger, and they'd have a direct line to a god."

For all the good that would do. Drager wasn't my pet; I couldn't just hand him over for a visit. "Did you see the way one of the troll boys was staring at me?" I asked, that dark gaze in my mind. "I don't think he likes humans, and that might be problematic. You know, with my humanness."

Lexie's expression was once again hard. "They're golems."

It took me a few seconds to rack my brain for a definition of this new mythical creature. "Golems... as in servants made of clay?"

Lexie flashed her proud smile. "That is where the myth originated from, yes, but they're flesh and blood beings who can harden their skin as needed, giving them a very strong defensive mechanism. Outside of the Fallen, I've heard of nothing that can pierce golem skin when it's at full strength."

"Are they obedient servants?" Myths were starting to mix in my mind, and I wondered if I had the wrong lore.

Lexie shook her head. "Nope. They make their own decisions, but if they do tie their loyalty to you, it's unbreakable. A bond like no other. As strong as the earth they are born from."

Shaking my head, I tried to wrap my head around all the new information. "If I survive, I'm going to write stories about this. I hope you know that."

Lexie all but rolled her eyes at me. "You're surviving. Non-negotiable."

With that statement, similar to what Drager had delivered this morning, she opened the office door and ushered me inside.

It was time to get my class schedule.

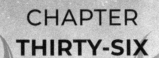

CHAPTER
THIRTY-SIX

Celeste was behind her desk, hair slicked back from her sharp features, and when she looked up to find us there, she pasted on a fake smile. "Rolta is waiting for you," she said, waving us into the next room.

I smiled politely, all the while knowing that I'd do everything in my power to never be alone with her. Hatred burned deep in her eyes; no amount of professionalism could hide it.

Rolta was writing in a large notebook with a feather-tipped quill, and when we walked in she looked up. "Oh, wonderful," she said quickly. "I've got the human's schedule worked out."

"Her name is Morgan," Lexie said shortly, but I honestly didn't give a shit at this point. It only bothered me when Drager used *human* with distaste.

Rolta ignored her. "We have four private classes, and one shared class where she can join the general students, since observing other fae might help with her knowledge of Risest. And then there's a special request for the end of today."

Lexie nodded, and reached out to take the heavy parchment

221

that must hold my schedule. Rolta resumed writing in her note-book again, and I took that as us being dismissed.

"Come on, Morgs," Lexie said slowly, her focus on the parch-ment, before she lifted her head and smiled. "First class starts in ten minutes."

"What's the first class?" I asked as we left, not sparing a glance for Celeste.

"History of the Fallen and Faeries," she said, eyes lighting up. "This is going to be a good one."

"This is one of the private classes?" I asked.

She nodded. "Yep. Most fae at this level are completely up to date on their story."

"What other classes do I have?"

She held up the parchment and read from it. "You have two private fight classes, one for attack and one for defense. They'll use weapons and other techniques."

My body hurt just thinking about it, but I also wanted to take part in those classes more than any other.

"You have a private class for Fact and Myth of Faerie Creatures and Races."

A snort escaped me. "Myth... okay. Good to see that there is myth even here in a mythical world."

Lexie continued. "You have a shared class on energy manipu-lation. This will be a purely observational class, but it'll allow you to see our strengths and weaknesses. Each clan is different, along with each race within those clans. I don't know the students at the academy this intake, of course, but there's usually a good mix across the five lands and various races."

"That sounds very cool," I said with a grin. "And what's that final special request class?"

Lexie looked again. "Right, okay. Looks like your final class is... *with the Fallen.*"

The last words were whispered as we both ground to a halt and stared at the parchment.

"Did you just say with the Fallen?" I managed to rasp around the lump in my throat. My voice grew higher. "Why? Seriously what? Why the fuck would I have a class with them?"

"I have no idea," she breathed. "This has to be Drager's idea, and if I had to guess, it'll be in regard to their discussion of the thief. Or maybe I'm completely wrong and it's about humans. I don't have a fae-ing clue. But we'll learn soon enough."

The energy of the five, when they were a dozen feet away, had been enough to almost knock me off my feet. How would I survive a class in close proximity?

There was also the little matter of one of them speaking in my head. Drager's shock told me that it wasn't him, and that he didn't believe any of his brothers were capable, but I'd heard the voice. Unless the mere presence of five hot gods caused me to temporarily hallucinate.

Weirder shit had happened. Already. To me. Just this week alone.

"Is there lunch in that schedule," I asked Lexie, desperate to focus on the normal. "Rolta probably doesn't know that I need to eat more than fae."

She let the parchment fall to the side as she used her free hand to hold on to my forearm, pulling me along toward my first class. "You'll be fine," she said. "I'm not going to let any of them starve you to death."

"Very funny," I drawled, giving into her demands to move faster so we wouldn't be late to History of the Fallen and Faeries.

We ended up in a small room on the main floor, off a very long hallway of classrooms. The hall was filled with fae on their way to their own classes, and as we entered my new history room I caught a glimpse of curious faces before Lexie closed the door behind us.

Inside it was one of those regular classrooms, with tables and chairs facing a large white wall. Nothing else lined the walls, giving this space a completely nondescript look. "Welcome to History of the Fallen and Faeries," a very high-pitched voice said, and I flinched before I could stop myself.

I'd thought we were alone, since there was no obvious sign of another in the room, but clearly I'd missed something. Like the teacher.

A shadow seeped out of the corner of the room, and I gawked, an action I'd have been ashamed of if I could form coherent thoughts.

"Sit down," Lexie ordered, shoving me toward one of the tables and chairs. All the while the shadow drifted toward the front of the room.

"This is Professor Malin," Lexie continued, taking the seat next to me. "She's a ghost walker from the Nightmare Realm on the Isle of Denille. This is one of her forms."

Her *form* was shadow and mist that occasionally morphed into the dark shape of a humanoid, before it would drift and trickle into a mess of shadows once more.

"Does she have a form that's more corporeal?" I asked quietly. "I have no idea where to look."

Professor Malin let out a chuckle, which sounded like one of those high-pitched whistles only dogs could hear. And in this case I was the dog, debilitated by her laugh. I managed not to cry out and clutch my ears, but only just.

"You'll get used to her," Lexie told me. "She's ancient and knowledgeable. The perfect teacher for our history."

Knowing I was being rude, I stopped gawking at the fascinating and terrifying professor, and focused on my reason for being here. Learning about the Fallen and the fae they lorded over.

"There's no point learning about the Fallen if we don't start a few centuries before that," the professor said, the shadowy form drifting near the white wall. This time I had no chance of stifling my gasp as images appeared across the white.

It was a map, displaying a large piece of land with oceans around it.

"This is the Eastern Realm of Risest before the Fallen," Professor Malin said, her voice already less jarring. "As you can see, there are no divided lands, and the clans and races were spread out in their own territories."

Small writing and images appeared: *Siren's Den, population eight thousand, Banshee Cove, population twenty-five thousands,* and so on, with a multitude of fae races.

"We used to live in our race territories," the professor continued. "And we all battled with each other for more land and resources. Mostly because select races are bloodthirsty like that. Fae have always existed in a dominance battle, and there was very little peace to be found."

"We didn't have enough room for all the races," Lexie added. "Because a large section of the Isle of Denille was occupied by the nightmares, and they didn't share their land at all."

Professor Malin nodded. "Correct. The Trench of Nightmares was centered across our realm, and any who got too close disappeared. Their deaths were brutal, and that kept the rest of this land battling for whatever territory remained."

A deep and dark trench appeared across the center of the world, and with it trickles of fear entered my gut. "You're from the Nightmare Realm?" I asked the professor quietly. "You lived in the trench?" Was that how she knew about the brutal deaths, since it stood to reason any other fae that knew was probably dead by those means.

"I was, and the scattered memories that remain of the mindless creature I was in my past is what causes nightmares for this nightmare fae."

"Was there ever peace in Risest before this?"

Lexie opened her mouth, as if to answer first, but Professor Malin didn't give her a chance. "Not in the Eastern Realm, but apparently the small lands to the west of us are more peaceful and prosperous. Superior to us."

"Until the Fallen," Lexie added, and the misty shadow bopped up and down as if she was nodding.

The map faded from the white walls, then reappeared, and this time it had five distinct zones marked by dotted lines. Center to all five was the moderately sized academy territory, right where the largest pit of the trench had been last time. The five zones were labeled, and this was my first time with a proper overview of the lands. I could now see exactly where Drager's territory was, and the size differences between the Fallens' lands. It had been this disparity in size that had Drager believing his brothers might be behind the infiltration of his library.

Ocheran was in the top right corner, surrounded on two sides by ocean, and the other two bordered the academy and other lands. The bottom left side was labeled *Craters of Lastoa*, which I remembered being Tylan's territory—the red dragon. It looked sparse and rocky from what was dotted on the map, where Drager's was lusher and green. A fact I already knew, having marched through a section of its forest yesterday.

Top left corner was *Seas of Verden*, and it was almost completely poked out into the ocean, the smallest of the lands, but it was depicted as very Bahamas-like. Made sense for Kellan, the green dragon with his surfy vibes.

Mid-top was the *Wilds of Santoia*, which looked like a mixture of deserts and forests, and I could see Emmen, the orange beast ruling over the expanse of his land.

Final, spanning up and through the center, was the largest of the five lands, the *Isle of Denille*. Zahak's territory, where the trench used to exist. "What happened to the trench?" I asked. "I mean, even if the Fallen sorted out the races and organized you all into territories, there should still be a trench there, right?"

"He filled it in," Lexie said simply.

Twisting in my chair, I blinked at her. "On his own?"

Professor Malin's shadow bopped again. "Oh yes. Zahak is unique in that he controls all the elements, and his power is an untapped resource. The Fallen might not know who they were before they fell, but based on their energy, I have my theories."

Sitting straighter, I faced the shadow's direction, hoping like hell she was about to impart those theories. After all, this was a class to learn about the Fallen, and my fascination with the beasts was at a peak right now.

Bring it on, teach. Tell me all the things.

CHAPTER
THIRTY-SEVEN

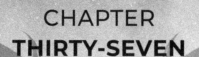

"The Fallen appeared in our world approximately two hundred and seventy years ago," Professor Malin started. "Give or take a few decades."

"Remind me to get their skincare routine," I breathed, trying to imagine those virile, gorgeous beings as near three hundred years old.

"It was the middle of the cold season, which only affects a few sections of the Eastern Realm," she continued, ignoring my humanness. "I remember because the moment they touched down on the land, everything stopped. Our warring, the pain within the trench, and the endless screaming in my head. It went quiet, and I was able to think clearly for the first time in my long life."

"I wasn't there, obviously," Lexie added. "But I've heard the stories. It was as if they caused a skip in time, and we all blipped. When we started again, every fae was different."

Professor Malin drifted closer to us, the current map of this world still behind her. "It was their energy. It was so foreign to the beat of our land that when they touched down, it disturbed the

228

balance. Not that we could call it balance at the time, since we were skewed so far to the side of war that the pendulum touched the ground there. But it was our current balance, and it needed to be disrupted more than anything else this world has ever needed."

"Like a jolt to the heart when it's in arrhythmia," I thought out loud, and there was a brief pause, before the shadow bopped again.

"Exactly. We were a dying nation, and they kickstarted us again. It wasn't instant of course. It took many years, at least a hundred if I remembered correctly, for them to divide and conquer. In the initial days, they worked together, and I still believe that was when we were at our strongest. Not that any accept or agree with me, but most of them weren't there at the time. I remember it very well, and we grow weaker again divided."

Lexie didn't argue with her, and I wondered if secretly more fae thought the same but were too afraid to speak against the Fallens' current way of managing their lands. "When the Fallen had their territories, they split most of the races," the professor continued. "So that there were no large clans in any territory. We all have our theori—"

"We couldn't have you rise up against us."

She stopped with a squeak at Drager's voice, and her shadowy form shrank as if she were disappearing, before she reappeared at full humanoid size again.

"There's power in numbers," he continued, stepping into the room, dressed all in black with scatterings of armor like he'd worn that first night I saw him. Examining him closer, I wondered why he looked so pissed off. I didn't like this mood of his. "When we separated the clans, you were all weakened. It also assisted in halting your fighting."

To give her props, Professor Malin recovered quickly. "Yes, that's the running theory. We appreciate the confirmation, Lord Drager." She paused, no doubt wondering what was about to happen next.

"What are you doing here?" I asked him, ignoring the gasp from Lexie and the professor. But seriously, he just kept showing up everywhere, and I had no idea why.

"Just checking in on you before we have our meeting," he told me, small smirk playing around his lips, even as his eyes remained dark. "Have you seen any of my brothers around?"

Making an exaggerated show of searching the corners and ceiling of the room, I shook my head. "Unless they can make themselves small or fade into shadows like Professor Malin, they're not here."

Drager's relaxed pose shifted in an instant, and he was standing before my desk, towering over me. From my seated position he was positively giant. "I'm going to have to work on that smart mouth," he murmured, his thumb brushing across my lower lip, grazing it roughly.

I forgot how to breathe, and maybe swallow, since a tiny dot of drool escaped onto his hand. That appeared to satisfy him, and he straightened, releasing my mouth.

"I'll see you soon, little human. We have class first, and then our date. Don't forget."

"I-I hav—" I cleared my throat. "I haven't forgotten."

He left as quickly as he'd arrived, and I could tell I wasn't the only one confused by his motivation. Why was he checking up on me? Especially during a private class. There was nothing to worry about in a room with only Lexie and one shadowy professor.

"That was odd," Lexie said, breaking the tension.

Professor Malin let out one of her high-pitched dog-laughs. "Yes. Yes. We don't often get visits from the Fallen." It felt like her energy was focused in my direction, and I imagined that if she had visible eyes, they'd be examining me very closely.

It was a mystery to me as well, she didn't need to worry.

"Time is up today for your class anyway," the professor added. "I'll see you back here soon, and we can continue with the history of the Eastern Realm and Fallen."

Pushing my chair back, I stood and smiled at the shadow. "Thank you, I'm really looking forward to learning more of this world."

She bopped her form once more, and I waved awkwardly before leaving. "Holy shit," I gasped to Lexie when the door closed. "She's a shadow. Like, I could see through her, and when she turned to the side it was almost as if she disappeared."

Lexie chuckled. "The nightmare creatures are unique in this world, that's for sure. Malin is so ancient that her power is an unknown entity, but most of the others hold their power in attack and fear. You'll understand what I mean when you spend more time in the general population of the academy."

I'd seen some of what had to be nightmare creatures yesterday during the gathering in the Grand Theater, and then this morning in the dining hall, but I'd avoided looking at them for long. All I saw were many eyes and limbs, along with fangs, claws, and other scary appendages.

"I've seen a few about," I told Lexie, "and for real, they'd never pass for anything other than a monster in the human world. But... and I mean this truthfully, they don't scare me as much as the highborn fae with their beautiful faces and deceptive hearts."

Like Greta. Her vibes were not vibing with mine at all, and I was happy that Lexie had dismissed the alliance near instantly.

Lexie beamed. "You, my friend, are correct as always. The trench might have meant death to any who stumbled into it, but other than that, the nightmare creatures let the rest of our land be

231

—unlike the various races and clans scattered about the Eastern Realm. That was the real death and destruction."

The Fallen had smoothed their sharp edges, but at heart, all of this land was still at war. It was just less obvious now.

"Drager popping in like that was odd, right?" I started tentatively.

Lexie didn't answer, but her expression told me she was worried. He was checking up on me for a reason, and the fact that he'd asked about his brothers was concerning.

But there wasn't time to worry about it, I had classes to get to. "Okay, so what's my next class?" I asked her.

Lexie didn't have to glance at the schedule again—I'd have had to look at it ten times and I'd still have forgotten the order. "You have your class on the faerie races."

Excellent. Not that all the classes weren't useful, but I really needed this one, considering I almost lost my arm to a bunny. This class was at the farthest end of this very long hallway, and we made it through with only curious looks from a dozen or so other students. "Most of them are still in class," Lexie explained when we reached a huge wood and steel-lined door. "Yours are shorter, at least for now."

That made sense since my human brain could only contain so much new information. Lexie didn't just open the door to the Facts and Myths of Faerie Races classroom. Instead, she pressed her hand against it, and closed her eyes briefly. "Safe to enter," she told me a beat later, and the door swung open, slowly, as if it was almost too heavy to carry its weight.

The inside was as far removed from the previous classroom as one could be. The floor was cobbled stone, the walls also stone, and there was an earthy scent as we stepped into the well-lit space. "As you've no doubt guessed," Lexie said as she led me over the uneven ground, toward a building off in the distance, "this room is used for a more practical style of teaching. At times, the creatures we studied roamed freely. Always safe to check before opening that door. I'll never forget the time a unicorn caused havoc through Main Hall, with hundreds of students trying to get to class."

She laughed, while shaking her head, and I couldn't tell if the memory was funny, scary, or tragic. Her emotions weren't clear, but what was clear was that…

"You have freaking unicorns?"

Giving me the side-eye to end all side-eyes, she had to shake her head again. "Are you seriously losing your mind over that? You saw a dragon. You saw a troll. Hen, you saw Calendul, and let me tell you, she's far more terrifying and mystical than you imagined."

"But unicorns," I said with reverence, clasping my hands tightly before me. "They're so magical."

Lexie's sigh was greater than was necessary. "You're going to get yourself killed. It's only a matter of time."

I took that to mean unicorns weren't quite the majestic magical horsies I was painting in my head. Oh well, at least I had this class to get me up to speed.

We stumbled across the rougher grounds to reach a large hut. It was made from wood, metal, and blocks of concrete, as rustic as everything else in this room. The scent of livestock was even stronger here.

"Professor Druin should be out in a moment," Lexie said, glancing around. "He lives in this hut, so he's always around."

A second later the front door, a heavy structure like the one at the entrance of this room, swung open. Secretly, I'd been expecting a giant of a man to emerge, some very buff, outdoorsy type who would be able to wrangle whatever creatures he brought into this room.

I was half right.

Professor Druin's head emerged first, and that was humanoid-ish, followed by his body, which was very much not human. At all.

"Centaur," I breathed.

Lexie's nod was discreet, and I shut my mouth after that, taking in the professor as his four legs skillfully traversed the few steps from his front door. His head and upper body were covered in more hair than a human, the same dark coat as his lower half. His face was mostly clear, with just scatterings of hair on his neck and chin. His skin was light yellow, his eyes very dark and a little bulbous like a horse, and his lips were nearly non-existent. As he stopped before us, he smiled broadly at Lexie. "My favorite pupil returns," he said in a rumbly voice. "Always keeping me on my hooves, Lexical."

She chuckled and leaned up to hug him. He stood a good two heads above her, so she managed to wrap her arms around his waist, the part which met the lower horsey half. Here, he had a deep brown coat, four legs, and the rest was shaped like the back of a horse, including the tail.

The class hadn't started yet, and already I was getting an education.

When Professor Druin pulled back, he gave me his full attention, eerie eyes examining me closely. "And you must be Morgan Starrer, my new student."

The urge to curtsy overcame me, but I fought it down. The last thing I needed was to look like any more of a bumbling human fool. "Thank you for teaching me," I finally said, only sixty percent awkward.

"It's my pleasure. I feel we have much to learn from each other. I've always been curious of my counterparts in the Earthly realm."

Counterparts...? "Horses?" I said softly, hoping I wasn't offending him with that one word.

He smiled again, and lipless smiles while cute on animals in the human world, were not as cute on him. It was almost scary, but I managed not to react.

"Horses," he agreed. "We don't have them here, and I would like to know about their role in the human world."

Shit. He probably wouldn't like what I had to say, but I'd give him the truth.

Here's hoping we made it through the first class before I was kicked out.

CHAPTER
THIRTY-EIGHT

Professor Druin led us around the back of his hut, and on the other side there was an arena. It was a fenced-off area, with loose dirt on the floor, and seating to one side.

"Please sit," he said, waving his hand toward the rows of stone seats terracing up from the arena floor. When Lexie and I were seated, he remained in the arena facing us. "Normally in this class we'd focus on one creature or race at a time. But you are not here for the full two years, and this is not for your future in the Eastern Realms. With that in mind, I'm fast-tracking my class. I'll focus on the most dangerous creatures first, touching briefly on the races you'll come across, and give you one or two pointers for each. Sound okay?"

"Sounds perfect," I replied.

"Excellent," he continued. "Let's get started, then."

The next few hours with Professor Druin were intense. He wasn't kidding when he said he was giving me a crash course, and even though I asked Lexie for a pen and paper to keep track, my head still spun with everything I'd learned.

In messy sprawling writing, I'd managed to jot notes about at least twenty creatures, including:

Yonters: birds of prey. Strong enough to take down five highborn fae. Solitary, but with intense family ties, their loyalty will never be broken. Their beak can pierce through all but the strongest material, and they eat meat.

Thank the gods Cal had been on Lexie's side and considered her a friend, because she was truly terrifying.

I'd also learned about: *Dunedins, ground dwelling scavengers. Able to move rapidly across land. They live in burrows with their clan. On average, each clan has a few thousand members, and the fae-eating entity spends most of its time hunting. Drawing in the unsuspecting with waves of energy that call the weak.*

It was apparently a huge positive that I didn't pet the bunny. It must have been the fear emanating from Cal that masked the *call of the dunedin*, because I hadn't felt a pull to move toward it.

I'd also learned more about the sabre, which really was like a giant forest kitty, and the concors, which were very much not forest kitties. There was more here to fear than not, if my current list of animals was anything to go by—though the professor had said he was focusing on what could kill me first, so it was a skewed list.

"So many new fears to add to my nightmares," I muttered to Lexie as we left the room, the scent of livestock vanishing as soon as the heavy doors closed. "We have *lochen* in the ocean, *presfn* in the skies, and *klagour motems* under the ground with the damn dunedins. I'm not Australian, girl. I don't have experience living amongst dozens of creatures that can kill me with a thought."

Lexie's laughter was low and relaxed, and I hoped that meant my odds of crossing most of these fae killers was low. "You'll be safe. Firstly, you're with me and I'm not letting any bunny eat you, and secondly, most of the time avoiding is all you need to do.

As you've probably noticed, there's a bit of a pattern in the creatures having to draw you in first before they take you. It's kind of our M.O. If you can resist, you'll be safe."

My track record in resisting wasn't strong, but then again, Drager wasn't really a fae creature. He was from some alien planet, or the sky, or whatever. And he sure as shit didn't wait for permission before touching.

"What's next, then?" I asked. We were back in the hallway, and while my brain was fatigued, I was also buzzing with all this new information.

"Next we feed you before you turn into a creature we should all fear," Lexie said, managing to keep her expression neutral, even as her eyes laughed at me. "Then you have fight training for the afternoon."

The hall was busier now, and Lexie walked the entire way to the dining hall with one hand over her right shoulder. Outside of all the stares—some curious and others downright loathing—we didn't have any trouble, and I wondered if Greta was keeping them off our backs for the time being, as a show of how smooth an alliance with her might be.

Or maybe it was Lexie's presence.

The stares she got were different, filled with respect and reverence… along with a healthy dose of fear. She was well known here, both through her family name and her own achievements.

"It surprises me, you know," I said suddenly when we started up the stairs.

She didn't look at me, her focus on everything else around us. "What surprises you?" she said, distracted but still listening.

"That you appeared so content just shelving books with me. We did that for years, and I saw no indication that you were restless or had all this waiting for you somewhere else."

Now I had her full attention; she blinked rapidly, shocked.

238

"Morgs, are you being serious?"

It was my turn to blink rapidly. "Uh, yeah, of course I am. It's clear that here you hold a position of respect and power, both from your family name and own achievements. There, we were minimum wage workers who barely saw sunlight or other people. Our big decision every week was which pub we went to on a Friday night. It's a mundane life, you know."

She hugged me fiercely and I almost fell down the stairs. "Morgan Starrer, I could shake you." Her arms tightened and I fell into her hug, needing the comfort more than I'd realized. When she pulled away, she met my gaze. "My time with you on Earth, at Dragerfield, was the best years of my life. The absolute best. You showed me warmth and family, unconditional love, and I was never bored or dissatisfied. I promise. I'd give anything to go back to when we sprawled across our living room, buried in books, eating pizza and drinking wine. Those are the core memories I'll keep with me always."

Tears spilled from my eyes, and there was no chance of stopping the flow. "Mine too," I choked out.

I hugged her again, and thanked whatever gods existed—*not Drager*—for Lexie in my life. Despite our issues lately, the core of our friendship remained the same. As strong as ever.

"Come on, Morgs. Let's get some food," she finally said.

I nodded, wiping my face as she continued up the stairs and I followed her.

Lunch was very much like breakfast, but with far fewer students in the room. "Most fae eat once a day," Lexie said as she looked around. "But I've grown quite fond of multiple meals, let me tell you."

She proved that by hoovering her plate like it was the only meal she'd get all week. "Same," I managed to say around a mouthful of bread. "Second breakfast is my favorite though."

Lexie snorted, spraying me with some bread, and then we both dissolved into laughter. "Shit, sorry. I was just remembering the time you went on a date and asked him about second breakfast, and when he had no idea what you were talking about, you picked up your stuff and left."

More laughter spilled from me. "I have hard limits, okay. And that's one of them."

"I don't disagree," she said with a shrug.

After lunch, Lexie led me back downstairs, and when we entered the main hall we continued along the path we'd taken yesterday, out of the building and onto the velvety grass. "Outside class?" I asked, looking around for where we might be going.

"Yep. First thing is the obstacle course, so we can assess your abilities."

"What the fuck did you just say?" I gasped, missing a step. If that didn't prove my abilities without need of an obstacle course, nothing ever would.

"Come on, Morgs. You'll be fine. I've seen you leapfrog a table in the bookstore to get the last copy of a special edition hardback."

"That was life and death," I shot back. "Like mothers lifting a car off their child. This is a completely different situation."

The bitch just rolled her eyes at me, and now I was wondering if I was fast enough to run away and hide. As I had that thought, we rounded the corner of the academy to find a dozen or so fae out in a field, kicking a round object around. It didn't look like a ball from home, but it was similar, and they zipped and zapped around the field so quickly, confirming that there was no chance I'd ever outrun anyone here.

Might as well resign myself to this fate, and maybe... just maybe, I'd find some improvement in my athletic ability. Or die trying.

Beyond their field, we ended up in another section which was clearly the obstacle course. I could see a range of climbing, crawl-ing, and jumping stages. Even with tendrils of Drager's power inside me, there was no way I could get through all that unscathed.

"The panic on your face…" Lexie said with a laugh. "Don't stress. If you can't do it, you can't. But as your instructors, we need to know your abilities. So we don't push you harder than your body is capable of handling."

"I can already tell you that I'll be at level one, which is the lowest, and that you should push me as hard as you would a newborn. But if you insist I give this a shot, I will not let you down."

"That's my girl."

I stuck my tongue out at her. "Just remind me to stretch," I said with a huff. "Because I can already tell you're about to work the fuck out of me."

Her lips twitched but she was in professional mode now. She stepped away from my side and joined the two fae already waiting at the head of the course. One female and one male.

"Welcome to fight classes," the female said. She had a purring lilt to her voice, that matched the sexy black catsuit she wore. Her hair was dark, slicked back in a high ponytail, highlighting blue eyes and light brown skin.

She was stunning.

Scarily stunning.

This faerie world bred a type, and I had a sneaking feeling that by the time these fae were done with me, I was going to be crawling back to Earth.

Oh well, as I'd said to Drager many weeks ago: break me.

I can take it.

241

CHAPTER
THIRTY-NINE

T he obstacle course had a clear path. You had to complete each section before you could move on to the next one, and they were all designed to test different skills and abilities. The only issue I could see on immediate inspection was that some sections were clearly designed for fae who had extra abilities. Like… the ability to jump eight feet in the air and catch a small ledge on the side of a wooden wall, and then pull themselves up and over the wall.

"We understand that there are sections that will be beyond your capabilities as a human," Lexie told me, standing next to the pretty brunette. "So we're sending Mika here with you, and he'll be the extra boost you need."

Mika was the silent male, who stood a head taller than me, so well over six-feet, and had the broadest shoulders I'd ever seen in real life. Except for those on the Fallen.

"You'll be safe with me," he said in a smooth, pleasant voice. He had curled brown hair flopping messily around his head, matching the smooth, boyish lines of his face, giving him a very boy next door look—only jacked up on fae-juice, because he packed a lot of muscle and was clearly lethal and well-trained.

Maybe it was the focus in his dark eyes, or maybe it was just instinct, but I felt as if I could trust him to get me through this.

"Just follow my lead," he said, flashing perfect white teeth.

Staring at the wall now that we were closer, it was worse than I'd expected. The wall itself was at least twelve feet tall, and the handle was almost at the top. If I did manage to make it up this side with Mika's help, would I break a leg landing on the other side?

Mika nudged me. "I voted against this, but Tasha has a set way of teaching, and she's acting as point on your training."

Tasha. The sexy chick in the catsuit.

"Let's get it over with, then," I muttered, forcing my gaze away from the height of the wall.

Mika took a step from me, and with what appeared to be zero effort, launched up the wall, gripping onto the small ledge with both hands, before he dropped his right off and held on with just the left. "Come on, Morgan," he called, reaching for me with that free hand.

The fact he used my name and not *human* gave him a few brownie points, and I refrained from glaring at him as I sucked in a deep breath and stared up. "I'm not light," I told him honestly. "You might want to brace yourself."

His smile was slow and cheeky. "You're tiny. Your weight will barely even register."

Yeah, I'd heard that before. Human men weren't the only ones to overestimate their muscles, it appeared. Stepping a few feet back, I gave myself a run up, and then without overthinking it, I sprinted for the wall and threw myself up as high as I could manage.

My legs were strong from carrying books up and down the

stairs at Dragerfield Library, and that helped me find the power to boost up the wall. I honestly didn't expect Mika to catch my hand the first time—or maybe any time—and I sure as shit didn't expect him to haul me up in one swing, but I was wrong on both accounts.

As our hands gripped, his felt like being encased in steel. I had no fear of slipping, and without showing any strain he just lifted my entire body, before jerking me high enough to grab onto the same ledge he was already hanging from.

"Holy shit," I gasped, holding on. I was higher than he was, my elbows wedged on top of the ledge. It was the perfect position to push myself up, but of course I'd never lifted my own body weight, and it was harder than it looked.

"If I might be so bold," Mika said conversationally, still hanging there like he could hold on with one hand all day, "I can help you with the distance again."

Yeah, what the hell. I'd come this far. "Sure, do your best."

A low gasp spilled from my lips when a firm hand landed under my ass, and once again I was moving up faster than expected. Mika almost threw me over the wall, but I grasped the edge at the last moment, saving myself from a broken neck.

Hanging half over the wall, I tried not to panic at how far away the ground looked on the other side. Mika flipped himself over a moment later, landing smoothly below, staring up at me. "Hang over the edge and let yourself fall," he said. "Your body will know what to do."

"My body knows how to read and eat," I called back, inching farther over, until my legs were dangling down while the top half of me remained perched on top of the wall. "It doesn't know how to fall without dying."

Mika chuckled. Stupid fae thought I was kidding.

With a sigh, I lowered myself until I was hanging by my

fingertips. Closing my eyes probably wasn't the smartest move, but it happened by instinct, and even bracing myself for impact, it felt like my legs snapped as I hit the ground. My cry was small and lost in Lexie shouting out to me, "Yes, Morgs. Killing it."

I was not killing it. I was so far from killing anything except myself that it wasn't even funny, but as I straightened and tested out my lower limbs, I was relieved to find that there wasn't any lingering pain. I'd landed okay after all.

"Great job, Morgs," Mika said, mimicking my best friend. "Shall we move on to the next obstacle."

No, we shall not. "If I must," I replied with fake sweetness. "I wouldn't want Tasha mad at me."

Mika's smile didn't falter. "It's not pleasant."

"Ex-girlfriend?" I guessed.

His brow furrowed slightly, and it was the first kink I'd seen in his affable armor. "Something like that. But we're long over, and now I'm just here to follow her orders and do as I'm told."

"All with a fake smile on your face," I added, before realizing that was a touch personal and should have remained inside my head.

He regarded me closer than he'd done up until now, finally nodding. "Something like that," he repeated, and that was where the conversation ended.

Section two was a series of steps between obstacles, dodging right and left. It wasn't difficult, but Mika told me it was about how fast you could get to the end. He took off first, near a blur as he stepped in rings, swerved through poles, and flipped over some small hurdles at the end.

Showoff.

I followed at my human pace, and my first priority was to not breathe as heavily as my lungs wanted me to, while my second was to not trip and fall on my face.

245

I succeeded at one of those priorities, making it to the end without tripping. My breathing, on the other hand, was just short of embarrassing. But damn, it was farther than I'd expected, and there was so much jumping.

Mika's smile almost felt real when I huffed in next to him. "So fucking... simple," I gasped out. "Sad it's over."

"There's plenty more, don't worry yourself."

"Zero worries," I said, between heaving breaths.

Turned out I had a lot of worries as I crawled, leapt, and rolled my way through a dozen more obstacles, each of which was designed to test me to my fullest ability, and break three nails. I wouldn't have made it through at least half of them without Mika's help, and by the end he was my new best friend.

Lexie, who made me take this stupid class, was out, and Mika was in.

When my former best friend pranced over to me and attempted to hug my heaving, sweaty ass, I shoved her away. "You are dead to me," I gasped, jabbing my finger with a much shorter nail on it at her. "How dare you."

Lexie laughed, because she was a psychopath. "Come on, Morgs. You did amazing. You made it through the entire course. Many of the students here don't manage that."

Tasha also wandered over, slower, and I didn't imagine the derisiveness of her stare. "You did adequately, with help. We will adapt our training plan for your... shortcomings."

I'd show her *shortcomings*. Mika caught me as I lunged forward, his steel-band arms that had been hauling me around for an hour stopping me in my tracks. "Hold on there, killer," he said with a laugh. "Save that for training. If you work hard enough, maybe you'll do us all a favor and kick Tasha's ass."

Tasha's snort said everything about her worry over me *kicking her ass*.

"We'll see you back here tomorrow, human," she told me, before turning and marching off, leaving me with Lexie and Mika.

He released me, and I glared daggers, before my anger cooled and I realized that attacking a fae, who had done nothing wrong and was clearly adept enough at fighting to be teaching a class on it, wasn't the smartest move. He'd saved me once again. "Thanks for today," I told him, rubbing at an already forming bruise on my arm. "I might not be able to walk tomorrow, but I'd never have made it through that course without your help."

He shrugged, running a hand over his curls, as they flopped back into the same perfect placement. "It was fun. I enjoyed every minute. See you tomorrow, Morgs."

With that he shot me a grin and left me standing with Lexie, who was staring at me with the strangest look on her face. "Shut up," I snarled, clutching my side. Now that the others had left, I could fall apart at leisure. "You got me into this mess."

Her laughter was louder than was necessary. "You did so much better than I thought. Though I wasn't expecting Mika of the *Henlenson* clan to be your obstacle course buddy. He's hot stuff, Morgan."

He was hot stuff, and I'd genuinely liked him, even when he'd been encouraging me beyond my body's capabilities. "So, I still have my energy manipulation class today?" I asked, wincing as I straightened.

"Yep. You're supposed to have a defense class as well, but we'll leave that until tomorrow. No point breaking you on day one. You won't recover fast enough."

"Especially since we have no idea what to expect from this random class with the Fallen," I reminded us both.

Lexie nodded. "We have some time before energy manipulation. Let's go back to the room so you can shower, because no offense, Morgs, you kinda smell."

I more than *kinda* smelled. When you bothered your own nose, it was time to rinse off and change clothes. It was a rule, and it existed for a reason.

"Let's do it," I said, hoping my wobbly legs would sort themselves out on our journey back to our dorm. A shower and new clothes was all the incentive I needed, and as we set off I gave myself a silent pat on the back.

I'd made it through their obstacles. With help, yes, but I didn't give up.

That was worth a lot to me, even if snobby Tasha didn't feel the same way.

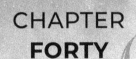

CHAPTER
FORTY

E nergy manipulation was held inside another room off the main hall. Lexie led me in, and we weren't the first inside, but no one looked our way as they got ready.

"We can observe from here," Lexie said, turning away from the arena to climb a set of stairs. The stairs didn't lead anywhere, so I could only guess that they were generally part of a training exercise and would be the perfect seating for us.

As we settled down to watch, more students entered the room, each of them dropping their bags and heading into the middle of the arena. The teacher, a typical highborn fae with aristocratic features, silky black hair, and beautifully tanned skin, appeared a few moments later, stepping from a shadowy area at the back of the room. We were too far away for me to see what was over there.

"Everyone gather in," he said, waving the fae closer until they were all collected in the center of the arena, which looked to have rubbery material on the ground with wooden fences encircling it. "Today we're going to work on pushing our will into inanimate objects and having them shift to your desired needs."

There were twenty or so fae in this class, and they ranged from highborn, a satyr, a troll—single eye was a giveaway—one of the golem boys... and Greta. First time I'd seen her since this morning.

Right behind them was a nightmare creature, shadowy like Professor Malin had been, but completely corporeal. I could see all eight tentacle legs which hung from its round waist. These *legs* pushed its body up and down, almost flexing. "It's an orcale," Lexie whispered. "They came from deep in the trench, but they're fairly harmless."

"Where is its face?" I murmured back, searching closer. It looked like an egg with tentacle legs.

"When we get closer, you'll see its eyes are on top of the dome, and it moves them in a full circle around itself."

"Okay, then." I had no desire to get any closer than I was right now, more than happy to take her word for it. "Did all the nightmare creatures assimilate into the five lands?" I asked as the professor got the class moving around the arena.

"Parts of the trench still exist," she told me. "In Zahak's land, right near where the deepest cavern was originally located. Most left, of course, having awoken from their raging as Professor Malin said, and they did move across all five lands, claiming territory in what suited their disposition the best. We have many races here, and none are considered superior or inferior. We're just different. And different has different requirements, you know?"

I nodded. "Yeah, even on Earth that's true. I had a friend, Katy, who was a twin. She always used to joke that her parents liked her brother better, but I sensed that deep down she really felt that way. One day she said something to her mom about it. I wasn't sure if it was the first time she'd ever expressed this or not, but it was definitely the first time her mom addressed it."

This was a longer story than I'd anticipated when starting, but I was committed now, so I ploughed on.

"She told Katy that they loved both of them exactly the same. More love than any heart could hold. Then she told us that Austin had autism. We didn't know that word at the time, so she went on to explain that he had additional needs, and that was why, at times, it felt like he got more time and attention, and maybe grace. They let Austin get away with actions they'd never allow Katy to do, and that made her feel that she was second best."

By the time I finished, I realized how the story might sound, so I hurried to add.

"And I don't say any of this implying that any faerie has autism or additional needs, I'm just saying that no two humans are alike, and that means no two needs are alike. I'm assuming it's the same for fae, even amongst the same race."

Lexie surprised me when she reached out and hugged me hard, holding on for long beats like she might never let go. "I know what you meant, and your story works," she murmured against my shoulder. "Fae are more animalistic in how we approach life and situations, but we are all unique as well. It's been a huge learning curve assimilating under the rule of the Fallen, but we needed their energy. We needed their order. We cannot be left to our own devices."

I wasn't sure how I felt about it all. My own opinions and feelings toward a totalitarian control were complex and based on Earth and humans. Here, it wasn't my place to comment. The fae weren't rebelling against them, and that had to mean that in some way, their lives were better now.

Unless it was mass brainwashing.

Couldn't rule it out. But until I knew more, I'd take their words for everything being better now.

The class got underway, and I focused on learning what

powers these fae possessed. Each of them had a rock before them, probably about the size of a tennis ball. The professor was explaining how to draw energy from their bodies, while also remaining grounded to the energy of this building and the world around them. "Never just use your own power," he said forcefully. "You can burn yourself out in an instant. Especially if your natural abilities don't lead toward energy manipulation."

Greta got it the first time, lazily waving her hand so the rock lifted and hovered chest height in front of her. Her brow furrowed briefly after that, and then she leaned in closer, and I blinked as the shape of her rock started to change, stretching, forming a point on one end, and what was a roughly hewn handle on the other.

"Emerelsos get the same training as Lightsbringers," Lexie said, leaning toward me. "Anything can be turned into a weapon if needed."

Apparently so, since Greta had made herself a rock dagger.

A few of the other students achieved new shapes in their rocks, but most were left with a ball at the end. A ball that hovered mid-knee, but it remained the same.

"As I told you," Lexie shot me a smirk, "we're not really that different power-wise to humans."

My snort was loud, and sure enough, a few faces turned our way. I lowered my eyes and pretended to be invisible. "Not a single human can make a ball hover at their knees," I reminded Lexie. "Not even the strongest."

She shrugged. "The way your professional sportspeople juggle the ball, it looks like energy manipulation."

"Looked like, but it's not." They had skills and training, but this was magic.

When the class was over, and the students had left, we stood, and I winced at the protesting of my muscles. Between the sexercise, walking, and now fight classes, I was either going to develop some muscle definition or I was going to end up bedridden.

"Do we have time to grab some food before Fallen Gods class?" I asked as we left the room, with no more than a curious stare from the professor. I felt a little rude not having met him before class, but I was following Lexie's lead, and she'd gotten me out of the way straight-up.

"I don't think so," she said. Apparently the fae instinctively knew what time of the day it was in their world. A skill that didn't work for her on Earth. "We only have about ten minutes to get there, and it's back outside."

A long breath escaped me, and I forced myself to remain calm. "I don't understand what class I could possibly have with the dragons," I muttered. "This makes no sense."

Lexie didn't even attempt to reassure me, and that was terrifying in and of itself.

The halls were the busiest we'd seen so far in the academy. This time we'd finished class with many others, and there was gridlock as we attempted to maneuver through the main hall and out the front door.

"*Ew, human. They smell weird.*"

"*Ugly ass face with bug eyes.*"

Two of the many comments I heard as Lexie pushed through, creating a path for us. No one touched me, but there were dirty looks, and I sensed that if I didn't have a Lightsbringer warrior at my side, my journey would have been a lot rougher.

By the time we stepped out onto the grass, my heart was slamming hard in my chest, fight or flight mode all but activated. "That felt hostile," I said, swallowing roughly to clear my throat.

"Don't let them bother you," Lexie added, sounding far less stressed. "They're testing your ability to handle this world. They don't know your strength. You've dealt with far worse than a few mean comments. You endured years of psychological bullying and came out stronger on the other side."

She was talking about my mom again, and as an extension my father, and I loved her for the pep-talk, but the truth was... I didn't feel particularly strong. Not on Earth and not now.

"It doesn't bother me that they think I'm ugly and have bug eyes." Ironic, considering the being that said that did have a slight praying mantis look, with green skin and antennae. "It's just fear in not knowing who might attack, and what weapons they might use."

Lexie clasped my hand. "It's smart to be cautious. Your body knows how to react, and you should always listen to it. Some of those students did mean you harm, and your instincts were spot on."

"And now I'm even more terrified." It wasn't a huge shock that my presence here was unwanted, but knowing they were actively meaning me harm did change that entire interaction. Humans weren't welcome here, and it was in my best interests to remember that.

As we stood there in the fresh air, though, the sun descending through the pink sky, my emotions calmed. I'd made it this far, and I wasn't alone any longer. I had Lexie at my side, and Drager was still an ally at this stage—an ally who required my presence, so we needed to start moving to his class.

"Let's get this over wi—" I was cut off by a scream.

Lexie's weapon appeared in her hands almost instantly, and I ducked lower by instinct.

"Back inside, Morgs," she shouted at me.

Crouched as I was, the ability to move quickly was impaired, and by the time I stood Lexie was in full battle mode, swiping through the air at the sudden influx of yonters sweeping over the academy grounds. "Calendul?" I called.

"Not her clan," Lexie shot back.

The entire flock—at least twelve—of these attack birds swooped over the academy grounds, sending the screaming students scurrying. Only a couple, like Lexie, had weapons and were fending off lethal beaks and claws.

On my feet, my body's aches were forgotten as I sprinted toward the entrance of the building. I hated leaving Lexie out here, but I was useless in helping her, and she wouldn't race inside until I was safe.

Five steps was all I made before two yonters descended on me. "Lexie," I screamed, but there was no way for her to get to me when she was battling three of her own.

Five out of twelve attacking us? There was no way this was a coincidence; we were the targets.

Claws wrapped around my right shoulder, cutting into my skin as one of them yanked me up into the air, well above Lexie's reach. Screams spilled from me as I fought best I could, the pain increasing in my shoulder as its talons dug in harder. I had no idea what to expect, but after Professors Druin's class where he described their feeding patterns, I figured it was taking me back to the nest to eat.

The yonter went higher and higher over the middle of the lake, before heading toward the forests, only to come to a dead stop in the air, hovering and screeching.

"Please," I called, right before it opened its claws and let me fall.

Into the deadly lake.

CHAPTER
FORTY-ONE

I was high enough to have time to scream, cry, and pee myself a little. I mean, it's not every day I'm dropped five stories into an icy lake, filled with deadly fae creatures who could kill me faster than the yonter. Oh, and there was just that small issue of me not being able to swim.

The yonter couldn't have known that when it dropped me, right? Had that been its intentions all along? Questions I would never have answered if I died here today.

Hitting the water, when it finally happened, hurt like a bitch. I'd managed to enter feet first, but I'd let my right arm and leg drift away from my center, and they were jerked to the side. The pain was instant, and even as the water numbed me and panic took over, I was aware I'd done some damage to my limbs.

As the water grew darker above my head—I'd landed deep—a sliver of light remained above, and I focused on that speck. Kicking my legs, I tried to push up through the water, wishing I wasn't completely clothed. My jeans and boots were weighing me down. My injured arm screamed at me as I tried to paddle through the water. All the while, dark dots danced on the edge of my vision as my lungs screamed for air. Hitting the lake had knocked all breath from me, and I'd had no chance to take another before slipping below the surface.

The light grew a little brighter, but I was still too far from the surface. Weakness filled me, and even though I wasn't giving up just yet, the reality of my situation was growing more apparent.

Come on, Morgan! You've survived worse than this before.

I counted in my head, each stroke and kick. *One… two… one… two… one.*

The rhythmic counting kept me going, but it was always going to be a losing game. Everything was stacked against me: I wasn't a strong swimmer, I was hurt, and I'd landed too deep. The darkness took over as my arms stilled, no longer able to move.

My frantic struggle to get to the surface eased.

Lexie was my last thought. She'd tried so hard to protect me, and I was so grateful to have her in my life. I hoped she was okay and had been able to fight off those yonters. As long as she was alive and well, then I'd die a happy human.

I'd see her again one day, I had to believe that. Not even death would break us apart.

As the final threads of consciousness slipped from my grasp, I was jerked from the water by thick bands wrapped around my waist. When I left the lake, I went into convulsions, choking and coughing water from my lungs. It spoke of how close to death I'd been that I didn't realize a dragon had me until we were flying across the academy, over the buildings, and off into the distance.

Drager took me away from the lake and into a forest, not as dense as the one we'd walked through to get to the academy. When he finally landed, the adrenaline had died off in my body, and I hung in his grip like a limp doll. I was placed gently on the forest floor, his beast form stepping away as if afraid to squash me.

After a minute, I managed to push myself up to sit, my body shaking, limbs in pain as the injuries I'd sustained made themselves known. The dragon let out a roar so loud it shook the land around us, and my ears ached.

"Drager," I groaned, my voice raspy from coughing as I propped myself back against a log. "Too loud."

He roared again, even louder, and I finally focused long enough to see the giant black beast before me.

Holy. Fuck. A shot of adrenaline kickstarted my brain in an instant.

Unless Drager looked identical to Zahak, then I had the wrong Fallen.

Zahak had rescued me.

And he was pissed.

My heart slammed so hard in my chest that I wondered if he could hear it between his roars as he paced back and forth, destroying trees and shrubbery with his huge body. I held both hands up before me, placating the beast, even though I had no real idea what had him so riled.

"Zahak," I called, before remembering we didn't have the same relationship as Drager and me, and this scary Fallen would no doubt expect a *lord* at the front of that title. "Thank you for saving—"

"Morgan!" Lexie's shout was close.

"Zahak! What the hell have you done with my human?" Drager added, even louder than my best friend, confirming who the dragon before me was.

Zahak ignored both, his huge head coming closer. I flinched as his snout, five times the size of my head, prodded me, sniffing

258

around my right shoulder. The press sent a shot of pain down my arm, and I remembered that I'd been clawed.

As I looked down, it was to find watery blood seeping from the wounds. Zahak could clearly smell the blood, and he wasn't happy about it. Hopefully it didn't make him want to eat me in one gulp.

"It's just a minor flesh wound," I rasped, having no idea if that was true or not. "But it's okay. It's not going to kill me."

A hot snort of breath encased me, and that dark glossiness of his eyes grew closer.

"Morgan, holy fae babies. Do not move an inch." Lexie had found us, her voice coming from right behind the dragon.

"Are you okay, Morgan?" That was Drager, who sounded like he was at her side.

Neither moved any closer to the furious dragon, and I didn't blame them.

"Totally fine," I said, and trusting my gut, as Lexie told me to do, I pushed myself up to stand. I stifled a moan as I put pressure on my right arm, which had the shoulder injury and a possible broken limb from hitting the lake.

"Brother, what the hell are you doing?" Drager growled. "Let her come to me."

Zahak shifted his weight, moving his head away from me, revealing a pair of worried faces on the edge of the trampled tree line.

"He saved my life," I told them. "I think he's just concerned about me being injured." Logically, it made no sense, but it was also the only explanation for why his dragon was acting this way, and why he'd saved me for a second time. The first could be considered a coincidence, but when it happened again, it was definitely a pattern.

Zahak remained in front of me, so I started to edge around the giant dragon tail wrapped around my legs. The second I moved, his body rumbled. I paused and the rumbling stopped just as quickly. It was clear that Zahak did not want me to leave his protective presence.

"Let me go to her," I heard Lexie say. "I'm her best friend. I love her as family and would die for her in an instant. There is no other here who can say the same. She needs me."

There was a long pause, but Zahak must have agreed somehow, because Lexie was racing around the side of his beast, her pretty face strained. The evidence of tears remained on her cheeks, and I hated that I'd worried her. Speaking of, there were multiple injuries scattered across her face, neck and arms. "Are you okay?" I burst out, throat protesting the volume I'd used.

"Totally fine," she said quickly, gaze darting across my face as she took me in. "Except for my heart attack when that froggin' yonter took you."

"You and me both," I muttered. "Why did they attack?" I had my theory that Lexie and I had been the main targets, but a part of me hoped I was wrong.

"You were the target."

Hope. Dashed.

"Why didn't they just fly off and eat me?"

Zahak's dragon started to rumble again, and without thinking I put my hand on the huge section of tail I was near and brushed it soothingly. The heat of his scales near scorched me, and I was reminded that this wasn't a pet lizard. This was a scary beast, who oddly hadn't tried to eat me.

"Zahak flew in at the last second," Lexie told me. "When he arrived on the scene, the cowards fled. You were just lucky you were over the lake when it dropped you."

Holding my injured arm closer to my body, I stopped stroking the dragon. "Lucky, but not completely unscathed."

Lexie's concerned expression grew. "Right, so we need to get you to the healers. Can you tell your guard dragon that he's hurting you by not letting you leave."

"Zahak, you saved my life and I'll never forget it," I told him. "I'm so grateful for you, but Lexie is right... I need medical attention." More rumbles from the beast, but this time when I attempted to move out of the barrier of his tail, he let me.

Slowly, Lexie and I edged around Zahak, and I caught a glimpse of dark eyes and gilded wings, before he launched himself up into the sky above. In the next beat, Drager was at my side, his arms around me as he hauled me up into his chest.

"Ouch, ow-ow-ow," I cried, as his strong grip pressed on my aching body.

He eased up his hold, and I sank into his warmth, my eyes fluttering shut as if I could finally let myself relax. "Who organized the attack?" I murmured against him. I didn't want to examine why I felt so comfortable in his hold.

Especially when a part of me mourned the loss of the black beast.

"I don't know," Drager bit out. "But I'm going to find out, and I'm going to destroy them."

He was sweet and psycho, which bothered me way less than it used to. I was growing accustomed to the greater intensity of emotions in this world. To Drager's intensity.

Drager carried me back to the academy, as I drifted in and out of consciousness. My brain was frazzled, and I was exhausted after attempting to swim from the depths of the lake. I had always been a weak swimmer, but this was the first time I'd almost died from it.

In the academy, I was taken to the healing wards, which were a series of ten rooms on the second floor. Here, fae who were naturally skilled in manipulating the energy of a body closed up the gashes on my shoulders and infused healing into my bones so it would hopefully be back to full strength in a few days. Lexie refused help since she was already healing on her own.

"You need to rest up," the tiny pixie told me. She stood about two feet tall, thin, with wispy blond curls and huge opaque wings. "Don't overexert yourself until full healing is complete."

"I won't," I promised. "Thank you for your healing."

She smiled brightly, and her hair grew brighter with it. "You're most welcome, kind human."

Drager, who had spent his time as a silent bodyguard in the corner glaring at every fae who touched me, joined Lexie and me as we made our way to the dorm. "I'll have food sent to your room," he growled, the first words he'd spoken in an hour. "Don't leave tonight, and tomorrow I will escort you to class."

The healing energy had me feeling floaty and free, with most of the injuries already gone, but I wasn't about to argue with him when he was in this mood. "Sorry about our date," I said softly. "I was looking forward to it."

He glanced down at me, expression hard. Part of me wondered if he'd even remembered the date. "We'll reschedule," he said, and that was the end of that conversation.

When we made it to the room, Drager took a quick look around before he left, but not without delivering his warning once more to remain in this room until he returned tomorrow.

Lexie let me shower and change for bed first, and when the tray of food was delivered, I ate only a few pieces, too exhausted to do more than that. When I couldn't keep my eyes open any longer, I crawled into bed, which was surprisingly warm, like someone had been lying under the covers already.

As I drifted off, Lexie called, "I love you, Morgan. Sleep now. I'll watch over you tonight. You can rest without fear."

"Love you, Lex," I mumbled, wanting to tell her to get some sleep, but I was too far gone.

Just as I slipped farther into the land of dreams, I felt a soft lick across my cheek, just like that time in the cream hallways of Lancourt, but I was too asleep to do anything about it.

My imagination wasn't keeping me awake tonight. That was for sure.

CHAPTER
FORTY-TWO

My sleep that night was the most restful I'd had in a very long time, helped along by the energy boost from the pixie in the healing center. My dreams were filled with the giant black dragon who'd saved my life, *again*, and I had many confusing thoughts about Zahak.

Consciousness returned slowly, and as I opened my eyes and went to stretch my arms, I found one of them pinned with a heavy weight. Glancing down to see what had happened, a scream ripped from me.

Lexie leapt out of bed, reaching me at the same time I managed to scramble back against the headboard, both of us staring at the sabre draped across my bed.

Draped across my bed!

It wasn't like the sabre I'd seen in the forest; this one had a glossy black coat with hints of red and was six feet long at least, as it took up half my bed.

"What. The. Fuck?" I whispered frantically as the creature stretched and yawned. "What is it?"

Lexie's eyes were wide as she gestured for me to get off the bed. "It's an ocher sabre," she bit out. "I didn't even know they existed anymore. They're ancient ancestors of modern sabres."

I crept off the bed, and the sabre yawned and stretched once more, seemingly in no rush to attack. Not that I expected it was going to—it could have taken us out while we slept. There was literally no reason it would wait until we were awake and could fight back.

At least one of us could.

"How did it get inside?" I asked Lexie.

She spared a second to glance at the front door, before returning her focus to the sabre, weapon clutched in her hands. "The door remains secure. The only ones who could have broken my ward without alerting me, would be Rolta, or… the Fallen."

The black panther-like beast rolled over on the bed, all four paws in the air, lethally sharp claws visible as it stretched and flexed. The tentacle-like whiskers were thicker and longer than the one in the forest, and I swore serrated along one edge, as if they too were weapons.

"Uh, excuse me, nice kitty. What are you doing here?"

The words hadn't even fully left my mouth and it was off the bed, all pretense of it being nothing more than a lazy housecat gone, as it prowled right up to me. Lexie shifted between us, and that was when the sabre let out a mighty rumble.

"Lex," I said softly. "I don't think it likes you blocking me. Maybe just ease up a little and we can see how it reacts."

"Not a froggin' chance, Morgs. It could rip your guts out in a heartbeat, and I'd be too slow to stop it from beside you."

"Trust me here," I whispered back. "It reminds me of Zahak's dragon. You're making it worse." Before she could roll her eyes at my naiveté, I darted to the side, and the sabre jumped as well, as if it had known all along what I planned on doing.

"Morgan!" Lexie raged, her sword glowing brighter as she teetered on her toes, unsure of her next action now that the sabre stood between us.

"It was in Lancourt," I told her softly, my gaze locked firmly on the beast. "It licked my face."

Everything was making sense now, especially remembering that lick last night as I drifted off. A lick that contained the same texture, scent, and energy as the time in the hallway. I'd been too out of it to notice last night, but this morning it was all clear.

A purring rumble rocked its chest, and in a flash it licked me again.

"Can you go invisible?" I asked the creature.

With another rumble, it faded into a zip of light and energy, similar to Professor Malin's shadows. "No wonder I couldn't see you in that hallway," I said with a started laugh. "You would have blended right into Drager's white and cream monstrosity."

When it reappeared, I asked, "Why are you here?"

Lexie relaxed her warrior stance, her sword vanishing into its magical sheath. "It's protecting you," she said simply.

"Why?"

A much more important question, really.

"Zahak," she breathed.

I'd said that it reminded me of Zahak, but just in the way the creature was acting. I'd never expected that this sabre was his. "Zahak?" I repeated faintly.

Her wide-eyed look didn't fade. "It's the only truth that makes sense. These creatures were rumored to have been lost in the trench, and he's the one who closed that chasm. Not to mention, if this creature was Drager's pet, I'd know about it."

The sabre growled, and she cleared her throat in a hurry. "My apologies. Not pet, but ally."

That seemed to please the beast, who sat on its haunches and proceeded to lick a paw. How it went from menacing demon to cute kitty in a heartbeat was fascinating.

And terrifying.

Terrifyingly fascinating.

"Do you think Zahak plans on retrieving his *friend*?" I asked carefully.

Lexie didn't reply, and I took that to mean she had no idea.

The sabre remained docile as we spent the next half an hour getting ready for the day. As I showered and dressed, I was relieved to find very few aches and pains remained. The gashes in my shoulder were only a faint pink mark now, and the deep-seated fatigue I'd felt was all but gone.

"Your healers are amazing," I told Lexie when I emerged from the bathroom ready for the day. "I feel completely normal."

Sabre was back on my bed, lazily grooming itself, while we continued to act like it was normal to have a giant panther in the room with us.

"I'm glad to hear that," Lexie said, "but let's not forget that someone did try and murder you yesterday. You need to be even more careful until we figure out who that someone is and take care of them."

I hadn't been alone once yesterday, except when I'd showered, but it wouldn't hurt for us all to be a touch more observant. "Sounds like a plan to me."

Drager knocked on the door a few minutes later, and Lexie went first to open it. "I've cleared the hallways," he said roughly, not entering the room. "You're fine to head for class. I'm off to follow a lead about the attack yesterday."

I waited for him to check on me, see if I was okay, but he just delivered his message to Lexie and then left without sparing a single glance for those of us inside the room.

The pain that followed wasn't the sort any healer could fix, and I reminded myself to harden my damn heart one more time. I'd grown complacent with almost dying, falling into his arms once more and relying on his strength.

If I wanted to survive, I had to stop that.

Lexie waved me out of the room, but before I made it to the door, Sabre launched into action.

"I think she wants to go first," I said drily. In my mind she was female, and her name would be Sabre until I found out otherwise.

Sabre stuck her head out into the hall before she stepped out, indicating we could do the same. The hallway was cleared, as Drager had informed us, and we had a seamless run to the dining room.

The rest of the day followed a similarly smooth process, thanks to Sabre at my side, a very intimidating bodyguard. While I ate breakfast, during the morning classes with Professor Malin and Druin, and when we headed for my first fight class, not a single student came our way.

"What in the gods is that?" Tasha looked horrified as we approached, her face paler than yesterday as she stared at Sabre. "I thought they were myth."

She'd asked *what* but she clearly meant *how*. I understood her confusion, having met many mythical creatures since leaving Earth. It baffled the mind.

"This is Sabre," I said, running a hand across her velvety fur. "She's my bodyguard to prevent a flock of yonters stealing me away again."

Tasha's expression didn't change, remaining wary and concerned. Mika, on the other hand, who stood at her side dressed in black and rocking every inch of his badassness, just smiled. "Life is never boring when you're around, Morgs," he said, shifting his stance. "I can't wait to see what happens next."

"Glad my near-death experience and the consequences of that

entertains you," I said with a snort. In truth, I did miss aspects of my *boring life*, but here in Risest there was a part of me awake and excited by the unknown elements in my future. Yeah, I might be murdered tomorrow, but I also might discover a new and magical reality.

I felt more alive than I had in a very long time.

"Please ask your *friend* to step aside so we can teach you," Tasha said shortly.

"You need to go easy on her," Lexie added. "Under healer's orders."

Tasha didn't look impressed by that, but she also didn't argue.

Turning to Sabre, I smiled reassuringly. "I'm going to learn how to fight and defend myself. Please don't kill the nice fae teaching me, okay?" She rumbled and purred, before strolling off to the side and settling down to watch.

Lexie faced me first. "Okay, so after your obstacle course yesterday, it's clear that your speed and reflexes are slower than the average fae, but your body has great capabilities. We'll just need to start slowly."

"Very slow," I confirmed.

"Let's run," Mika shouted, and then he was prodding me into a jog along the grassy area. We were training behind the academy, not quite where the obstacle course was, but in the same vicinity.

After ten minutes, when I couldn't breathe, my lungs screaming for air, Mika continued to jog and bounce beside me as if he'd barely even warmed up. "That might be enough for today," he said as we headed back to where Tasha and Lexie waited. "We're taking it easy, and you'll need some time to get your stamina up."

Spots danced before my eyes as I leaned forward with my hands on my knees. "I… will ki… ll y—" A cough overtook me before I could finish.

Mika just laughed, like the smug fucker he was, flashing me perfect teeth and a sweat free face. "I hate you," I managed to groan, which only made him laugh harder.

"You're going to love me. I've always wanted a human friend."

At least he didn't say pet. One step up from how most fae saw me.

The rest of the class consisted of me getting my ass handed to me over and over by the three of them. If this was taking it easy, then I'd be dead when they went full throttle. They didn't attack with weapons, or even really attack at all, but they did test my reflexes in a series of blocks and strike moves. By the time we were done, I felt like I'd been used as a boxing bag, covered in bruises. I also had a puffy lip from where I'd missed a block and Tasha cracked me in the face. "I pulled my punch," she said shortly when I cried out.

Sabre growled menacingly, and that was when she wrapped the class for the day.

"That was a disaster," I told Lexie as I hobbled away. "I'm like a newborn foal finding my legs for the first time."

"It wasn't too bad," she lied. "Lots of room for us to improve, and for you to start learning awareness of your surroundings."

Sabre purred extra loud at that sentence, and I took that as her agreement.

Personally, I could never imagine being aware of my surroundings like Lexie was. Not just Lexie but Tasha, Mika, and Sabre. While I had learned through the years to watch my words and actions, so as not to trigger my mother, I was nowhere near the level of these fae warriors.

If I didn't sort my mindset out soon, I was going to get killed. The yonters might have failed yesterday, and with my bodyguards that might fail the next time as well.

They might fail a hundred times.

But it only took one success.

At some point, it was up to me to take my safety into my own hands. Whether I liked it or not, I needed to step out of my comfort zone and find a new normal.

One that included jogging apparently.

Dammit.

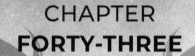

CHAPTER
FORTY-THREE

Maybe it was the slivers of healing still going on inside of me, but by the time dinner rolled around, I was wrecked. Lexie got me food, happy to leave me at the table under the care of Sabre. The giant, mythical, ancient beast drew all the attention, but also kept the students away.

It was nice, actually.

At one point Greta paused about ten feet from me, but then she moved on without a word. When Lexie returned, more protein than I'd normally eat piled up on the plate, my eyes were fluttering closed.

"Come on," she nudged me. "You need to eat before you sleep, otherwise it'll take longer than ever to finish up healing."

A yawn overtook my face, and I muttered around it, "Bossy."

Her smirk was brief. "You have no idea how bossy I can be, friend. I'll bully you all the way back to health. Now eat!"

I'd have saluted her, but I honestly didn't have the energy for more than one task, and I decided that eating did have to take precedence. Lexie had placed the plate with the bread farthest away, as if she knew that'd be the first thing I'd reach for. It was her way of encouraging me to pick up the smoked meats first.

Joke was on her, I had more than enough energy to reach for the bread, even if my eyes were half closed when I did so. She rubbed her hand over her face, probably counting to ten, but she didn't reprimand me again. She was happy to see me eating, whatever the food group.

As I finished the first slice of bread, the heavy weight of a sabre head landed in my lap and I jumped about a foot in the air. Sabre rumbled a purr, as if she enjoyed scaring the shit out of me. She didn't remove her head though, and I had a sense of what she wanted.

Selecting a few pieces of fruit, I offered them to the giant housecat. A huge purple tongue swished out between those lethally sharp teeth, and she hoovered the melon right down. "Why are they born with teeth and claws like a predator," I wondered, "if they hunt plants and fruit?"

Lexie eyed the cat, shaking her head at how it was begging in my lap for food. "They're designed to be predators against fae, but since they don't eat the meat they hunt, they're smarter about it. They can be trained not to randomly attack, because they're not doing it when they're hungry. We aren't food to them, we are targets."

As if they'd been designed for fae to use without worry of being their dinner.

Rubbing my hand over the soft and thick fur on her head, she rumble-purred again, and I fed her another slice of melon. When Lexie glared at me, I also fed myself, and soon we'd eaten through everything on the plate.

As I relaxed into my chair, the noise around us died off unnaturally. Lexie's weapon appeared, but Sabre didn't move from her spot on my lap, purring and nudging my hand for more pats.

If there was real danger, she'd have reacted, right?

My unasked question was answered a moment later when Zahak appeared from the other side of the rotating food buffet. He walked with purpose, eyes never wavering from where we sat in the back corner.

"Frogs," Lexie cursed. "This can't be good."

"Maybe he just wants his kitty back," I suggested, giving Sabre an extra little scratch. "I'm going to miss her though."

"It's Zahak," she hissed, like I wasn't hyper aware of his presence. "He's as kitty-like as a sabre, and you have to stop claiming them all as pets."

Sabre rumbled, but she was too blissed-out on ear scratches to do much more.

I'd only seen Zahak's human form one time, from a distance, so his dragon felt more familiar to me as I gazed up at him. Heat and energy swirled strongly around us, and I noticed that he was again dressed like a high-level SWAT officer: black fitted shirt, black cargo pants, and heavy boots.

Dragging my gaze slowly over his impossibly long legs, heavily muscled thighs, and trim waist, I found a body so similar to Drager's it was disconcerting. Broad shoulders, thick, muscled arms, and... his face.

It was Drager's, and yet it wasn't.

Drager was sunlight, with his blond locks and arrogant expression.

Zahak was midnight, those eyes so dark with flecks of gold— focused on me like there was not a single other student in the room.

In the world.

"Astra," he rumbled.

Sabre bounced to her feet, and I mentally slotted her real name into the picture I had of her.

"Astra?" I repeated with a question in my tone.

He tilted his head, examining me closer, sending trickles of unease through me. He was dissecting me, and I wasn't sure I liked the sensation of being under his full attention.

"What can we do for you, Lord Zahak?" Lexie asked respectfully, attempting to draw his focus.

She was on her feet, but the weapon was once more sheathed, even as her expression remained wary. She wasn't the only one either; every student in the vicinity was on their feet.

Except me.

For that reason alone, I decided not to stand, even if it was uncomfortable as hell to have him literally towering over me.

"We've apprehended some students under suspicion of orchestrating the attack yesterday," he rumbled. "I thought you might want to be there."

I barely managed not to gasp as his voice, even deeper than Drager's, blasted through me. It was filled with fire and ice, sending both heat and cold into my essence. Drager had created a similar reaction inside me with that first phone call, but Zahak was even more intense. If that was possible.

When I attempted to reply, the words just didn't appear, leaving me gulping like a fish out of water.

"Rolta's office," he added, and with one final press of his giant hand to the top of Sab— Astra's head, he turned and left the dining room.

It took many minutes before the sound picked up around us, and I sucked in deep breaths, hoping to stem the dizziness plaguing me. It was only after my pulse stopped going haywire that I realized Astra was still with us. She hadn't left with Zahak, and I wondered what he was up to.

"I don't like this," Lexie said, still on her feet, gaze locked on the doors Zahak had exited through. "I don't like it at all. Why do you keep drawing their attention?"

"I wish I knew. I'm not doing it on purpose," I assured her. "And it's only Drager and Zahak. The other three haven't made an appearance."

Lexie turned aghast. "Zahak and Drager are the worst two, Morgan. I don't think you're comprehending the trouble you're in here. I didn't have a chance of defending you against one of them, let alone two."

"There's no need to defend me," I reminded her.

"Yet," she shot back, letting out a sigh. "Come on, we should do what he said. Lord Zahak might sound like he's asking, but it's an order."

When I stood, I was relieved to find my fatigue from before had eased. Lexie might be a drill sergeant, but she knew what she was doing—the food had made a huge difference. Or maybe it was the shot of adrenaline in the form of one devastating Fallen god.

Astra remained with us as we moved between tables, and I wondered why Zahak continued to save my life. He wouldn't do that if he planned on killing me in the end, right?

That made no sense, because if he wanted to murder me today, no one could stop him.

Which meant one of two things: he was saving me because of a connection to Drager and their brotherly bond, or, and this was the worrying part, he wanted to keep me alive for a reason only he knew. A reason that might get me killed in the end, when the time was right.

No doubt these were the thoughts that had Lexie freaking out, but I couldn't worry about a possible future that might never come to fruition.

Lexie remained on my right side as we exited the room, Astra on my left, and every single gaze burned into our backs on the way out. *So much for staying under the radar*. The Fallen had ensured that was never going to happen. Down the stairs and into the main hall, we entered the reception, which was unfaed at the moment. Celeste's shift must be done for the day, since it was evening and classes were mostly over.

Rolta's door was closed, and Lexie approached it first, knocking firmly and announcing herself.

"Enter," a deep and familiar voice called—Drager was inside.

I hadn't expected that, and the thought of Drager and Zahak in the same room together had my pulse doing that stupid surge. How the fuck could I ensure I didn't embarrass myself in front of both of them? My humanness was going to let me down here, and I had no idea how to prevent it from happening.

When Lexie entered, Astra nudged me forward. I'd already run out of time to get myself together. Feeling frazzled, I pasted on an expression of calm as I stepped inside.

Green and gold eyes met mine. "Come here, little human," Drager rasped, holding his hand out to me.

The room was more crowded than I'd expected. Rolta sat behind her desk, with six fae across from her, seated as well, but in a more *strapped down and forced to be here* kind of way. Drager was in the right corner, gesturing for me to join him, Zahak in the left, leaned against the wall, observing everything with those dark as sin eyes.

Astra left me and joined him, and I went to Drager, his energy seeping into my body as soon as our hands touched. He swept me closer, tucking me against him, and I found myself relaxing. I'd only been thinking earlier it was dangerous to start relying on him like this, and yet I couldn't help but take the small comforts he was offering.

"Now that everyone is here," Rolta said, her voice high, "it's time to get the questioning underway."

The six, strapped to their chairs by what looked like glowing *energy chains*, remained somewhat motionless. The headmistress stood, not as tall as the Fallen, but impressive all the same. Her eye was hard as she glared across the six, and I paid closer attention, noting that there were four females and two males. All of them were completely unknown to me except... the male on the end. He was one of Greta's, the golem that had glared at me during our first meeting.

CHAPTER
FORTY-FOUR

Rolta took the lead on questioning. "We have uncovered that all of you left the grounds yesterday morning and visited known whereabouts of yonter clans in the Isle of Denille. We need an explanation."

A harpy fae in the center leaned back in her chair, wings tucked in behind her as she snarled. "Who really cares which one of us it was," she chirped, her pointed face wreathed in annoyance. "The only one to get attacked was a human. Might as well be dirt that got hurt, it's that important in this world. Can we just move on and get back to studies."

Well, that was a rapid downgrade from animals.

Zahak took a single step forward, ripped up the harpy chair and all, and before anyone could say a single word, severed her head in one swipe of his hand. She'd had a head attached to her body, and then it was flying to land at my feet.

A scream died in my throat, choking me, as shock held me immobile.

"We won't ask again," he said, a whisper of death.

An unblinking harpy face stared up at me while I choked and struggled to get myself under control. Drager let out a huff. "Always so impatient and messy," he chastised his brother. "Can you at least wait for us to finishing questioning them."

Literal psychopaths—the Fallen were not mentally stable.

Zahak dropped the chair, and it landed exactly as it had been before, just minus one head. For some reason, a snort of laughter escaped me, and even though I stifled it almost instantly, Zahak stared at me. "Sorry," I spluttered. "Shock and... she's just sitting there still. It's..."

I shut up because I'd already done enough damage with my mental break.

His lips twitched, just a tiny movement. "They needed an incentive to answer the questions truthfully and without subterfuge. Now they have it."

The other five prisoners were staring at the headless body in the chair next to them, her dark gray blood still seeping from the gaping hole where her head had been a minute before. Zahak was right, and a part of me wondered if I should be repulsed or impressed that he was so invested in finding out who attempted to murder me.

Nothing said romance like an offering of your enemies' heads.

Wait, what?

I was losing my freaking mind. Not only was there *no romance* between me and this Fallen, but headless bodies *were also not sweet.*

Shut up, brain. Just shut the fuck up.

"It was Greta," the female next to the golem blurted out suddenly. She must have had some troll in her as well, because while she wasn't as tall as Rolta, she had the single eye and general brawny appearance. The golem growled, and slammed his shoulder into her, moving the entire chair with him.

"Shut up, or that death will look like a fantasy," he raged, but she was in a panic as words spilled from her lips.

"We were all forced to help as distractions, sent off to make it harder to figure out who had organized the hit. It was supposed to be an easy task, but clearly no one expected the Fallen to care enough about a human to get involved. I won't die when I did nothing except leave the grounds."

Zahak straightened from the wall again, and she flinched so hard her chair almost toppled over. "You were involved," he said calmly. "That's all I need to know."

She shook her head, gasping in and out, words strangled. "No. No. You don't understand. Greta would have killed me if I refused. I had no choice, but I have nothing personally against that human. Or any humans, in general. As far as I'm concerned, they can do what they want with their finite, powerless lives."

There you had it, folks. I'm free to live out my less-than-dirt existence, without interference from any superior race. This chick was the cheerleader humans really needed on our side.

"Greta is from a very powerful family," Lexie said, drawing attention to herself for the first time. I wondered how she'd reacted when Zahak removed the harpy's head, because right now she looked calm and confident. "It's not going to be that easy to tie her to this. No matter what these students say."

"It was all me," the golem shouted. He'd stopped trying to knock anyone over, his focus on Rolta. "I organized everything, and I will take the punishment for it."

Zahak smiled. It was the first I'd seen from him, and I'd thought his lack of expression was scary. This particular smile was so much worse. Drager tightened his hold on me, and I anchored myself to his energy.

"Are the others free to go?" Rolta asked as silence extended around us.

"Yes," I said quickly. "They shouldn't be punished for this."

Zahak's expression grew harder, but he didn't argue with me, and Rolta wasted no time freeing the three fae from their restraints. "That was the right action," the headmistress said as they fled the room. "They'll tell everyone what happened here, and that will be the final key to confirm that the Fallen are prepared to follow through with Drager's warning at the first assembly."

The heat against my back intensified. "My warning shouldn't have needed confirming," Drager snarled.

The golem snorted, uncaring now that he was slated to die in place of Greta, who he clearly loved. Why else would he offer his life for hers? "Firstly, you're not our god, Lord Drager," he said shortly. "We don't take orders from you. And secondly, we classify you are more reasonable. You've made no secret of the fact that you're not a fan of humans, and we figured that once she was gone, you'd be back to worrying about our lands. About *our* races. About finding out who the traitor is that stole from us."

Drager released me to stand before the golem. "I'm not even remotely reasonable when my orders are ignored," he hissed. "This human is the one helping me search for the traitor. You would have destroyed my only lead, and that in and of itself is all I need to know to ask for your death."

Who was he going to ask?

Zahak joined him, and I noticed that they were closer in height than I'd previously thought. While their coloring and facial structure differed—Zahak was harder in all ways—their resemblance as brothers was more than obvious.

"That's your problem, Drager," Zahak shook his head at his brother. "You hold that human like she belongs to you, and yet you don't destroy this fae who hurt her. Stop playing the good god. It doesn't work in these circumstances."

He swiped out, and as the golem saw what was coming, his skin turned much darker, and I got to witness the clay-like hardening Lexie had spoken about before his head rolled across the floor to join the first. Not even a golem could stand against the might of the Fallen.

I remained frozen in place, silent screams building inside me once more as the shock of another violent fae death held me immobile.

"We could have asked him more questions," Drager shot at Zahak. "Found out what he knows."

Zahak's chest swelled as his rumbles filled the room. "We know all we need to know from him. He was a puppet, and I will deal with the master."

He left, and the intensity in the room calmed. If only I could say the same for my insides.

"Well," Lexie drawled, "that didn't go the way I expected."

Drager shook his head. "Zahak has never been one to suffer deception. His loyalty never wavers, and he expects the same in return."

"Should I warn Greta?" Rolta asked as she fell back into her chair, eye locked on the two headless fae across from her.

Drager shook his head. "Don't get involved. Zahak will not rest until he uncovers every fae involved in this, and I don't want you caught in the crossfire."

Rolta held both hands up and nodded, her skin paler than usual. "I'll keep what happened here to myself, but you know the others will warn the Emerelso clan all the same."

"We're counting on it," Drager added darkly.

"Taking on the Emerelso clan is going to start a war," Lexie said, repeating her concerns from earlier. "They're a large and powerful clan. They won't take lightly to Zahak killing one of their daughters."

Drager laughed, sounding genuinely amused. "There'd be a war if I killed her, because she's not from my land, but Zahak is their god. Their leader. They will accept the punishment or they will all suffer, and in the end there's no point losing their entire bloodline for one fae who can't follow the rules."

Lexie didn't look convinced, and I hoped she was wrong. I really didn't want to create further unrest in Risest. "Maybe I should return to Earth," I said, sounding less shaky than I felt. "My presence here is creating more issues than it's resolving, and I'm no closer to finding the traitor. I'm not even sure at this point I'd recognize the voice if I heard it. It's been so long, and most fae have unusual tones compared to humans."

Why I finally felt confident enough to reveal this worry to Drager, I had no idea, but at some point in our journey together I'd stopped fearing him. I'd stopped fearing his reaction to me, and that gave me freedom to not only express myself, but to tell the truth.

Lexie, on the other hand, glared at me like she thought I'd lost my mind.

Maybe I had. Maybe Drager was about to swipe my head from my shoulders to join the other two all but at my feet, but my instincts told me he wouldn't.

"You will remain here in Risest until we find the traitor," Drager said, not angry, but there was no give in his voice. "We will keep you safe, even if I have to step in as your permanent bodyguard."

Lexie's head dropped, and I knew her well enough to know she was taking that statement as a personal dig, and I wasn't having any of that. "She fought off multiple yonters," I told him shortly. "It's definitely her presence that's kept most of the students at bay, so you should be grateful I have her."

The smallest of smiles played around Lexie's lips as she lifted her gaze and met mine. *Thank you*, she mouthed at me.

I nodded, ready to fight harder if necessary, but Drager decided not to push back. "Fine, you remain with Lexical and Astra, since my brother has seen fit to share his favorite beast with you. I need a word with Zahak right now, so you head straight for your room and stay there until I open that door in the morning. No exceptions. Do I make myself clear?"

Taking his orders chafed at my insides, but I knew it was futile and stupid to argue, so I reluctantly nodded. "Crystal clear."

He turned to Rolta, initiating a discussion for their next steps. "The bodies are not to be returned to their clan," he started, but the rest of their discussion was missed as Lexie ushered me from the room, Astra following close behind.

I let her push me along, my brain semi-fried from everything that had happened in the last few hours. The exhaustion I'd felt at dinner was long gone, replaced with panic and adrenaline that set my stomach to roiling. We'd figured out who had tried to kill me, or at least some of whom was involved, and I'd witnessed two fae losing their heads right before me.

"Why would Greta ask to be allies and then try and murder me before we answered?"

That part was the most confusing for me.

Lexie didn't slow her pace, still dragging me along, her steps loud and angry. "I suspect that the offer was only to get a closer look at you. To determine if you were powerful or any sort of threat. They saw me reach for my weapon and knew that I'd be able to prevent a normal attack. So they had to go big."

"What if we'd accepted her offer?" I pushed, swallowing against the acid rising in my throat; my stomach was not a happy camper.

"There was never a chance of that, and she knew it," Lexie bit out. "My clan and hers are too competitive for me to ever allow an alliance between us. I pretended to think about it, and she pretended that she wanted this union. This is part of my early warnings to you about the games fae play. It's never the hand you see… it's the one hidden under the table."

We were on the second floor now, and she was moving with even more determination.

"I expected more blood, you know?" The words slipped out, and Lexie jerked her head around to stare at me. "In the movies, when someone loses their heads, blood spurts everywhere. But it was just seeping. It was weird."

She blinked once as her forehead furrowed. "Have you been wondering that all this time?"

I shrugged. "Should I have been wondering something else?"

Lexie pulled me closer. "You should be running and screaming, all the while trying to find a portal to Earth. Fallen gods are killing fae for you, and we have no damn idea why."

Hmmm… was Lexie right? Was there something wrong with me or had I acclimated better than expected, and was now as bloodthirsty as the fae?

At that thought, the swirling in my stomach intensified and I leaned into the corner we stood near and puked up everything I'd eaten at dinner.

CHAPTER
FORTY-FIVE

Lexie got me back to our room and into the bathroom, and even as my stomach heaved I could no longer vomit because there was no food left inside me. "You're in shock," she whispered as I sobbed. "Your brain was trying to protect you, but it all catches up eventually."

Another sob shook me, and I felt cold and alone as I huddled against her. "At least we know I'm not a sociopath," I spluttered as more tears spilled down my cheeks. "This is a normal reaction to two heads rolling to rest against your feet."

"Don't mourn them," she said shortly, even as she continued to rub my back.

A snort of laughter broke through my sobs. "Oh, I'm not. I'm glad they're dead, because we're both so much safer than we were this morning. It's just witnessing murders that took me by surprise. I'm having trouble processing the emotions I feel."

Especially my confusion around Zahak, and his role in all of this. When that dragon stepped up and protected me like the rest of the world didn't matter, it broke a part of me. In a good way. In the way of a person who'd always felt like they were never truly loved and appreciated, finally having a moment of unconditional acceptance.

Lexie bobbed her head slowly, mulling my words over. "Yeah, that makes sense. Their deaths aren't bothering you, but the violence you witnessed stunned your senses." She took a seat on the floor next to me, the scent of my vomit strong in the air even after the toilet cleaned itself multiple times. "What's the deal with Zahak?" she asked me, and I wondered if I'd accidentally let my inside thoughts out again. "I mean, Drager is one thing, but he's at least known to enjoy sexy times with fae when the mood strikes him, but Zahak's a lone wolf. I've never heard so much as a whisper of him touching a fae."

Drager enjoying sexy times with other fae bothered me more than it should, considering I had no claim over his arrogant, bossy and controlling ass.

"You know as much as I do," I said, gazing out to see Astra perched on my bed, apparently sleeping. I wondered then if she could share our conversations with her god. "But I suspect it's to do with Drager, and the competitive nature of their relationship. Nothing more."

"Why do you think Astra was in Lancourt that day you got lost?" Lexie asked, lowering her voice.

Leaning in, I replied in barely a whisper. "I have no idea, and I'm wondering if she can pass information on to Zahak. We should be careful what we say around her."

Lexie glanced at the sabre and stopped asking questions, but the worried expression never left her face.

———

The next morning I woke feeling rested and less conflicted about what had happened yesterday. Those fae had tried to murder me, and the consequences of their actions caught up with them. Zahak didn't mess around, and I should be grateful for that.

This wasn't Earth, and fae weren't humans. Different races required different treatment; I had to remember that.

As I sat up and stretched, Astra yawned from her spot next to me on the bed and proceeded to lick my face in greeting. "Good morning," I rasped, clearing my throat. "You're in a good mood."

Running my hand over her head, I noticed a red dot on one of her tentacle whiskers, and when I pulled away, red coated my fingers too. "What did you get up to last night?" I asked her, fully awake as I examined my hand. "This looks like blood, Astra."

She was a herbivore, so there was no way she went out hunting last night. Not for food anyway. She purred and stretched again, before she rolled off and padded toward the doors on the balcony, where she paused, like she wanted me to open them for her.

I glanced across at Lexie's bed, but it was empty, so she was either in the shower—which I couldn't hear—or she'd had to leave and felt comfortable that Astra was with me. Making sure my boobs were in my tank top, where they never stayed at night, I followed the sabre. The stained-glass doors opened before I reached them, demonstrating no need for me to help, and I barely managed not to flinch. There'd come a day when I grew accustomed to this world and their abilities to manipulate energy, but it wasn't this day.

Astra exited onto the balcony first, and I was following when screams filled the air. It was clearly early, the first slivers of pink filling the gilded sky, so the sound of hysterical cries was extra jarring against the early morning silence.

One scream followed another, until it was all I could hear.

Freaking out that the world was ending, I rushed outside, wishing Lexie was here with us. Having no idea if she was safe or the reason for those screams had me near breathless with panic and fear. Astra didn't stop me from joining her, and that should have been my first warning that she knew exactly what had everyone in hysterics.

Drawing to a halt before the railing, I reached out and gripped onto the edge. "What the fuck...?" I breathed.

On the lawn, beside the lake, there was a row of spikes. Dug deep into the ground, they stood about seven feet tall—at least that's how it appeared from this angle—and on top of each spike was a head. A dozen heads displayed one after another. Their sightless eyes faced us, and it didn't escape my notice that most of them were pointed toward my room.

"What in the love of masochism is happening here?" I managed to say. Astra purred sweetly, prowling back and forth like a proud cat who'd dropped a dead mouse on her owner's pillow.

"You did this?" I asked her, desperately wishing she had the vocal cords to reply. "You killed all these fae? Why?" She purred again, a deeper rumble, and I turned back to the scene as more screams added to the macabre.

"Greta!"

That shout came from a balcony near ours, and the realization of why a dozen dead fae were facing my room hit me hard and fast. Leaning over the railing, I scanned across the heads until I found one that was somewhat familiar—Greta. Her hair was distinct, even as purplish-red blood stained the long, light strands.

Blood similar in color to what had been flecked across Astra.

"Are they all Emerelsos?" I choked out. Unlike last night I felt no queasiness. This didn't gross me out, but it was shocking.

The longer I stayed in Faerie, the more used to their violent

290

nature I grew. My future therapist was going to have a field day with me, but considering everything that had happened since the night I answered the phone and stumbled into a faerie party at Dragerfield Library, I wasn't doing too badly.

Steps sounded behind me, and assuming it was Lexie, I didn't turn until Astra let out a deep rumble.

Drager stood in the doorway.

"You did this?" I asked him.

Astra had been involved, I knew that for certain, which meant that Zahak was as well… but I had no idea where Drager stood on all of this.

The Fallen's expression remained dark as he shook his head.

"Zahak," I breathed. "This was all Zahak?"

Astra's purred loudly, and I turned back to the scene to find a massive black dragon soaring in over the lake. He settled on a patch of grass in front of the spikes and lifted his massive head to roar into the world, flames shooting from between his lethal jaws.

"My brother is forever the drama dragon," Drager spat. "The dead don't speak, so hopefully he thought to question them before bringing his kills back here to make a point."

"He killed them for me?" I whispered, pressing my hand to my chest where my heart pounded hard. "Why? And why are there so many? Are they all students?"

Drager's heat surrounded me as he moved closer. Astra didn't like it, if her grumbles were any indication, but she knew better than to try to stop him. Not that I'd have let the dragon hurt her. I'd stand between them to ensure my new friend didn't come to any harm.

"This is Greta's bloodline," Drager said softly. He wasn't looking at the heads or his brother, instead focusing on my face. "He tracked them all down as we slept and slaughtered them for their daughter's role in your almost death."

"Why?" This had to be asked again, because it was all so confusing. "Why is he doing this?"

Drager's laugh was dark, jagged. "He's always wanted what I had, from the moment we were born in the same pod. I don't remember much from our time before we fell, but I remember that much. Zahak is my bonded brother, and with that we have competed in all aspects of life. Power. Love. Control. We don't remember which one of us is the eldest, but we know it's only by a few minutes, and that few minutes has dictated our relationship for all eternity."

Astra remained silently at my side, but she was side-eyeing Drager. Hard.

What he said made sense to me though. From the similarities in their looks, to everything that was happening here. Probably even Drager's renewed interest in me, and *dating*, was all just a centuries-long competition with his brother who had saved me in Lancourt. It wasn't about me at all. I was just the convenient new toy to tug-of-war over.

"Right," I said softly, turning back to the scene. Deep inside, the broken parts of me churned slowly, anger building. Once again, I was nothing more than an object to use and abuse. My mother had the same mentality, believing I belonged to her as an extension of her being, and could be controlled. She never cared about me as a person with my own unique needs and desires. I was a weapon against my father, and a tool to make herself feel strong.

Her small sliver of power in a world that told her she was useless and invisible.

I couldn't believe it was happening again.

I should have seen it coming. I should have expected it.

Fae gods giving a shit about a human was beyond any fairy tale, and even having logically known that before now, I'd been falling into the magic of it anyway. I'd been giving away pieces of my heart even as I tried to harden myself against it. Just like the golem, there was no hardening that could stop the strike from a Fallen.

"Thanks for telling me," I said to Drager shortly. "But you can inform Zahak that there's no need to destroy my enemies any longer. This isn't a competition. I'm only here until you get sick of me, or I find the thief, and then I can return home. No need to waste his time any longer. Or yours."

Drager observed me for a long time, and I refused to return the look. "You're hurt," he finally said. *No shit, genius.* "Why?"

A derisive snort left me, and despite my inner pain and anger, I mostly felt tired. "I'm a pawn in a game between the two of you, and that's not exactly a dream come true. I don't like being the plaything of powerful men. It never ends well for the toy."

Drager's hand wrapped around my shoulder, turning me so I was forced to face him. If I'd fought, I'd have been hurt in that grip, so I didn't bother. "Who said you were just a pawn—play-thing—however you referred to yourself? That might be the case for Z, but we are not the same dragon. His free hand brushed down my cheek and gripped my chin. "You're the first woman to intrigue me in a century, and I need to know why. I need to know you, little human."

The point *human* had turned from an insult into an endearment happened so subtly, that I'd missed it. But when he called me that now, it felt comforting. As if my humanness was the part of me that he liked the most, versus the part that he wished to excise from my being.

"It's never going to work between us, Drager," I told him truthfully.

"It'll work if I say it'll work," he growled back.

Shaking my head, I found my gaze drifting between Drager

and the row of heads still presented for me. If there was ever a hope of knowing my true feelings here, I needed to get to the bottom of this feud between brothers.

I needed to figure out what feelings were real and what were born of their longstanding rivalry.

To do that, I had to remain in Risest, and alive, which meant back to classes today to learn their history and learn how to fight.

My future might just depend on it.

CHAPTER
FORTY-SIX

When Drager had enough of the scene outside, especially as more students filed out onto their balconies and lost their faerie minds, he dragged me inside my room. "Before Lexie returns, we need to reinforce our bond," he told me.

"Say what?" I shot back without thinking. "Our bond?"

We had a bond? First I'd heard about it.

Drager's laugh was low, wrapping around me as his husky tones did their job and seduced me with their beauty. "Every time we are together, and my energy infuses with yours, we're forming a bond. You know that."

Pushing back against his chest, I glared up at him. "I sure as shit don't know that. You've never mentioned it once, and I'd think forming a bond should have been the first conversation we had."

These dragons needed an updated class on consent—not that it appeared to be a huge concept here in Risest. They lived and died in a power structure, and for that, no consent could work. Because they weren't born equal.

"There was no choice, Morgan," he rumbled. "The fertility ritual required you to be able to handle my power—"

"And massive dick, yeah I know," I grumbled.

His eyes narrowed on me. "In that regard, it was infuse you with energy or you'd die. It has been the same every other time. You must have my power, or the energy of this world will destroy you. It was worse in Lancourt, but even here, eventually Faerie would eat away at your energy."

This *stuck between a rock and hard place* cliché was starting to get really old.

"I'm guessing that's why you're here this morning," I said shortly.

Drager nodded. "One of the reasons."

He didn't expand on the other reasons.

His hands pressed against my stomach, so large that they nearly wrapped around my waist. If I wasn't curvier than average, at least ten-fifteen pounds overweight, then his fingers would have touched. Drager didn't appear to mind as he caressed my bare skin beneath the skimpy pjs.

"We don't have time for what I want to do this morning," he rumbled, his grip tightening as he picked me up. My legs wrapped around him as his hands settled under my ass, holding me close. Our faces were near level, and all I could smell and breathe was the burning scent of summer that I would always associate with this fae god.

He'd called himself the sun god, and it was exactly who he was.

"How's my library doing?" I whispered, reminded of the first time I'd stared into his hazel eyes.

The gold grew brighter. "Your touch of ownership was all over that place," he rumbled back. "I've long been curious about the human who had enough energy signature that I'd recognize her in a crowd of thousands. My curiosity grew so great that the night I found a missing book, you were the number I reached for first. Not Lexical."

Well, that answered one of my longstanding and burning questions. Her phone might have been dead, but he'd never even attempted to call her first. And with that truth, the anger roiling deep inside calmed. His curiosity had started before Zahak was part of the picture, so it wasn't just about their competition.

"I'd have lived in the library if I could," I told him truthfully. "It bothered me to leave it, but of course Simon is a mean old bastard and would have smacked me in the legs if I stayed past end of shift."

Drager tilted back his head and laughed. "Simon is a very strong druid from your world. He enjoys a simpler life away from the internal struggles of his family, and he takes his job guarding the library during daylight hours very seriously. Even from those who love it."

Earth had druids? I had not expected that. I shelved it as a question to ask another time.

Drager leaned down and pressed his lips to mine, clearly done with questions too, but there was one more piece of information I needed. "What if Lexie walks in?" I whispered.

The Fallen's smile wasn't sweet, and it sent flutters down my chest and into my center. "I sent Lexical out on an early morning errand. I told her I'd get you ready for school."

Glaring my hardest, I leaned in very close so our faces were almost touching. "Despite your penchant for carrying me around, I'm not a toddler. I don't need help getting ready."

Drager's chest lifted beneath us as he rumbled out a laugh. "Oh, I know you're not a toddler, Morgan. Very well aware."

He slammed his mouth against mine, and I couldn't halt my moans. For all my doubts and misgivings, the moment we touched, the moment I tasted him, all rational thought faded. I forgot that we were from two different worlds with vast power imbalances. All I cared about was my next moment with Drager.

His energy flowed into me with that kiss, and as the heat trailed down between my tits and into my center, I felt the infusion of power bonding with my lifeforce. After Drager had so bluntly pointed it out, the bonding was more obvious. This knowledge made me feel uneasy, but for the most part I was too consumed by him to care.

The kiss went on for a long time. I was a panting mess by the time he lifted his face. "Astra, out," he ordered.

The giant panther prowled closer to us, bearing not a single resemblance to a sweet kitty. She looked like a killer, teeth on display as her body grew larger and more menacing. "You don't want to fight me, sabre," Drager snapped. "Return to your master and tell him his interference is no longer required. I've got it from here."

"Wait a minu—" I started to protest, because it was my decision if Astra was here with me or not. Drager didn't get to make those choices for me. If I gave up the last of my independence, I'd give up everything.

He kissed me again, and poured more power into me. I was drowning in his energy and heat. Unable to say anything further. Astra must have left, because my clothes were torn from my body, leaving me naked in Drager's arms. I felt achy and needy like we hadn't had sex in a long time. It was the dragon's power that did this to me, combined with my attraction to him—a truly lethal combination, and I could not fight it, no matter how much I might have wanted to at times.

With one hand remaining as a support under my ass, the other curled against my pussy as he slid his fingers along my slit, before two ended up deep inside. My back arched, and I was thrusting against his hand, chasing an orgasm. Heat spilled from his fingers as they stroked me, opening my body up to his, and it took him about ten strokes until I was coming hard, jerking against his hold.

"That's it, my little human," he rasped. "Lose yourself in me."

Bastard got off on the power and control, and I got off on him. It was a dangerous combination. "Drager," I groaned as he added a third finger, really pushing me to my limits, as more heat seeped into me until my body was on fire, burning and desperate.

Lifting my own weight, I slammed back down on his hand, and he was the one to groan now. "The scent of your arousal drives me crazy," he admitted. "I have no idea what I will do in these moments, and I have to work very hard not to tear you apart. My beast wants to keep you, little human."

The tightening of my stomach and thighs was the only prelude to the next rush of pleasure that had me crying out and shuddering against the dragon, my release near squirting around his hand as I came hard. He removed his fingers one by one, which sent aftershocks of pleasure through me.

He lifted that hand and slid his tongue across his index finger, tasting me, and as the gold and green deepened in his eyes, dark scales slid up over his neck and face, briefly, and then they were gone. "What color is your dragon?" I asked breathlessly.

"Like Zahak's but also different," he bit out. And that was all I got before he dropped me on the bed, the darkness in his gaze deepening as he spread my thighs wide on either side of me. "You're going to be screaming my name before this morning is done," he growled, gaze burning into me. He traced a finger down between my breasts, until he reached the junction of my thighs, and he swiped through my arousal.

When he lowered his head, I held my breath, waiting for the first touch. His tongue was more textured than a human, and when he swiped it across my clit, my groan filled the room. My hips came up off the bed, and instead of holding me down as he had before, this time he embraced it, settling his hands underneath me for a better reach.

Slowly, oh so slowly, he swiped from the top of my pussy all the way down to my ass. His chest rumbled as he buried his face deeper, tasting me like I was the last meal in the world, and as his tongue plunged inside me, fucking me as hard as his fingers had, I was panting and scraping my nails against the sheets. This time he didn't let the pleasure overtake me too quickly, slowing as soon as the swirling pleasure grew too great, dragging out the build-up.

He hadn't done this slow, torturous building of pleasure since the fertility ritual.

Back in the library, when I finally exploded, it was at times so intense that I'd blacked out.

"Drager," I panted. "Please. This is torture."

His laughter sent more vibrations and heat into me, and I recognized that he was using his energy to adjust my body so I'd fit his size—killing two kinks with one mouth.

I arched against him, straining, desperate. I was so wet that even held in the air I knew how soaked the bed was beneath us. Not that this greedy dragon let much of my arousal escape. He consumed it like it was necessary for life, and when I finally exploded, darkness danced on the edges of my vision as I'd anticipated.

Drager eased me back to the bed and shot me a satisfied smile. "Your body knows who it belongs to," he said with a nod. "It's clearer to me than ever."

I shot him a growl of my own. "Enough of this belongs-to business, buddy. We've already established I'm no possession."

He stared down at me and ignored my sad attempt at a growl. "You'll understand soon enough, Morgan Starrer. For now, let's just secure this energy inside you."

He crawled over the top of me, and the sheer size of him took my breath away. Leaving one hand beside my head as he held himself up, he used the other to remove his shirt, slowly. Once he'd stripped away the cloth, all we had left was glowing, bronze skin, rippled with muscles.

"Fuck me dead," I breathed.

His head tilted, and I had a feeling that expression wasn't familiar to him. Or it didn't easily translate in the faerie language. "There will be no death," he replied. "But I will fuck you."

His pants vanished in the next heartbeat, and I wondered if I'd forgotten the sheer size of his cock, ribbed with scales, and jutting out before him proudly.

It was still a mystery how it fit. I mean, I knew women had babies, and they were much bigger than Drager, but certain hormones were released for that to happen, and bones shifted and everything. Drager just used his magic tongue and managed to fit. Without pain. Only pleasure.

The anticipation of having him inside me grew stronger as he hovered, and I ended up reaching out and wrapped my hands around his shoulder, trying to pull him down. Of course, I'd have more luck shifting this academy a few inches to the left.

Drager never moved until he was ready.

"Let's switch it up," he said, a glint in his eyes that told me he had a plan.

He flipped our positions so fast my head spun as he pulled me down onto his cock. Still in control, even when I was the one riding him. "Hold on, little human," he rasped, thrusting up.

Usually, he gave me time to adjust to his size, but this morning he was waiting for no one.

He slammed into me so fast that I could do nothing except hold on, and cry little mewling cries as my body raced toward release with the same speed as his thrusts. It should have been too fast, but between the firm grip of Drager's hands on my hips, and the sheer size of him filling my pussy, the ridged sides scraping over every nerve ending, I had no choice but to close my eyes and let the pleasure roll through me.

It started in my gut and spread out through my limbs, until my fingertips were tingling, and I wished this feeling could last forever. In these moments with Drager, I understood and loved every part of the dragon as our bodies fused and energies bonded.

When he destroyed me with his powerful thrusts, I wondered how I'd survive when the day came that he was done with me. Or maybe that would never happen. I was human, with a finite life, and he'd live forever. I'd only be able to handle his size and power for probably another twenty years or so, and that was fine by me.

I'd take twenty years of this. Even if the rest of my life was alone.

CHAPTER
FORTY-SEVEN

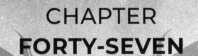

"Drager's put a pep in your step," Lexie commented drily as we made our way out to the front of the academy. A cool breeze has sprung up overnight, and I shivered slightly in my light shirt and black tights. I was dressed for fight classes, having just finished a history lesson with Professor Malin. This time she'd focused on the years of rebuilding after the Fall, and the time it took to split the lands and allow races to choose their *god* and future leader.

It was spoken about as a prosperous and joyful time for the Eastern Realm of Risest, and I had no argument based on what I'd seen here so far. Well, except for the issue of a thief and traitor, but other than that, the fae were content.

"His energy definitely gives me additional strength and speed," I confirmed. "The sex is just... I did not know sex could be like this, and each time I'm fucked up in more ways than one."

Lexie snorted. "Good thing you're heading to get your butt kicked, then. Work off some of that glow."

No doubt I'd be glowing by the end of my lesson, just not from multiple orgasms.

Astra grumbled from my side. Despite Drager's words from before, he'd allowed her back on protection duty, but she'd been far less cuddly. If I had to guess, she was a little pissed off. I really hoped she couldn't communicate with Zahak, because it was all going to get very awkward if that was the case.

We passed the row of heads, which remained on display. It appeared everyone was too scared to remove them in case they upset Zahak. Not that anyone knew for sure it was him, but the rumors were swirling.

It was all we heard as we walked between classes this morning.

When we made it around the side of the academy to the training zone, Tasha and Mika were there, but this time they weren't alone.

"Frogs," Lexie muttered.

Zahak stood apart from the others, looking like a giant in his black modern-day warrior ensemble. His ancient, terrifying, and disturbingly gorgeous face was expressionless as he stood statue-like. He looked as if he'd be able to stand for an eternity as he was, the world changing around him while he remained untouched.

"What's he doing here?" Lexie added as our steps slowed.

"I have no idea," I breathed back, feeling my pulse pick up as my feet all but ground to a halt.

Astra didn't have the same hesitation, racing over to Zahak. She broke through his stoic façade as he bent to greet her, and I had to say, men showing kindness to animals had no business being as sexy as it was. Legit aphrodisiac.

There was cruelty in all the Fallen, I knew that without having even met three of the five, but I'd never seen Drager show kindness like Zahak did with Astra—who was, for all intents and purposes, just an animal under his control. Sure, a rare and ancient animal, but at the end of the day she was not his equal. And yet he treated her as if she were.

When Lexie and I made it to Tasha, she wore a tight smile. "Lord Zahak has asked to observe today. He wants to see your progress."

Unable to stop myself, I lifted my head to meet his unreadable gaze. "This is only my third class. I'm as useless as I was yesterday."

Mika, who had been silent up until now, spoke up: "Not true. You didn't throw up yesterday. That's progress."

I had thrown up yesterday, actually, just by another means.

Zahak's expression didn't change, but the darkness in his eyes deepened. "Start the class," he rumbled.

Tasha swallowed roughly, and there was none of her usual arrogance as she faced me. "Okay, Morgan. Let's start with the warmup, as per usual. Mika will run with you."

Wanting to escape the tension, I nodded rapidly and bounced briefly on the spot. Today, when I took off, filled up with Drager's energy, I was able to keep pace with Mika for the first mile or so. "Well, well, well, what happened to you?" he asked.

"Incentive in the form of a giant Fallen god glaring at us," I suggested.

"Yeah, he's just a little terrifying," Mika whispered. "I'm from the Seas of Verden, and Lord Zahak scares us more than Lord Kellan ever could."

I pictured that blond haired, green-eyed, surfy looking Fallen. "Kellan appears to be more laidback than the others," I said with a shrug. "Less intense maybe."

Mika looked behind him again, no doubt checking Zahak wasn't close. "He is for the most part, but it's never wise to piss any of them off." He paused and added, "Do you ever call them by lord?"

I snorted, before shaking my head. "Nope. They already have too much power and control here. I'll have no part in adding to that." I glanced back as well, but Zahak remained exactly where he'd been when we took off. "Are they usually this involved in your lives?" I asked.

"Not at all," Mika said without hesitation. "I'm forty years old and I've never even seen two of the Fallen until this week. Lord Kellan has monthly rituals for energy that take place in our oceans, but it's not mandatory to attend. Most of us do for the boost of energy, and to catch up on world happenings, but the rest of the time we chill and do our own thing. If you don't make waves in Verden, then you don't get rolled by the gods."

Drager ran Ocheran in a similar manner, from what I'd seen. He had his gatherings at the library and allowed his fae to live in Lancourt for a time, but otherwise he left them to their own devices. Maybe the reason a single dictatorship-style leader worked so well here was their energy gave order, but then they didn't overstep in their control. They let their fae be fae and gave them no reason to rebel.

"There's darkness brewing on the horizon," Mika said suddenly, as we turned to make our way back. "I wasn't here before the Fallen of course, but I have elders who were, and they describe the feeling in the air when they knew that the tides were turning. They knew that the world was about to shift. That's when the darkness infiltrated us the first time, and we all turned to chaos."

"The Fallen righted the balance," I said, remembering my lessons.

Mika nodded. "Yes, they did, and it's been smooth sailing ever since, but there's a storm brewing out there. I can feel it."

Clearly the Seas of Verden fae lived and breathed the oceans around them, and I enjoyed hearing his unique way of referring to the energy he felt. I did not enjoy the worry in the undertone of those words though.

By the time we made it back, the burst of energy I'd started with was fading, but I'd finished the run without Mika having to prod, poke, and half carry me home. That was a step in the right direction.

"As you haven't made it to one defense class yet," Tasha said when we stopped before her. I worked hard not to breathe like I was dying, even as my lungs screamed for air. "Rolta cancelled the other class, and it will all be combined into your time here with us. With that in mind, we will start today with blocking."

Lexie and Tasha demonstrated the move I needed to learn first, and I paid attention as best I could, under the eye of a huge Zahak-shaped distraction.

"Got it?" Lexie asked me, after going over the series of movements.

"In theory yes," I told her. "Just go slow the first couple of times."

Lexie nodded, but the usual softness she generally displayed toward me was gone as we faced each other. "Sorry, friend," she whispered. "It's time to throw you in the deep end."

Tendrils of concern twisted in my gut, but knowing that Lexie would never truly hurt me, I didn't let them rise.

"Okay, we practice twice," Lexie commanded, "and then I'll attack and expect you to block."

Excellent.

She stepped in to hit me, slowing her movements. "Block me here and here," she said, before she spun and kicked out, again slowing her movements right before she hit me. "And here you will step as we showed you, and ready your position to return the attack. You got it?"

I nodded, even though I sure as fuck hadn't "got it." My nonexistent reputation was on-the-line though, and for that I'd figure it out. Or die trying.

Lexie got back into position across from me, and swung out as she'd demonstrated, and I barely managed to get my arm up in time. "I'm slowing my strikes still," she snapped. "You're going to have to move faster than that."

I nodded, and managed the first step when she kicked out, but I misjudged the second, almost tripping. When I righted myself, I wasn't standing how I needed to return attack. Lexie shot out another hit at me, and this one grazed my cheek because I didn't even lift my hand at all, let alone in time.

Don't look. Don't look.

I forced myself not to glance toward Zahak, uninterested in seeing his annoyance or even worse, disappointment. Drager never bothered to hide the way my *humanness* irritated him, and I expected the same from his brother.

I might not be akin to an animal to Drager now—hopefully, since he didn't mind having sex with me on a regular basis—but I was still a lesser being.

"Focus, Morgan," Lexie said sharply. "You're never going to get this if you're daydreaming."

She was right. I had to do better.

Forcing everything from my mind but the series of movements we were learning, I nodded to let her know I was ready to go again. We faced each other, and this time when she struck, I blocked just as she'd shown. Lexie was still slowing her hits, but it was a definite improvement. My footwork remained clumsy in the second part, but at least I didn't trip.

"Better," she said. "Now you can try with Mika. He's taller and broader. It's best you anticipate an attack from all sizes."

When he stepped in across from me, he ruffled his curls, flashed a boyish smile, and shrugged. "Sorry in advance if I smack you, but I promise not to hit hard."

"I can take it," I lied. I absolutely could not take it; I cried when I stubbed my toe. The pain I was most experienced with was mental pain. I could handle a lot of that, but physical, not so much.

Mika laughed, because he knew me well enough already to know I was the biggest liar.

When his smile faded, I prepared myself. I knew him now too, and he always announced his attack by the slight narrowing of his eyes. When he struck out the first time, it was so much faster than Lexie, but I'd anticipated right this time, blocking him cleanly.

I choked back a cry as our limbs collided though, the shock-wave ricocheting up my arm. There was no time to worry about that, as I swung myself around, blocked the next hit, and even got back into position to strike out. Mika blocked me easily, as if he was swatting a fly, but I was super proud of myself.

I'd done it, and against a fae moving much faster than Lexie had. No doubt she was struggling to hit her best friend, the frail human. Mika, on the other hand, had no such qualms.

"Again," he said in the middle of me mentally congratulating myself. "This time don't let the pain stop your movements. You froze up when our limbs collided. Use the pain, drag it inside and build your defenses stronger."

I nodded and got back into position, but this time I couldn't stop my gaze from meeting the god off to the side. He remained as he had been before, one hand on Astra's head, his focus on me, expression unreadable.

His presence made me uneasy, but in a different way to Drager's, and just as Mika went to attack, I held up a hand. "One second," I said. "I need to ask a question, and then I'll be able to focus."

Spinning, I strode over to stand in front of Zahak, tilting my head back to meet his gaze.

"Did you kill Greta and her family?" I needed it confirmed by the god himself.

The silence behind us was absolute, as if the three fae were afraid to even breathe.

"Yes."

I waited, but apparently that was the only answer I was getting.

"Why?"

He leaned in closer to me, coming way down from his lofty heights, until our faces were inches apart. I'd never been this close to him, and I sucked in a deep breath, his scent filling my senses. It was darker, filled with spice, unlike Drager's sunlight and summer. Zahak was the icy rains teamed with the rage of fire as you desperately clung to its warmth.

"Because they tried to kill you, *la moyar*, and for that they had to die."

La moyar... That triggered a memory of that first time with Drager, when I'd thought I heard him say those words. He'd never said them again, though, and I was suddenly desperate to know what it meant. Before I could ask, Zahak reached down and brushed his hand across Astra once more.

"Don't let them hurt you, even in training," he warned as he straightened. "I won't be responsible for my actions if they do."

With that, he turned and walked away from the field, disappearing around the corner of the academy. Astra remained where she was, watching me with what felt like a knowing stare.

Which made one of us, because I had no fucking idea what was going on.

CHAPTER
FORTY-EIGHT

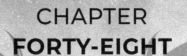

When I returned to my trainers, they eyed me warily. Lexie shook her head and mouthed *What the hat is going on, Morgan?* And I replied by also shaking my head because I had no explanation.

The next hour was spent perfecting defense techniques, and then they moved on to sparring, where I was expected to attack and defend. By the end, I was wrecked, covered in sweat, my hair half out of the braid I'd put it into earlier, lank curls everywhere.

"Come on, let's get you cleaned up," Lexie said, shaking her head. "You're a mess."

"Mika tried to kill me," I whined.

To which he laughed. "I barely even touched you. Now that I know Zahak is beheading anyone that makes the wrong move against our little Morgs, I'm on my best behavior."

They'd heard every part of the conversation with Zahak, and I knew by this evening the entire academy would be very aware of who was responsible for the spiked heads. Tasha looked like she was about to burst at the seams, not being able to spill this information already.

Lexie was quiet as we entered the academy, moving toward the stairs. My body was yelling at me, so I focused on moving one foot in front of the other, and not wincing with each step. Even the base of my feet hurt, along with many other parts of my anatomy. Astra remained a few steps behind us, and she barely made a rumble either, as if we were all exhausted, even though I knew it was only me.

When we were safe in our room, Lexie relaxed. "I'll get the shower going for you," she said with a cheerful note in her voice. "Then we can burn those clothes, because there's no saving them."

I playfully threw the shirt I'd just lifted over my head at her, which she dodged like it was moving in slow motion. She disappeared into the bathroom as Astra settled on my bed, and I followed Lexie, finishing undressing once I was in the tiled room.

The door closed without me even touching it, and I turned to find Lexie two inches away. "What the fae is happening, Morgan?" she rage-whispered, leaning in so close and talking so low I could barely hear her. "Zahak too?"

I waved my hands at her, hopefully highlighting my own shock. "I don't understand it," I whispered back. "I don't get what's happening. He killed people for me, Lexie. Killed. Murder-killed."

She all but rolled her eyes. "Murder-killed. Okay, Morgan. But seriously, this is a terrible situation to be in. Stuck between two fiery dragon shifters who want to destroy each other half the time. They'll tear you in half to prove their dominance."

"Drager already tried that," I muttered, and she shook her head.

"Not in that way, though I'm sure that's an issue too, but in a more metaphorical way. Having a relationship with both of them is going to lead to disaster."

It was my turn to roll my eyes. "I'm barely having a relationship with Drager and we're sleeping together. Zahak and I have exchanged about ten sentences, and eight of them was him rumbling at me. There is no relationship. It's just these odd exchanges."

"Odd exchanges like him saving your life multiple times and presenting you a range of heads to hang on your wall?"

I nodded and shrugged. "Yeah, like that."

She rubbed a hand over her face, her brow scrunched like she had a terrible headache. "I need to get you back to Earth, Morgan. Being here is going to get you killed."

"You know I can't leave," I said, exhaustion pressing down on me. "Drager would only drag me back, and I won't have you getting hurt... or worse, to try and save me from whatever fate has in store for me."

"Fate?" Lexie breathed, looking aghast. "You think this is more than just *wrong place wrong time* with the library?"

I nodded. "Yeah, I do. From meeting you, to the library, and that phone call... the odds tell me that there's more at play here than just a series of random events."

She stared at me, eyes wide and shiny, before a single tear escaped. "Fate is a fickle bison, my friend. Let's hope they're kinder to you." She shook off her sadness and forced a smile. "Okay, I'll let you shower, then we can eat."

She started to move toward the closed door. "Wait," I called. "Do you know what *la moyar* means?"

She looked back, brow furrowed. "La moyar... I've never heard that used before. It's none of the fae languages I know. Why?"

"Drager and Zahak have both called me that, and I'm starting to think I should know what it means."

"When did Drager call you la moyar?" she asked with a tilt of her head. She was as confused as I was about this term from the Fallen.

"In the library, when we were first together," I said.

Her expression didn't change. "And Zahak said it out on the training field?"

I nodded, and we both remained silent for a few seconds.

"Maybe ask Drager," she finally suggested with a shrug. "It has to be from their original language, if they're both using it."

My chest was tight as I considered it. "If the right time presents itself," I finally agreed.

She nodded and left me to shower. I spent a long time under the water, trying to clear my mind and failing miserably. The truth was, my life here in the faerie realm was rife with mystery and danger, and no matter how many times I ran the facts over in my head I couldn't figure it all out. It had to be fate, though, because how else would I end up here with gods and mystical creatures?

My attraction to Drager couldn't be denied. It hadn't happened straight away—I'd thought he was hot albeit terrifying—but during the faerie ritual our relationship had changed. A bond had formed, without my knowledge apparently, and it was only reinforced every time we were together. My one hope was that, eventually, time would reveal all, and I'd be able to move on with whatever remained of my nerves and sanity.

When I was finished and dried, I examined myself in the reflective tile above the sink. I hadn't worn makeup in weeks, barely brushed my hair these days because there was never time, and only had a selection of about ten outfits to choose from. None of which appeared to matter. My time out in the fresh air, running, and eating only fae food—no junk food in sight—had cleaned up my skin, toned muscles, and added shine and volume to my hair.

Drager's energy didn't hurt either, leaving me at the peak of health. I had even lost a little weight, or more likely toned up, so my curves were more pronounced than ever.

I felt good about myself.

My mother tried to raise a meek pushover who caved to the will of others. I'd fought back, and while I still faltered in my approach, I was finding the balance in being a good person while also holding tight to my own feelings and beliefs. It was a hard line to walk, but I felt like I was finally getting there.

When I emerged from the bathroom, Lexie already had one of my few outfits on the bed, and I shimmied it on in seconds. Jeans, white runners, and a fitted red shirt that hung low over the back of my jeans.

"Time for dinner?" I asked, starving.

Lexie nodded. "Yeah, but it might be a grab and run situation. Drager stopped by while you were in the shower and said that the Fallen are having a meeting about the library thief. He wants us there."

That caught my attention. "They haven't discussed anything yet?"

She shook her head. "Apparently tracking down whoever attacked you was first priority."

I didn't know what to say to that, so I said nothing.

Astra, whom I thought was asleep, leapt off the bed so quickly I let out a little shriek. "Holy crap," I gasped. "I almost peed myself. Can you at least stretch first."

She let out a rumble and then proceeded to stretch her huge body out before me. "Smartass," I muttered, and she gave zero fucks as she licked her paw.

When we entered the dining hall, there were a lot of fae

present, most of them mid-way through eating, but by the time Lexie and I made it to the rotating food bar, the hall was completely empty. It was like one of those cartoons where the characters leave so fast that only their outline and an animated cloud of dust remained in the air to show they'd even been there.

"Guess word got around about Zahak," Lexie said with a laugh. "Looks like we have our pick of food."

She remained relaxed, but I felt like I'd just walked into a storm of lice. My skin itched, my face felt hot, and the energy that wasn't mine churned in my stomach. Still, I couldn't deny the truth: Drager's warning hadn't worked quite as well as Zahak's.

Which was no doubt his entire point. He'd told me that he would do whatever it took to keep me safe, even if it made me uncomfortable.

A truth to remember when moving forward and dealing with that dragon shifter.

CHAPTER
FORTY-NINE

S tudents continued to disappear as we walked from the dining room with our plates, strolled down the stairs casually eating food, and exited the academy. Even on the outside, when the sun was still quite high in the sky, and I knew that classes were on, there was nary a soul in sight.

"It's as if we suddenly developed a superpower to make fae disappear," I said with an uneasy laugh, picking up my last piece of melon and sharing it with Astra.

Lexie didn't seem to mind. If anything, she was excited that keeping me safe had just gotten that much easier. Girl was going to be sending Zahak a box of chocolates and a small bouquet of rodents for his dragon to eat.

We made our way around the lake, toward a pocket of trees that I'd only seen from the balcony of my room but had never been into. It wasn't on Drager's land, but it was closer to his than anyone else's, which told me that this meeting spot was his idea. The control freak dragon shifter would leave nothing to chance, not even when it came to his brothers.

Maybe especially when it came to his brothers.

When we stepped under the trees, it immediately grew cooler, and I shivered, wishing I had a heavier sweater. Drager, for all his infinite wisdom as a "god" here, hadn't included any clothing for those of us less warm blooded than a dragon shifter.

Lexie took my plate, placing it with hers on a large gray rock. "We'll grab them on the way back, if they're still there," she said.

"They might not be there?" I wondered, glancing back at them one last time.

Her smile was slow, and not particularly cheerful. "They're made from the soil of this land, turned into clay, and heated by the fires of underground geysers. It's not unknown for the land itself to claim back what belongs to it. Including fae."

Well, okay, then. A completely non-disturbing image followed that statement.

We continued, and I expected Astra to start prancing and bouncing around like the other sabres I'd met when we first made our journey to the academy, but she didn't. If anything, she grew more serious and darker, moving faster so we had to hurry to keep up.

I felt their energy before we even caught a glimpse of the Fallen, a blast of heat against our skin, and just like that I had no need for a sweater.

"It's going to grow more uncomfortable when we get closer," Lexie warned me.

"We're not close now?" I asked, wiping away a bead of sweat from my brow.

She shook her head. "Nope. They're still a few hundred yards away. I'm worried about how you might react to such a strong burst of elemental and *other* energies. Don't hide it, okay. If it's too much for you, I'll get you out of there, even if Drager demands you stay."

That would be him, demanding I stay where it might kill me. Wouldn't be the first time.

"I've got a decent amount of his energy still inside me," I reminded her. "And the last time the five got within a dozen or so feet of us, it was *hot*, but not unbearable."

"It's going to get hotter," Lexie said. "I can feel the pulse of their power through the forest."

Determined that I wouldn't show my humanness today, I forced the faster pace now. I had to marvel that even in such a short time of working out and fighting, I felt stronger. My legs didn't even complain as we jogged through the forest in heavy boots.

Another few minutes passed, and I had to slow. Not from fatigue, but because it felt like we were wading through soft sand. The energy wrapped around and held us near stationary. Except for Astra, of course.

"Little human." I jumped at the low rumble from beside me, stepping back as a Fallen moved from the shadows and into the light. It was Tylan, of the red beast variety. "Seems we're both late for the meeting."

His presence sent the heat around us skyrocketing, and I wasn't sure what to do as he joined us on the makeshift path through the forest. "Little human?" I finally said. "Drager has everyone calling me that now?"

Tylan shrugged, and I marveled at the fact that I'd thought he was smaller. I mean, he was a little shorter than his brothers, but he still towered over me. "What can I say, our fearless leader commands and we follow suit."

There was no obvious disdain in his tone, but it was implied.

"We should keep moving," he said, waving us along the path.

He still reminded me of a woodsman with his beard and style of clothing. Today he was wearing a red checkered flannel shirt, which set off the deep brown of his hair and eyes. He was pretty, that was for sure, but not in the same way as Drager and Zahak. They were destructive. Tylan's energy was not as intense, thankfully.

"I'm not calling you Lord Tylan, I hope you know," I said, falling into step with him. My defiance over their title had become a thing now, and I couldn't give it up so easily.

His smile grew as he crossed his arms to emphasize the sheer breadth of his chest. "I hate being called lord. Ty is just fine."

Ty. I like that, and I wondered if maybe we could be friends eventually. It didn't hurt to have more allies, just in case Drager decided to kill me when I got to be too much effort.

The fact that I didn't trust him not to eventually destroy me was a decent indicator that I shouldn't be sleeping with him. But who could say they'd never made a bad choice even knowing it was going to be bad.

"Are we safe in this meeting?" Lexie asked him, her first words since he'd stepped from the shadow.

"Yes," he replied without hesitation. "You're not the ones who need to fear us. At least not today."

Ty's energy grew easier to deal with as we walked along, and I wondered if he was helping somehow. Whatever it was, by the time we arrived at the meeting place—a huge opening between the most ancient looking trees that I'd ever seen—I was calm and barely sweating.

The trees caught my attention first, at least ten of them spanning around the clearing. Their trunks looked to be six-plus feet wide, and they were too tall for me to see the tops. I'd seen this patch of forest from my balcony the other day, wondering at the trees that towered above all the others.

Reaching out, I pressed my hand to one, jumping as a spark hit

320

my palm. "This is the spot we first fell," Ty said softly. "Our sacred spot. We've never brought an outsider into it before."

Blinking rapidly, I tried to understand what he *wasn't* saying with that statement, but all my thoughts ended up weird and scattered.

"I voted not to allow outsiders in, if that counts," a cold voice said. The other Fallen made their presence known, and that snapped statement had come from Emmen, his light eyes drilling into me.

I swore the air grew chillier under that icy gaze.

"Nice to see that you remain eternally late, brother," Kellan said to Ty before anyone could address Emmen. "I enjoy the tradition of these meetings, and hope that never changes."

Ty laughed, shrugging. "What can I say. The party doesn't start until I arrive."

The pair clasped hands in greeting, a flash of energy between them, and then Ty joined his brothers, leaving Lexie and me standing there, feeling very out of place. Astra even joined Zahak, who was leaning against one of those ancient trees, clearly uncaring it was filled with electricity—or whatever had sparked me.

"Little human," Drager drawled as he approached, reaching out and wrapping one arm around my waist as he dragged me into the middle of the clearing. Lexie made a small sound but she didn't stop him. "Meet my brothers," Drager continued. "Zahak, the interfering bastard you know, and then there's Kellan who controls the Seas of Verden." The blond dragon nodded; his face filled with curiosity as he eyed me.

"Nice to meet you, little human."

"It's Morgan," I replied drily. "Unless you'd like to be referred to as *Giant Lizard*."

Kellan didn't react, but I saw Ty's smile grow.

"I see that you've already met Ty," Drager continued. "Perpetually late, and cheats at basically all games. He's the lord of the crater lands in Lastoa."

"Winning and cheating are not the same thing," Ty said with a shrug. "I'm crafty."

"You're a fucking cheat," Emmen growled.

"And that's Emmen," Drager pointed toward the snarly dragon. "He controls the Wilds of Santoia, and his nature is just as wild."

"We're dragons, brother," Emmen shot back. "We're all wild, even if you lot wear the veil of civility."

Emmen didn't bother to greet me, and I was fine with that. Four out of five dragons having manners was four more than I expected. I was only bothered by Drager's penchant for calling me *little human* being passed on. I'd thought that would just be between him and me, but apparently not.

Zahak had never used it though, and as he remained the silent and scary observer in the corner, I fought the urge to approach him. Not that I could with Drager's arm holding me tightly to his side.

"Can we get this assembly started," Emmen said as he took a seat on another fallen log. Multiple logs lined the inner circle of the trees and had clearly been placed there as seats for the Fallen's meetings. "Some of us can't leave our lands for too long, and I need to make the journey home."

Ty took the next log on his right. "You can leave it, you just don't want to."

Emmen didn't argue the point.

The others sat, even Lexie, until it was only me, Drager and Zahak standing. I sensed that a dominance battle was silently occurring, but I wasn't about to play that game. It had been a long day, which included getting my ass handed to me in fight class, and I needed to rest my legs.

I attempted to pull from Drager's hold, but his grip briefly tightened on my arm. Was he about to force his will on me? Now. In front of his brothers.

It could only be to prove a point to Zahak, and I wasn't cool with games like that.

This was a pivotal moment here between the three of us, and I wondered which way it would all play out.

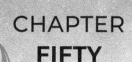

CHAPTER
FIFTY

Zahak moved fast, knocking Drager's hand off my aching biceps. The heat grew more intense as I was freed, and I scrambled away from the raging pair to join Lexie. "You overstep, brother," Drager seethed, and from my spot on the log I glanced his way to see dark eyes and scales appearing.

"You were hurting her again," Zahak growled back. "And we don't have time for your games. We have a threat in our midst. That's our focus."

Tylan let out a rumble, deeper and more intense than I'd heard from him before. "Zahak is right, we don't have time for this. We've had three attempts at a meeting without bloodshed, and we can't fail again."

Drager shrugged. "I'm already the winner, so I can let this go."

"This is not a competition," Zahak said with a nod. "You'll learn soon enough." With that, he sat on one of the logs across from me, stretching his long legs out before him. He appeared calm, though his eyes blazed, and the heat remained intense in the clearing.

Astra sprawled at his side, nudging against his hand, which he placed on top of her massive head and stroked softly. Drager sat as well, not by my side as I expected, and the tension eased. As discreetly as I could, I mopped up some of the sweat on my face with the sleeve of my light cotton shirt, and hoped this wasn't going to be a long meeting. Sitting in this clearing was akin to sitting in a sauna.

"We're here to discuss the fact that all of us have been chasing a threat or traitor in our midst for the last two cycles," Emmen said, getting it started. "If we'd have had the regular meetings that I suggested the last time we parted ways, we wouldn't be dragons chasing our tails. That must stop, because now we're two steps behind."

"Not only behind, but we know that divided we're weak," Ty added.

"Weaker," Kellan shot back, sprawled out as he brushed his right hand over some of the plants near his log. Those plants grew larger and brighter under his touch, and I remembered that he had an affinity with water. "Weaker but never weak."

"Goes without saying," Ty said with a scoff. "But I don't like being even a sliver weaker. We control hundreds of thousands of fae between us, and just because none have ever risen against us doesn't mean they won't. Proven by the fact that we're all sitting here now, looking for a threat. At some point, we grew complacent, and now there are fae working to sabotage all we've built here."

The knowledge that many of those *hundreds of thousands* of fae would kill to be right where I was, amid a Fallen meeting, hadn't escaped me. Maybe it was the slightly awed expression on Lexie's face as she looked between the brothers, or maybe it was Drager's power roiling inside of me, but this felt *epic*. Change worlds and create history sort of epic.

"What have you noticed happening in your lands?" Drager said, getting to the crux of the conversation. "The big and small happenings. We'll never get to the bottom of this with only one fifth of the information."

He was correct. We'd been searching for a threat in the land of Ocheran, which had probably been a colossal waste of time. If this thief was hitting all five lands, there was a more than better chance that it wasn't even one of Drager's minions.

"I'll start," Emmen said, and I noticed that while he was gruff and hard, he was also super focused. "In the Wilds, there have been a multitude of incidents. I didn't notice at first when occasionally some of my creatures would disappear. You know I have the most animal life in the Eastern Realm. It wasn't until, in my private reserves, I had one after another of all the different species vanish. Animals don't just disappear. They fight and there's blood and mess left behind. But there's no evidence these creatures even existed."

"He knows every animal in his land?" I whispered to Lexie. "Like, down to individual ones in each species?"

She nodded her head briefly.

"Next it was books," Emmen continued. "Information tomes I've been using to document our history were taken from my lair. My beast should have picked up on someone entering our domain, and yet we knew nothing until I found the empty covers. All the interior pages were gone, with only the cover remaining to hide their tracks for as long as possible."

The Fallen's faces grew grimmer as he went on, and I wondered if this information meant more to them than it did to me. No doubt I didn't know everything that had been going wrong in Drager's land, and how it tied into the other four.

Tylan went next. "Large holes have appeared around my craters," he said. "The lava base is disturbed, and the fire-ants have been screaming for weeks. They only do that when their family unit is damaged. I also lost a few books, those that give detailed information about the fae under my command, and their unique ability to deal with the heat of our territory."

The picture grew clearer for me, and I was hit with a thought that hadn't occurred me to until this very second. "You all lost books," I burst out.

Five hard stares turned my way. "We did, little human," Ty said. "What does that mean to you? Drager brought you here for a reason, and he hasn't seen fit to provide us with that reason yet, so I'm asking you directly. What do you know?"

"I worked in Dragerfield Library with Lexie," I started hesitantly. "I used to shelve all the books that were borrowed by the fae at night. I heard a voice the night one of those books vanished, and Drager has kept me around to identify that voice if I ever hear it again." Clearing my throat, I met Drager's gaze. "Have you ever noticed any other missing books?"

He was on his feet in a beat, striding over to tower above me, and I fought the urge to jump up too. There was no real point, though, since he towered even if I was standing.

"What other missing books?" he growled, glaring down at me.

Refusing to cower, I shot back my own *fuck off* expression. "I never thought they were missing, you know, but there have been a couple of books that have been checked out for weeks. I mentioned it to Simon, and he told me to *mind my damn business* and then whacked me with his stick and took off."

Drager's eyes were darkening with each word from my mouth. "Why did you never mention it to me?"

I shrugged. "Because I didn't connect those books with the one you claimed was missing. If the others were stolen and not just checked out, wouldn't you have noticed as well?"

"You withheld important information from me," he seethed,

ignoring most of my statement. "How can I trust you? Maybe you're the traitor?"

Despite the stupidity of my next action, a snort of laughter escaped me. I wasn't the only one, with Ty throwing back his head and laughing. "Brother, you've lost your damn mind. We've just established that this threat has been making the rounds on all our lands. Morgan could not achieve that. She's a human who was struggling just walking into our energy this evening."

"Was not," I replied with confidence, even though my legs still felt like jelly.

Ty shook his head, smile firmly in place.

"Drager, sit the fuck down," Zahak drawled. "We don't have time for your dramatics today. Morgan has revealed a very important detail, and we need to discuss the implications of what it means."

There was a moment when the other Fallen grew silent, all signs of amusement fading as they looked between their two brothers—the two strongest, with a rivalry that I'd been dragged into the middle of.

Drager surprised me when he swung around with no more than a chest rumble and retook his seat.

"Continue, human," Emmen said.

Gritting my teeth, I forced words out. "If they're stealing books, they want information on all of you. Now, if it had just been Drager's library hit, then we could assume it was someone from Risest who planned on taking his land down. But since it was all of you..." I looked between the Fallen who hadn't revealed their land's issues yet, and when they nodded, I continued. "All of you had information lifted. Information about the creatures or fae from your lands. If I had to guess, this is an outside source, and they're planning an invasion."

Had I read many sci-fi stories about alien invasions? Yes. Yes, I had. But that didn't mean I was wrong.

"Where is this outside source from?" Kellan asked.

"There are clearly two options," Zahak replied, calmer than I expected given the gravity of the situation. "One of the other lands of Risest want to invade. Southern or the deep." His brothers nodded as they considered his words. "Or there are more from our world, hoping to take what we've built here."

"Our world was destroyed," Drager snarled. "That's the one truth we all remember."

I had not known that about their world, and I could see from Lexie's face she hadn't either.

"We're the last of our kind," Tylan confirmed.

Zahak shook his head, hand stilling on Astra's head. "Why would we remember that one detail, and yet everything else is a blank. It makes no sense, and I've long thought that everything we remember was manufactured. I don't trust any of it to be the truth."

"It might be other aliens too," I suggested. Hard gazes locked on me, and I clamped my lips together once more.

"Stands to reason," Lexie continued, taking the attention from me. "That if you fell from another world, that there are more worlds than just yours out there."

Despite their frustrated expressions, they didn't argue with our logic. It was often hard to argue with logic, despite my mother giving it her best shot.

"We have wasted so much time plotting against each other," Drager bit out, the rumble of his deep tones filling me. "I thought for a long time that one of you were plotting against me, and that stopped me from attending our meetings. We've given them exactly what they needed to stand against us."

"Morgan heard them speak," Ty reminded him. "We aren't as

far behind as we thought. Maybe if we could hear that voice again, one of us would recognize it."

"But I haven't heard anyone who sounds like her," I said softly. "How are you going to hear the voice when I only have a memory to go on?"

Zahak stood, drawing everyone's attention. "I can pull the voice from her mind," he said in a low, inflectionless voice.

"You can *do what the fuck now?*" I said, feeling my body grow tight as tension filled me. "How could you pull a voice from my mind?" My confused brain was trying to process his ludicrous statement, and in that, I remembered the voice in my head that first day in front of the academy. "Were you the one who spoke in my head that day in the clearing?"

He stepped toward me in a slow, almost predatory prowl, and I found myself desperate for air as if he was inhaling all the oxygen with each step. I struggled to my feet, needing to meet him in a less vulnerable position. "How?" I demanded, when he stopped a foot away.

"La moyar," he rumbled. "Fated mate."

Darkness crowded me as the lack of oxygen got the better of me. Zahak caught me before I fell, and my entire body burned as he swept me into his strong arms. "Mate?" I croaked out, and Drager's energy roiled inside me until it all became too much, and I passed out.

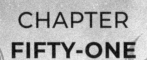

CHAPTER
FIFTY-ONE

I awoke to bedlam. The echoes of raging dragons filled the air around me, and I tried to jerk up into a sitting position, only to find Lexie crouched over me, holding me down. From the little I could see around her, including an unimpeded bronze and gold sky above, I knew we were no longer in the secret Fallen clearing. We were out in the open, beside the lake—a wing of the academy was visible behind Lexie's arm.

"Lex," I rasped. "What the hell is happening?"

She didn't release me as expected. "Drager and Zahak are working out their little issue with you. I tried to get you completely out of the way and into the academy, but when you're out of their sight, it grows way worse."

Pushing against her hold, she finally allowed me to sit up.

Holy fae gods. Give me strength.

Two dragons filled the sky above us, smashing into each other. Drager had told me that his beast was similar to Zahak, and while I could see that, they were also quite different.

Drager was more gilded than Zahak, his scales tipped in black rather than gold. His wings were darker though, with thick, dark veins racing through the gold edges.

"Yin and yang," I breathed, mesmerized. Those two, more than any others, looked alike in both their humanoid and dragon forms. "Drager told me they were born in the same pod, and I see it so clearly now."

Lexie blinked at me. "Same pod? We've never heard that before. Odd, the few memories they have of their birth and home world. Maybe Zahak is right, maybe it's all manufactured."

"Or maybe some memories were just too strong to be erased," I said, wincing as Zahak's claws scraped Drager's stomach. I forced myself up on wobbly legs, keeping my eyes locked on the sky. "We have to stop them."

Lexie joined me as I moved closer to the lake. "How do you plan on doing that?" she asked. "Last I checked, you're a human without the ability to fly or fight. Especially not against gigantic dragons."

"Okay, true," I grumbled. "No need to say it like it is." Lexie snorted, but the stress didn't fade from her face. "Where are their brothers?" I asked, looking around. We both winced as the pair clashed above us again, before she pointed.

I followed that line and saw the three of them standing close, arms crossed and heads back as they observed the fight. "What the fuck?" I snarled. "They're not doing anything."

They almost looked like they were enjoying the show.

Fury had me taking off in a sprint toward them. "Morgan, are you out of your mind?" Lexie shouted, racing after me. I'd taken her by surprise, but she caught up to me in about three seconds. "You need to stay out of danger."

"We'll all be in danger if they kill each other," I said, choking on those words as the pain of a world without them filled me. As confusing and messed-up as it all was, there was a web tangled around the three of us, and I needed to unravel it. I needed the truth.

When we reached Kellan, Emmen, and Tylan, they casually turned toward us. "There you are, little human," Ty said with a smile. "Thought you'd never rejoin us."

I didn't return his smile. "Why the hell are you guys not stopping this?" I jerked my hand up to the beautiful beasts intent on destroying each other.

The three of them looked at me, and then at each other, before looking back at me. In sync, they burst into laughter, losing their shit like I'd just told the funniest joke in the world. I almost punched them. But since Emmen was the closest, I refrained, because he had been the least tolerant of me since I'd ambushed their meeting.

"Only a fool would get between those two," Ty finally said when he managed to calm. "There's not a being that we're aware of strong enough to break them up."

"For fuck's sake," I muttered. Since no one else was going to break it up, then that left me to figure out a way.

Unfortunately, there was a clear and obvious solution to this mess.

I had to die.

Again.

Well, at least put myself into danger and hope that one of them cared more about rescuing me than they did about tearing each other apart. Surely if Zahak thought I was his true mate, and possibly so did Drager, one of them would sense me in danger, right? There was no way a true mate bond would exist without a warning sign of your mate's impending doom.

It made perfect logical sense to me, and with that, I left those three clowns and turned toward the lake. Except there was still one fae standing in my way, who was not going to risk me, even if I asked her very nicely.

"Lex," I said softly.

"Not a frogging chance, Morgan Starrer," she shot back before I said anything else.

"I have to stop them."

There was blood sprinkling down from wounds that both dragons had sustained, and it was killing me to watch it happen.

"You can't risk yourself. I won't let you get in the middle of a dragon battle."

Emmen stepped closer, as serious as he'd been the first time I saw his face. "You need help?" he asked me.

"I need to get their attention, and Lexie is a touch overprotective."

Faster than I could track, he wrapped his arms around Lexie. She'd seen it coming, but her speed couldn't match the Fallen. "Morgs, please," she begged, still fighting his hold, even as she appealed to me. "Please don't do this. They're not going to notice your attempt to stop them. You will literally just die trying."

"I can't lose them, and they're not stopping," I replied, desperate. "I'll just get their attention in the most dramatic way possible."

"I can help with that," Ty added, no longer laughing either.

Snarling at him, I waved him off. "It's too late to bother helping now. Why don't you go back to watching your brothers kill each other like it's a football game."

His face fell. "Aw, come on, Morgs. It's not like that. We're dragons, and violence is used to settle disagreements. But you and I are friends, aren't we?"

"Nope," I shot back. "Definitely not."

He grinned and then I was in his arms, thrown over his shoulder as he shot us up into the air. My scream was loud, espe-

Zahak, who was shifting back, if the burst of light burning my retinas was any indication.

"You can't do that so close to her," he snapped at his brother. "She's human. They're fragile."

Zahak returned to his human form so much faster than I expected, completely dressed in his black ops gear. "She's stronger than you give her credit for," he replied gruffly. "She's more than human if she carries the gene for a true mate."

I lifted my hand in the air. "Uh, excuse me. Firstly, I really hate when people talk over my head like I'm not here. And secondly, I'm human. There's been not a single sign in almost twenty-six years of anything other than human in this body. Thank you."

Zahak shrugged like that didn't bother him. Drager's reaction wasn't quite the same, as his brow furrowed. He covered it up quickly, but I saw it.

"Then humans are stronger than we've been led to believe," Zahak said as he pushed in closer to Drager. "And if they're not, that's why they have us. That's why Morgan has me. I'm her protector. Not you."

"It was *my* knot," Drager snarled back. "You can't claim anything other than the occasional mental connection."

His knot. I'm sorry. "We're just announcing knots here, in the group setting?" I said with a startled laugh. "Well, damn. Are we measuring—?"

"Morgan!" Lexie gasped.

"What?" I shot back. "Apparently we're cool to discuss our sex lives."

"I'm totally cool with it," Kellan added. "I've been trying to work out the logistics, and the math is just not mathing for me."

"It was also one knot during a fertility ritual," I continued, like Kellan hadn't spoken at all. "I don't think that's proof of a mate bond. I didn't get pregnant."

I hadn't gotten pregnant in all my time with Drager, and there was no way I'd be a true mate unless pregnancy was involved, right? I'd read the books. I knew the rules.

Books wouldn't let me down like that.

"This is the weirdest faeing day I've ever had," Lexie whispered, eyes wide as she shook her head. It was the Lexie equivalent of rocking in the corner.

"I have a theory about all of this," Emmen said, speaking up for the first time in a while. Ty had also remained quiet, but he looked amused, as if he was just enjoying the show. Emmen on the other hand, hadn't cracked one smile.

"And what's your theory?" Drager drawled. He clearly wasn't super excited to hear his brother's next words.

"We don't remember our lives before we fell, right? Outside of knowing we're blood brothers, there's not a lot else we can recall. What if we were sent here for a reason—"

He never got to finish his sentence as an orchestra of thunder rang out above us. All gazes shot to the clear skies above, and I wondered if it was a storm rolling in.

Drager and Zahak backed in on either side of me, and Lexie had her sword in her hand as we all stared up.

"Do you sense anything?" Emmen said, turning his head rapidly to take in the entire gilded sky.

"Nothing," Drager shot back. "No fae would stand against all five of us."

The boom sounded again, and with it, an amplified voice filled the air above and around us. *"Letmina trifarna conqueta le tarn."*

The voice, speaking a language I didn't understand, was so booming I had to cover my ears and squeeze my eyes closed against the pressure. It wasn't until she said, "It's time to face the consequences of your actions," words I understood, that I heard a familiar lilt.

"That's her!" I screamed, still covering my ears and eyes. "That's the traitor."

Another boom rang out, and as Zahak's arms wrapped around me, energy exploded, and we went flying. The last thing I saw were huge beasts descending in the skies above, and another blast sent us far across the land.

CHAPTER
FIFTY-TWO

Darkness surrounded us, so complete that for a second I wondered if I'd passed out again.

I felt conscious, and yet I couldn't see anything.

Zahak's arms were still around me, his spicy scent strong, along with the heat of his energy. All of my senses were working except sight, and that freaked me out, because I had no idea what the hell happened.

"Hello," I whispered. "Z?"

"I've got you," he rumbled. "Sorry, I was trying to figure out what the hell happened."

That made two of us.

"The voice in the sky was the same voice I heard in Drager-field," I told him, unsure if they'd heard me yell that out before the blast.

Zahak pulled me closer. "I know, la moyar. I know. And I remember now. I remember who she is and why we're royally fucked."

"Who is she?" I gasped.

A low glow spread across his skin. It had been so dark in here that it hurt my eyes for a few seconds until they adjusted. As they did, I realized why he'd been keeping us in the dark—he didn't want me to freak out at the fact that we were clearly surrounded by rocks, buried deep underground. A low purring rumble at my side had me jumping, and I looked down to see Astra. She'd made it with us.

"Who was the voice?" I asked him, knowing I should step out of his hold, but I needed comfort, so I wouldn't freak out about our stone surroundings.

"It's our mother," he said simply.

Blinking, I waited for him to expand on that. Only, he didn't say another word.

"Your mother?" I pushed. "You remembered her?"

"Her energy broke through some of the locks on our minds," he grit out, voice growing deeper. "Bits and pieces are coming back to me. We need to get out of here and find my brothers. They're in huge danger. We're all in danger."

"Dragons were falling from the sky, right?" I wasn't sure whether I'd imagined it or not.

"Yes, they were."

He finally released me, and I tried not to mourn the loss of contact. This cold, dark area contained an energy I didn't like, and without Zahak's power blocking it, I was seconds from running and screaming. "Where are we exactly?" I asked, voice wavering.

Zahak's expression was serious as he looked around. "We're in the trench, Morgan. She threw us into our lands, separating us."

"Trench?" I squeaked. "Like, where the nightmare creatures existed?"

Zahak nodded.

"But you closed it up," I replied in a rush. "Professor Malin told me that in history class. It's gone."

His expression did not fill me with hope. "I never got a chance to update you all about what has been happening in my lands. Along with losing books, as you so cleverly deduced, there have been movements in the trench. Cracking. I was planning on dealing with it when I returned, but for all intents and purposes, parts of the trench are once again visible to the land above."

I choked on my next words. "How do we get out of here?"

"We have to travel through the tunnels to the beam of light," he said, sounding pissed. "That's the only way to leave it now, unless we discover a large enough crack on the way."

Fuck my life. Maybe the fates were fickle bitches, just as Lexie had warned me. "Okay, great. I can last about two days without water. Can we make it to this beam of light in two days?"

Zahak's chest rumbled, his left hand shaking as he rubbed it over his face. A face with scales trailing along cheeks and across his forehead... he was on the brink of losing control, and no way would I survive if he shifted into his dragon under here.

"We can't," he bit out. "There is water in the trench, though, and I will find it for you. I will protect you, mate, even if it's the last thing I do."

We'd deal with this whole *mate* thing at another time. For now it seemed we had a mission.

"Okay, we should get started then," I said, looking around. "We can't waste any time, not if there's danger out in Risest. Lexie and your brothers are out there."

Zahak straightened, and I noticed a streak of blood that he'd swiped before from a cut seeping deep blue blood from near his hairline. "You're hurt," I exclaimed, stepping forward.

He didn't stop me from touching him, but I was a foot too short, so he had to bend down to assist me. "How is this possible?" I asked. "You're a god."

Zahak laughed. "*God* is a title, but even the most powerful have weaknesses. The universe demands a balance, and our mother knows exactly what to hit us with to hurt us. Until all our memories come back online, we'll be vulnerable to her attacks."

Gently brushing against the wound, which was already healing, I found myself unnaturally angry. "Well, in that case, our second task as we travel through the trench is to unlock your memories. She cracked them, just like she did this trench, and that was her second mistake."

I was running on adrenaline and hope at this point, but with very little other options, I would take what I could get.

"Second task is to stay alive," Zahak rumbled.

For some reason, I knew this wasn't just about food and water for me. "What do you mean?"

His expression was grave. "When I sealed up the trench, not all the nightmare creatures wanted to leave. Some of them have remained in the tunnels, and I'm not sure they'll appreciate my presence."

Astra let out a low growl, reminding us that she was one of those creatures.

"Are you serious?" I whispered.

Zahak's hands wrapped around my face as he pulled me closer. So close I wondered if he was about to kiss me. So close I breathed in his scent and lost all coherent thought for a beat. "I won't let anything happen to you," he promised. "Where you're concerned, if a threat comes at us, I'm death before they even blink. You have nothing to worry about."

As I stared into his eyes, deep and emitting a similar light to his skin, I felt reassured. "Okay, I believe you," I said.

Zahak was satisfied with that as he straightened. "We need to move now. The longer we sit here, the worse it will get."

With a gentle push in the center of my back, I found myself setting out on a path of stone, darkness surrounding me on all sides. Dragon at my back, sabre by my side, and with fear and hope intermingling in my chest, I really hoped I lived long enough to make it through this trench.

I had a lot of questions that needed answers.

Oh, and we also had a world to save.

A world now *filled* with fallen fae gods.

———

To find out what happens in the final book of Morgan's story, you can pre-order Crimson Skies here: LINK

AFTERWORD

STAY UP TO DATE:

The best way to stay up to date with all of my worlds and new releases, is to join my Facebook group here:

www.facebook.com/groups/jayminevenerdherd

We share lots of book releases, fun posts, sexy dudes, and generally it's a happy place to exist.

Next best place is www.facebook.com/JayminEve.Author

And my newsletter at www.jaymineve.com

xx

ALSO BY JAYMIN EVE

JAYMIN EVE

Fallen Fan Gods (Dark Romantasy dragon shifter/fae romance 18+)

Book One: Gilded Wings

Book Two: Crimson Skies (Release early 2024)

Boys of Bellerose (Dark, RH rock star romance 18+)

Book One: Poison Roses

Book Two: Dirty Truths

Book Three: Shattered Dreams

Book Four: Beautiful Thorns

Demon Pack (PNR/Urban Fantasy 18+)

Book One: Demon Pack

Book Two: Demon Pack Elimination

Book Three: Demon Pack Eternal

Shadow Beast Shifters (PNR/Urban Fantasy 18+)

Book One: Rejected

Book Two: Reclaimed

Book Three: Reborn

Book Four: Deserted

Book Five: Compelled

Book Six: Glamoured

Supernatural Prison Trilogy (Complete UF series 17+)

Book One: Dragon Marked

Book Two: Dragon Mystics

Book Three: Dragon Mated

Book Four: Broken Compass

Book Five: Magical Compass

Book Six: Louis

Book Seven: Elemental Compass

Supernatural Academy (Complete Urban Fantasy/PNR 18+)

Year One

Year Two

Year Three

Royals of Arbon Academy (Dark, complete Contemporary Romance 18+)

Book One: Princess Ballot

Book Two: Playboy Princes

Book Three: Poison Throne

Titan's Saga (PNR/UF. Sexy and humorous 18+)

Book One: Releasing the Gods

Book Two: Wrath of the Gods

Book Three: Revenge of the Gods

Dark Legacy (Complete Dark Contemporary high school romance 18+)

Book One: Broken Wings

Book Two: Broken Trust

Book Three: Broken Legacy

Secret Keepers Series (Complete PNR/Urban Fantasy)

Book One: House of Darken

Book Two: House of Imperial

Book Three: House of Leights

Book Four: House of Royale

Storm Princess Saga (Complete High Fantasy 18+)

Book One: The Princess Must Die

Book Two: The Princess Must Strike

Book Three: The Princess Must Reign

Curse of the Gods Series (Complete Reverse Harem Fantasy 18+)

Book One: Trickery

Book Two: Persuasion

Book Three: Seduction

Book Four: Strength

Novella: Neutral

Book Five: Pain

NYC Mecca Series (Complete - UF series)

Book One: Queen Heir

Book Two: Queen Alpha

Book Three: Queen Fae

Book Four: Queen Mecca

A Walker Saga (Complete - YA Fantasy)

Book One: First World

Book Two: Spurn

Book Three: Crais

Book Four: Regali

Book Five: Nephilius

Book Six: Dronish

Book Seven: Earth

Hive Trilogy (Complete UF/PNR series)

Book One: Ash

Book Two: Anarchy

Book Three: Annihilate

Sinclair Stories (Standalone Contemporary Romance 18+)

Songbird